ABOUT THE AUTHOR

Jo Middleton is a writer, mum of two grown-up children and servant to three cats and a golden retriever. Jo began writing 20 years ago, and in 2009 created her award-winning blog *Slummy Single Mummy*. Jo published her first novel, *Playgroups and Prosecco*, in 2019 and has since gone on to work with her good friend Gill Sims, hosting her 2022 theatre tour and co-hosting a podcast, *It's Five O'clock Somewhere*.

You can follow Jo on Instagram @jomiddletonauthor and find her on Substack @jomiddleton.

Happy BLOODY Christmas

JO MIDDLETON

avon.

Published by AVON
A division of HarperCollins*Publishers* Ltd
1 London Bridge Street
London SE1 9GF

www.harpercollins.co.uk

HarperCollins*Publishers*
Macken House,
39/40 Mayor Street Upper,
Dublin 1
D01 C9W8
Ireland

First published by HarperCollins*Publishers* Ltd 2024
1

A catalogue record for this book is available from the British Library.

ISBN: 978-0-00-871110-8

This novel is entirely a work of fiction.
The names, characters and incidents portrayed in it are
the work of the author's imagination. Any resemblance to
actual persons, living or dead, events or localities is
entirely coincidental.

Typeset in Bembo by Palimpsest Book Production Ltd,
Falkirk, Stirlingshire

Printed and bound in the UK using 100% Renewable Electricity
by CPI Group (UK) Ltd

MIX
Paper | Supporting
responsible forestry
FSC
www.fsc.org
FSC™ C007454

This book contains FSC™ certified paper and other controlled sources
to ensure responsible forest management.

For more information visit: www.harpercollins.co.uk/green

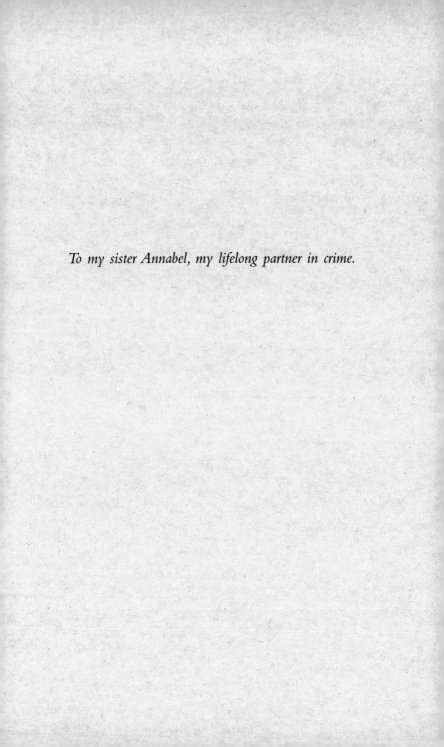

To my sister Annabel, my lifelong partner in crime.

CHAPTER 1

There is a brief moment with a hangover, just after you wake up, when you think perhaps that everything is going to be okay. And then you move and realise that it isn't.

I wonder if perhaps I can go back to sleep and start again later, or better yet go back in time and not drink the amaretto? It's so festive and delicious though and felt like such a very grown-up and tasteful addition to the Christmas party.

Oh Christ. The party.

I tentatively roll over and take my phone from the bedside table: 9.41 a.m. Fuck. At 2 a.m. last night when we were ushering out the final guests and I was looking around at the chaos of empty wine bottles, an abandoned game of Twister and a liberal quantity of crisps trampled into the carpet, it had seemed like such a good idea to clear it all up in the morning.

I'd set an alarm for 8 a.m., imagining that by that time I would feel delightfully refreshed and festive. At least I thought I had. I check my phone. Yes, there is an alarm set. For 8 p.m. every Thursday. Excellent.

I roll back, carefully, and stare at the ceiling, waiting for the nausea to pass, but immediately my brain starts replaying the never-ending list of things I need to do before Oli's judgemental parents arrive tomorrow for Christmas lunch. I wish sometimes that my brain would fuck off and leave me alone, honestly.

I look over at my darling husband, sleeping the sleep of a *man*, untroubled by thoughts of how best to arrange the table to avoid a repeat of the gravy incident of 2019 and how to stop his mother making comments like the ones she made last year about people who eat marzipan fruits.

It reminds me of those early weeks when the kids were babies. Every night without fail they would wake me, screaming (them not me, at least initially), and every night Oli would be oblivious. The next morning he'd wake up with one of those elaborate pantomime-style stretches, yawning, and say something that made me want to punch him in the face like: 'The baby slept well, didn't he?'

No, Oli, I would think, *the baby did NOT sleep well. The baby is a demon baby from hell who I suspect is trying to drive me slowly insane by waking at hourly intervals and then waiting until I have* just *drifted back to sleep to start mewling like a possessed tiger cub.* I never said this though, because I was too tired to form recognisable human words. I actually overheard him last night telling Georgie how lucky we were that Ben and Lily both slept through the night at such a young age.

I look at him now. A pool of drool has formed beneath his half-open mouth. I give him a kick.

'Wake up,' I say. He groans, wipes his mouth with the back of his hand and goes back to sleep. I kick him again. 'It's Christmas Eve,' I say, 'the house looks like Ben's room on a bad day and your family are going to be here in . . .' I check my phone again '. . . twenty-six hours and sixteen minutes.'

He opens his eyes and farts loudly, keeping eye contact the whole time, and then leans over to kiss me on the cheek. 'And they say romance is dead,' he says, smiling broadly, like he genuinely thinks he's being witty. The stench is enough to drive me from the bed. I pull on my dressing gown, and brace myself to assess the damage downstairs.

I cross the landing and hear the familiar iPad beeping that tells me that Lily is awake and playing her current favourite game. It's one of those cooking games where the aim is to prepare as many meals as possible whilst keeping your kitchen clean and tidy. It always strikes me as hugely ironic given that in real life she groans deeply at the mere suggestion that she might clear away her own plate. It really is true that the teenage years begin at seven.

Part of me wonders if I should do something about the iPad but another part, the part that has been parenting for fifteen years and is quite tired, thank you, tells me not to bother. That part wins. I've learnt to choose my battles and this is not one of them.

I poke my head around Lily's door. She's sitting up in bed, iPad resting on her knees, eating crisps from a bowl.

'Where did you get those?' I ask, eyeing the crisps suspiciously.

'From downstairs,' she says, pulling back the duvet along one side of her to reveal four more half-empty bowls of party leftovers, including one that looks like M&S wasabi peas.

'I see,' I say, as she tucks her spoils back under the duvet and ignores me in favour of her virtual restaurant guests. Unless I have ordered a hamburger with no tomato and two portions of fries then I am dead to her.

I leave her to it. The crisps are one less thing for me to clean up I suppose. And wasabi peas – are they technically one of your five a day? I decide that they are. Just like a fruit salad for breakfast if you think about it, which I choose not to.

I pause briefly at the door to Ben's bedroom but all I can hear is snoring. I know better than to wake a fifteen-year-old boy when I don't have to – I don't need the hand-made 'authorised personnel only' door sign to tell me that. God knows what time he went to bed. I have a little sit-down on the step outside for a minute, for the hangover.

There were a lot of things – like iPads and bedtimes – that I felt strongly about before I became a parent. I was never going to let my children have dummies. They were both only ever going to eat organic chicken, or at the very least free-range. I wasn't entirely sure why, but I appreciated that there needed to be an element of outdoor pecking involved for it to be wholesome. They were going to introduce themselves politely to strangers, develop a passion for a musical instrument from a young age and their favourite food would be something like chickpeas or asparagus. Screen time would be limited to half an hour a week, when we would sit together and watch videos about dolphin migration or space travel and they would be fascinated and engaged and afterwards want to start a project.

Whatever happened to projects? I swear when I was a kid I was always starting projects. I remember the summer holidays when I was ten, getting massively into badgers. I copied out all the badger entries from the encyclopaedias at the library and drew pictures of badger tracks and my project cover had BADGERS written in my best bubble writing, albeit with the R and the S slightly smaller than the rest because it was always so hard to judge, wasn't it? I doubt millennials or Gen Z or whatever they are now have ever truly appreciated the joys of bubble writing.

'Anna, bring a coffee up when you've got a minute,' shouts Oli from our bedroom, shattering my rose-tinted reminiscing.

I bristle. When I've *got a minute?* It's Christmas Eve. I've got an entire house to clean, his judgemental family coming for Christmas and I've still got roughly *one million* things left on the to-do list, including taking the children on a wholesome outing to forage for holly for my tablescape.

The whole tablescape thing has got a little out of control if I'm honest with myself. I've been trying very hard indeed to make my centrepieces look effortless yet elegant, but I just can't seem to make twigs look chic. I've convinced myself that fresh holly is going to be what brings it all together. I haven't actually got any

5

fresh holly yet, but it's okay because they have a holly bush in the front garden at number 13 and they're away for Christmas.

My phone pings in my pocket. It's Jennie.

'How are you feeling?! I have made medicinal tea and toast and chocolate spread and have taken it back to bed. Almost glad to be without the kids this Christmas!' The message is followed by a series of emojis – the vomiting face, a poop and a glass of red wine. That sums it up pretty nicely.

My phone pings again.

'Oh and I think I lost an earring last night so if you find a big gold hoop while you're clearing up then it's mine, thank you!'

I'll reply when my eyes can focus properly but for now I need to be cleaning up. Somehow ten minutes have passed since I sat down? I grab the wall, lever myself off the step and head downstairs to the living room. I will make Oli a coffee, but I'll use the Aldi instant we got for the builders – that'll teach him. I wonder how many happy marriages are based on simmering resentment and petty acts of revenge. Quite a lot I expect. My marriage is actually perfectly fine generally, apart of course from me being responsible for ninety-five per cent of all of the thoughts and planning required to do anything properly, but there is something about being hungover that makes everyone extra annoying.

It doesn't even matter because Oli can't tell the difference with the coffee, but I will know and that's the main thing. I hear him whistling and the noise of the shower going on in our en suite. Oli must be feeling a bit more human than me.

I only pause once on the way down the stairs for some hangover-induced deep breathing and to press my cheek against the cool wall, which is not bad at all. The living room, however, is very bad. It's worse than I remembered – a sea of dirty glasses and empty bottles and puddles of mulled wine on the coffee table, like a sad-looking festival site when everyone has gone home. It's fine, this is what dishwashers are for, and Lily has taken care of the crisps. I just need a couple of bin bags and to sneak some of the bottles into next door's recycling and it will be fine. All completely fine.

I decide to start by packing away the Twister. I don't know what we were trying to prove with the Twister honestly: that we are still university students and that playing Twister will be kind of fun and sexy because we're all so lithe and supple? Hardly. I can barely touch my toes nowadays. Whenever I go to the yoga class in the hall at Lily's school I wear loose trousers so the instructor can't see when I sneakily bend my knees. She's very intense and I know she'd be disappointed in me. She's one of those vegans who likes everybody to know about it, which, come to think of it, is all the vegans I've ever met. Suffice it to say that seductive straddling is definitely off the table. I hope very much that there is no photographic evidence of me trying to reach over our neighbour Marcus on all fours to get my left hand on a blue.

I bend down to pick up the plastic sheet and instantly a thousand ball bearings rush to the front of my head. I have a second where I don't know whether it's better to stand up again or let myself fall all the way onto the floor and stay there, but I think of Oli's mum

7

Pamela and the triumphant look on her face if she were to turn up and see me lying in my dressing gown on the floor surrounded by empty bottles and I opt for standing up.

Twister packed away, I head to the kitchen, fill the kettle with water and put it on to boil. I get out two mugs – Emma Bridgewater sausage dogs for me and the chipped one we got from the garage when we last had the car serviced for Oli – and the milk from the fridge. I go to get the coffee and bin bags from the walk-in larder (my pride and joy and envy of the entire PTA).

I open the door and am nearly knocked off my feet by Tommy erupting from inside. He makes a dash for the cat flap in the back door opposite the larder and is gone. Stupid cat, how did he get himself shut in there? I look around the kitchen and realise I haven't seen Tuppence yet either. Normally they'd be on the bed, clawing at my hair, petitioning for breakfast by about 6 a.m. The festivities must have sent her off somewhere to hide.

I turn back to the larder, reaching up to the bin bags, and see Father Christmas slumped against the cereal shelf. I close the door again. That can't be right. I blink twice, reopen the door and he's still there. He's knocked some things off the shelf and he's covered with a light dusting of flour. It's actually very festive, as though it's been snowing. It's the spelt flour that was £3.75 from the farmer's market, which is a shame. I should probably stop going to the farmer's market. I find it very difficult NOT to buy something once I've made eye contact, which I guess is what the stallholders rely on. I think the spelt stand is actually run by a cult though, so I must be careful as they are always inviting people to visit their 'bakery' and 'enjoy a meal' with them.

I notice that as well as the flour, Father Christmas's lap is covered with ketchup, which is weird because I keep the ketchup up here on the left and it's still there. I look again and realise that in the middle of the ketchup is the handle of a knife, at right angles to Santa's body.

Weird.

Time seems to slow and it takes my amaretto-soaked brain longer than it should to realise why I can't see the blade of the knife and that the ketchup isn't ketchup at all.

It's congealed blood.

Fuckety hell. Someone has killed Father Christmas.

CHAPTER 2

I close the door again quickly and lean back against it, breathing hard. I feel last night's amaretto trying to resurface, burning the back of my throat. What's happening? There can't really be a dead body in my larder surely? Not in my precious larder. Not when I spent such a ridiculously long time choosing the flooring. My floor! There will be stains, won't there?

I open the door, peer more closely at Santa, realise Santa is my boss Colin, and close the door again.

Fuckety fuckety fuck.

I reach for my phone to call the police and suddenly have a moment of panic. Shit. What if it's Oli? Is he the sort of person who could *kill Father Christmas*? Not that it *is* Father Christmas, but there's still something about the suit that would make you think twice, right? It would be like when you see a policeman and automatically feel guilty, like you've just shoplifted an Impulse body spray. Hypothetically.

Oli always gets rid of spiders by putting a glass over

them, and he carries them all the way to the bottom of the garden 'just in case', but that's exactly the sort of thing the wives on *Criminal Minds* say when the pitying woman from the FBI tells them their husbands are serial killers.

Oh God, what if I'm that woman who naively lives in a beautiful house and has designer handbags and never questions all the chest freezers in the garage because her husband tells her he has a thriving frozen pea business? 'Oh yes he works away a lot,' she tells the FBI, 'but you wouldn't believe how much money there is in peas.' And then they open the freezers and they are full of *heads* and he has forty-two trophy credit cards in women's names.

It's fine, I remind myself, beginning to hyperventilate, because I actually don't have a single designer handbag and I'm always complaining that I don't have enough freezer space. We do have the little one in the garage that we bought when I thought I was going to get into batch cooking, but it's such a trek to get anything from it. I would love a fridge freezer like Jennie's with a full-length freezer down one side. Jesus, FOCUS, woman, focus. Colin – remember? I wish I wasn't so hungover.

Freezer space aside, surely Oli isn't a cold-blooded killer? He cried at the reboot of *Sex and the City*, I don't think he has it in him to plunge a knife into someone. Plus he asked me to make coffee and the coffee is in the larder, and he wouldn't want me to see the body, would he? Unless he was having a last hoorah and was planning to do away with all of us in a twisted Christmas massacre. He didn't look like he was planning a massacre when he farted.

I open the larder for a third time and force myself to look at Colin. He looks one hundred per cent dead to me, but then I've never seen a dead person in real life before, only on the television, so I'm not sure how I'm meant to know. On *Death in Paradise* they always have a helpful indicator like a trickle of blood from their mouth. Colin doesn't have that. I'm trying desperately to think about what a sensible grown-up person would do next, but it's at this point in *Death in Paradise* that the jolly Caribbean theme tune starts, and so inevitably that's all I can think of now, which feels pretty disturbed. I suspect I am a Very Bad Person.

I know not to touch anything, but what if he's not dead and all this time I could have saved his life? I should check for a pulse, but there is flour and blood everywhere.

Think, Anna, think.

I look around, wondering how best to get to the body, when I notice something – a pattern in the flour near his left foot. It's a shoe print. A boot print maybe? I feel a tiny surge of excitement and immediately chastise myself. A man is dead, remember? Not a very nice man admittedly, but still, this isn't the Famous Five. I take a picture of it though. Just in case.

I decide that if I am very careful, I can hold on to one of the shelves (pasta and rice) with my right hand and lean over and check the pulse in his wrist with my left and avoid stepping into the larder. Perhaps that Twister was useful after all. I press two fingers against where I think a pulse should be but there's nothing. He's cold too. I snatch my fingers away. They leave a white patch on his skin that fades after a few seconds.

I try to stand up but my balance is off and I wobble. For a horrific moment I see myself falling face-first into his bloody lap, but I manage to claw it back and stand upright. He's definitely dead. I think I might be sick. I close the door again.

I try to take a deep, calming breath but it comes out as a strangled wail. I've just touched an actual corpse. Shit. I touched a corpse. Was that stupid? Have I left DNA?! I'm pretty sure Colin will have tried touching me up enough during the party for any DNA to already be on him, but who knows nowadays? I saw an episode of *CSI Miami* once where they caught the murderer by zooming in on some blurry CCTV footage that showed their reflection in someone's eyeballs. And that was before AI. Everyone knows the power of AI. I mean, I don't really to be honest, not in these circumstances, but that's why it's so worrying, isn't it?

I hear myself and realise I'm freaking out. I don't actually give a toss about AI. Is this what being in shock feels like? I hold out my hand. It's a bit shaky, but that could be the alcohol.

Tuppence appears through the cat flap and I pick her up and take a big sniff of her lovely head to calm myself. How nice to be a cat and not have to have a larder to maintain or a dead body to deal with. I hear the kettle come to the boil and click off and I picture the chaos this is going to cause. Pamela is going to have an absolute field day with this. I've never been good enough for her precious son and I can see her now, the raised eyebrows and pursed mouth that says, 'I could have told you from her liberal use of Bisto that Anna was the sort of woman to have a dead Santa in her larder.'

And all my Christmas preparations! I think about how long I spent spray painting those bloody fir cones for the Christmas window swags. I can almost see Kirstie Allsopp turning in her grave at the thought of them covered in fingerprint powder. Okay, so not her grave, but whatever it is people do when they're not dead. Not like Father Christmas Colin.

I need to make a decision. I need to call the police, but there's part of me that is very aware that I am well known for hating my boss, and that he's dead in *my* larder, with my finger DNA on him. (Gross.) Plus I've not entirely discounted Oli having done it in a moment of drunken rage and I don't especially want to dob in my own husband if he was defending my honour or protecting one of the children.

I'll call Jennie instead. Jennie is my oldest and best friend. We met at primary school and she has always been there for me. She'd have definitely told me if Oli was a serial killer.

I think about going into the utility room where no one will hear me but the last thing I want is one of the children going into the larder for Coco Pops and instead finding their childhood hopes and dreams dead under a paste of blood and spelt flour. I'll have to stand guard and talk quietly. She answers after two rings and I launch in before she has a chance to even say hello.

'Jennie,' I say quickly, my hand cupped around my mouth like a 1950s housewife arranging a rendezvous with the milkman, 'Father Christmas is dead in my pantry.'

'THE Father Christmas?' she asks in an awed whisper.

'What the fuck? No, not THE Father [Christmas,]' I say, looking around furtively in case Li[ly] [is] somewhere. I swear that girl pops up w[hen you don't] expect her. She once pretended to go to [bed, but] snuck out and hid under *our* bed to spy on Oli and me. It was unfortunate timing as I'd had a glass of wine and been watching *Poldark* reruns all evening. If we hadn't seen her Squishmallow sticking out from under the vallance it could have been very traumatic for all of us.

'You know Father Christmas isn't real don't you?' I say, a little concerned.

'Oh yes, sorry,' she says. 'It's that amaretto. Start again?'

'Father Christmas, NOT the real one,' I say, just to be clear, 'is in my larder and he is dead. Stabbed to be precise. With one of my Sabatier knives.'

'Oh, Anna!' says Jennie, 'not the set we got in John Lewis? I don't know if you can replace those individually. That's gutting.'

'Sure,' I say, feeling like she's missing the point somewhat, 'but also there's the MURDER?'

'Oh bloody hell yes,' she says. 'Who is it?'

'It's Colin,' I tell her.

'Your sleazy boss Colin?' she asks. 'I'd forgotten he came dressed as Santa. That was a bit weird, wasn't it?'

'It was so he could ask women to sit on his knee,' I tell her with a shudder. I'd managed to avoid his lap, or spending much time with him at all after the repulsive comment he'd made to me in the kitchen about 'my tasty-looking hors d'oeuvres'.

'I'm coming over,' she says. 'I'll bring a spade.'

'Why are you bringing a spade?' I ask, crouching to

15

check that no blood is seeping out from under the door. I could use the draught excluder, I suppose, if it came to it.

'I've always said I'd help you bury a body,' says Jennie, 'should the worst ever happen, and I'm not about to let you down. We pinkie promised, remember?'

I did remember. We were both nine years old and I should never have been allowed to take the class hamster home when I had three cats.

'You don't have to tell me what happened if you don't want to implicate me,' she added, 'although actually please do tell me. But we can worry about that later. The first thing to do is get rid of the evidence.'

'Whoa,' I say, realising what she was implying, 'it wasn't ME! I didn't kill him! Yes, I thought he was a smarmy bastard and I would very happily have done something like let him eat out-of-date olives—' (I had done that last night) '—but I've not suddenly lost it and stabbed him to death in my own larder, for Christ's sake. Not on Christmas Eve. I haven't even decorated the cake yet.'

It occurred to me that she had played the 'I'll help you bury a body' card pretty quickly.

'It wasn't you, was it?' I checked. 'He did make that pass at you at my work do. You were fuming about that.'

'Jesus no!' she says. 'Christ, Anna, you think I stabbed a man in your larder? I was wearing the embroidered heels I got from Russell and Bromley for Tash's wedding. I'm hardly going to risk blood spatter on those.' She paused for a second or two. 'And the morals of course. Murder being wrong and all that. No, if I was going to do it I'd have given him a quick and tidy bash on the back of the head with one of your Kilner jars.'

She's right of course. She bloody loves those shoes – and those Kilner jars are really weighty.

And then I have a worse thought. What if Ben did this? He seems like a sweet enough kid, but you hear of these things with teenagers – research showing that computer games turn them into violent maniacs.

'Oh God, Jennie,' I say, lowering my voice even further, 'what if it was Ben?'

'Ben as in your son Ben?' she asks, sounding highly doubtful.

'Yes!' I say. 'Because of the video games! What if my inability to impose the Mumsnet-recommended screen time restrictions has created a monster?'

'I'm not sure how much murdering there actually is in Minecraft,' says Jennie. 'I think they normally mean the games where you go around assaulting prostitutes and shooting gang members, not the sort where you chat with your geeky friends online about your latest quest and who is going to gather the coins today.'

'You never know,' I say, 'there are *studies*. Do any of us really know our children and what they get up to behind closed doors?'

'Do any of us really want to? Honestly though, Anna, I think you're safe with Ben,' she reassures me. 'Also when you went into the larder were there loads of cereal boxes left open, a dirty PE kit emptied on the floor and the lid off the jam?'

'No,' I say, confused.

'Well a teenager had definitely not been in there recently then. You'd know.'

That made sense. The last time Ben had made a sandwich it had taken me five minutes to get all the cheese off the floor and he hadn't even *had* cheese.

'Okay,' I relent, 'not Ben. And not me or you. What about Oli? Have you ever heard him talk about peas?'

'Peas?' she says. 'Not that I remember. Is that important?'

'Probably not.' I sigh. 'I just don't want to be the wife who thought her husband was a pea salesman and never questioned the freezers.'

'Anna, I think you might be in shock,' says Jennie. 'You're not making a lot of sense. Let's get back on topic. Ooh, did you find my earring?'

'Your earring?'

'Yes the gold hoop, remember?'

'No,' I say, 'I've been a bit preoccupied with finding the corpse so far, sorry. Look, I should probably go. I need to call the police.'

'No wait!' Jennie jumps in quickly. 'Let's not be hasty here, Anna, this could be our *chance.*'

'Our chance for what?' I say. 'To go to jail for concealing a crime?'

'Our chance to be heroes!' she replies. 'We could leave Colin where he is and solve the mystery ourselves! We could be like what's their name from the TV, the one with the great accessories!'

'Gok Wan?' I ask, confused.

'No!' says Jennie. 'Agatha Raisin! She's always doing things like casually breaking into people's houses to solve murders, then she gets away with it by flirting with the local policeman and having such great accessories.'

'I don't remember Agatha Raisin hiding bodies in her larder,' I point out.

'You're not actively hiding it,' she says, 'you don't need to even touch it. You just close the larder door and pretend like you've not seen it yet, while you take stock, maybe interview a few suspects, do a bit of light investigating.'

'Jennie,' I say, 'I am not going to hide a body in my larder indefinitely so that you can play detectives. I have two children in the house, one who still believes in Father Christmas. If she sees him dead in our larder it might take some of the magic out of Christmas for her, and possibly traumatise her for life.'

'Hmm yes okay, there is that,' she concedes.

'Anyway,' I add, 'I already touched the body.'

'Whoa!' she says. 'What?! Everyone knows you don't touch the body! Why did you do that? What if the police think it was you? I'll get the spade. Don't touch anything else.'

'Don't get the spade! It's fine, I had to check he was dead, but I did it carefully and didn't disturb the footprint.'

'Wait, there's a footprint? That's so cool! Maybe we can test it and it will turn out the footprint is red paint and then we'll discover an upturned can of paint in the murderer's shed and solve the crime! Hurrah!'

'It's not red paint,' I say, 'it's spelt flour.'

'The murderer is from the bakery cult at the market? That's a plot twist!'

'No, the flour fell off the shelf in the struggle and there's spelt flour everywhere. The footprint's in that.'

'You should take a picture,' Jennie says, 'and measurements. We'll need those for eliminating suspects.'

'We're not Rosemary and Thyme, Jennie. I'm calling the police in a minute and they will deal with it.'

'A footprint though, Anna!' says Jennie. 'It's a literal SIGN! I'm googling spelt. Maybe it reacts with something.'

I think about the moment of excitement I had spotting the footprint and waver momentarily, but no, obviously I can't investigate this myself. As fun as it might be to solve a murder, and as appalled as Pamela is going to be at the thought of Christmas at a crime scene, I have to call the police.

I make a mental checklist in my head:

Call the police.

Have dead Santa removed from precious larder.

Gather holly.

Create magical Christmas for all.

I add 'measure footprint' under 'call the police'. I tell myself that's me being useful. The police might thank me for it if they forget to bring a ruler.

'We're not solving the crime, Jennie,' I say. 'I have holly to gather and Christmas magic to create and I don't want Lily to ever know Santa died in her own home.'

'Okay, okay, that's fair,' she says, 'but at least take a minute. I really think you're in shock and you need a bit of fresh air or a brandy or something. You need to take stock.'

The thought of brandy makes me retch but maybe the fresh air isn't a bad idea. Take stock. Okay, I could take stock. I *need* to take stock, at least until I make sure none of my family are Father Christmas killers. That makes sense. I can do that. I need to get everyone up and outside, away from the festive corpse. We'll go for a walk and gather holly and I can clear my head. I'll talk to Oli and if he's not acting murdery we'll call the police and sort everything out, and Christmas won't be ruined and my tablescapes will come together and it will all be fine.

'Excellent,' says Jennie when I explain the plan. 'Keep in touch. I can be your woman on the outside.'

'The outside of what?' I ask. 'I'm not in prison.'

Not yet anyway.

CHAPTER 3

Okay then, get everyone up and out of the house. That sounded doable when it was just a *thought*, but I'm not sure how achievable it is realistically. Lily will be fine if I dangle the promise of some kind of treat, but I'm less convinced about Ben. Normally I'd leave well alone until he dragged himself downstairs for six rounds of toast. He's definitely going to be suspicious.

I've always found it funny that we spend so long when our kids are little trying to get them to go to sleep longer, spending our days in a half-zombie state from being woken at 5 a.m. to watch the same three favourite episodes of *Paw Patrol*, and then when they finally start sleeping in, so many parents seem desperate to wake them up again.

Sheila at work is always complaining about her boys sleeping in until midday whenever they don't have school. She likes to drag them out of bed at 9 a.m. on weekends and during the holidays to do ghastly things like play team sports or trim the hedges. Seriously, Sheila, what are you trying to prove? Why would you want them hanging around all morning when you could be having a nice quiet coffee in the garden with the supplements and a crumpet?

I can't wait until Lily starts sleeping in. I am going to bloody love finally getting to take the weekend mornings at my own pace. I'll probably start listening to Radio 3 and grinding my own coffee beans. I might even take up watercolours and take my freshly ground coffee down to my studio to capture the morning light. I don't have a studio, mind, and more likely I'll take a mug of Kenco Millicano back to bed with me and scroll Instagram until I am full enough of self-loathing to get up and go to Tesco, but you never know. I could have an as-yet-undiscovered artistic side, just waiting to be free of the shackles of motherhood.

The cats rub against my legs and meow, shaking me out of my fantasy and back into the real world. The world where Father Christmas is in my larder with one of my Sabatier knives in him. My poor knife.

I wonder if maybe it wouldn't be easier to call the police right now and be done with it, but then I picture them trampling through the house and Lily coming downstairs and seeing dead Father Christmas and I can't bear it. I have to get them out of the house. That's the most important thing. I have to protect them. I cannot let this ruin Christmas. I fill one of the abandoned coffee mugs with water and take two paracetamol and then two ibuprofen as well for good measure. I have to start thinking clearly.

First things first, I rummage around in the paper recycling, find a flyer for gutter cleaning (another thing to add to the mental list of 'jobs I haven't done that mean I'm failing as an adult human') and scrawl a note on the back.

Don't go in here. Cat has been sick.

I tape it to the larder door. That should put everyone off for now. If there's even a hint that they might be asked to clean something up they will all steer well clear. I casually lean the mop against the door to ram home the point.

The noise of the water has stopped so Oli must be out of the shower. That's good. I head upstairs and go for the easy target first.

'Lily!' I say, wide-eyed and in a weird sing-song voice that makes me look and sound like a woman most definitely on the edge. 'Time to get dressed! We're going for festive Frappuccinos!' I settled on Starbucks as the one thing that might appeal enough to both of them to make this work.

'Cool!' says Lily, almost looking up from the iPad. 'Can I bring the iPad?'

'Yep yep!' I chirp back. 'Bring anything you like! Just get dressed!'

She gets out of bed, still tapping at the screen, and props it up on her dressing table where she can keep an eye on things while she gets her clothes on. One down.

I stop at Ben's door. I can't hear snoring anymore, so I give a tentative knock. 'Ben?' I say, pushing the door gently open. Ben is up, shoving laundry into his basket in the corner of the room. He jumps and looks almost as guilty as the time I walked in on him doing something we've all silently agreed never to speak about.

'Oh you're up!' I say. 'Excellent! We're going to Starbucks.' I look again and take in the scene more clearly. 'Wait, you're up? And sorting laundry? Is this some sort of Christmas miracle?'

He scowls at me. 'Don't take the piss, Mum, I'm tidying up. You know, ready for Christmas, like you keep banging on about.'

I narrow my eyes but I don't have time to question him. 'Thank you, now get dressed – we're going out.' I leave the room and shut the door before he has time to protest. Two down.

'Where's my coffee?' asks Oli when I go into our bedroom. He's out of the shower and dressed, sitting on the bed putting on his socks. He's wearing jeans and the black roll-neck I got him a couple of birthdays ago and he looks pretty dishy. I have words with myself for the use of 'dishy', which is what my mum uses to describe Monty Don. 'There's just something about the way he handles the soil,' she likes to say.

'I thought we could all go out for coffee instead,' I say. 'To Starbucks. As a treat.' He looks confused. 'For Christmas,' I add.

'Go out?' he says. 'But we have the house to clean up, Anna. Remember the twenty-six hours and whatever it was until everyone gets here? And all the jobs and the cake decorating? I was going to get the Vax out.'

'Oh there's loads of time!' I say, in a high-pitched voice. 'And the most important thing about Christmas is that we all spend lovely precious family time together!' Of course what I really think is how nice that he was going to clean the carpets. I wonder if the police will approve of vaxxing a crime scene?

'In Starbucks?' he says.

'They have a tree up,' I say, as though that settles it.

'Was this the kids' idea?' he asks, clearly bemused as to why I've not leapt on the comment about the Vax.

'It's my idea,' I say. 'I want to do something nice together before everyone gets here and your mother *starts.*'

'Starbucks it is then,' says Oli. He stands up and rubs his hands together, like we've decided to sail the world and he has to go and organise supplies and hoist important things on the boat. 'I'll wake up Ben.'

'Oh he's already awake,' I say. 'He was sorting laundry.'

'Sorting laundry?' says Oli. 'Are you sure?'

'Definitely,' I say. 'He had a big armful of it when I went in. He was looking a bit suspicious if I'm honest. But he's up and that's the main thing, so let's not question it.'

It takes me about ten minutes to round everybody up and get them into shoes and coats. There's a tense moment where Ben heads to the larder muttering something about Pop-Tarts, but I make promises about toasties and muffins and placate him enough to get him into the car. Starbucks isn't far, so it's only five minutes later that we pull into the car park and we all trek inside.

Now we're all here and out of the house I'm not entirely sure what happens next. We can't stay here indefinitely, so I need a plan. I'm going to have to talk to Oli, but I don't know how to manage it with the kids here. Perhaps I should have done this at home? *The corpse though, Anna, you're protecting the children from the corpse.*

26

'You two go up and have a look,' I say to the children, 'decide what you want, and Dad and I will find a table.' I shoo them towards the counter and scuttle off to the table in the farthest corner. Oli makes to go with them but I grab his sleeve.

'I want to look at the sandwiches,' he protests, but I drag him with me.

'I need to talk to you,' I whisper.

'What's the matter, Anna?' he says. 'You've been acting really weird. All this family time stuff – what's going on?'

I'm a bit affronted that he thinks it so unlikely that I would want to spend quality time with my family on Christmas Eve, but I know I'm not going to get long on my own with him so I let it go.

'Something has happened,' I say, 'at home.'

'What's happened?' he asks.

'There's no nice way to say this,' I say, 'but there's a body in the larder.'

'Oh no,' says Oli, 'which one is it?'

I don't know what to say. Which one? How many *are* there?! I bloody knew it. I'm the pea salesman's wife, aren't I? They say it's always the quiet ones but you never really imagine it will happen to you. He's being so cool about the whole thing too, like it was only ever a matter of time, and now I've discovered his secret he can progress to stage two – kill off the wife. He's probably got a kill kit in the boot. Thank God we're in Starbucks; maybe I can get a message to Jennie if I pretend to go to the toilet. I blame myself of course, if only I hadn't insisted on that freezer for the garage.

27

'I did think Tommy was looking a bit iffy yesterday,' he says. 'He left half of his dinner.'

Wait, what?

'Tommy?' I say. 'What's he got to do with anything?'

'Is it Tuppence then?' he asks. 'Shame. She was my favourite. Don't tell Tommy mind.'

I realise what's happening. He thinks one of the cats has died. I feel a sense of relief, mixed with guilt that I was so quick to accept the notion of my husband as a serial-killing pea salesman.

'Oh the cats!' I say.

'Of course the cats,' he says. 'What did you think I meant?'

'Oh nothing!' I say, laughing quickly in what I hope is a very casual and relaxed sort of way. 'Ha-ha! Definitely nothing at all! It's not even a big enough freezer!'

He really does look confused now. I lean in closer to him.

'It's not a cat,' I say. 'It's Colin.'

'Colin?' he says. 'As in your boss Colin?'

'Yes,' I say. 'And he's dead.'

He exhales loudly and leans back in his chair. 'Shit, good shout getting the kids out while the ambulance comes. Heart attack was it? I wonder what he was doing in the larder though.'

'It wasn't a heart attack,' I say. 'He's been murdered.'

He runs his hands over his face and through his hair. 'Fuck me, Anna,' he says, and then, more quietly as he leans back in, 'You killed Colin?'

'What the fuck? No!' I hiss. 'I haven't killed him!'

Why does everyone keep assuming I killed him? Am I giving off serial killer vibes? Do people look at me and think, *Ah yes, there's a woman who has it in her to take a life for sure.* I haven't even told Oli any details and yet his first thought is that I'm a murderer? Really, there should be a lot more trust than this between a husband and wife.

'I'll get an iced white mocha with peppermint syrup, oat milk, an extra shot and foam,' says Ben, slumping down into a chair and getting out his phone. 'And a bacon roll,' he adds.

'I'm not ordering that,' I say. 'I'll never remember it, and since when do you have oat milk?'

'Since *forever*,' he says, rolling his eyes at me. 'Don't you even *know* about the dairy industry?' Then he mutters what sounds like 'baby boomers' under his breath.

'Of course I *know* about the dairy industry,' I say. I mean I know *of* the dairy industry, so that's basically the same. 'I've been having oat milk for years,' I remind him. I don't add that that's more to do with my wind situation than animal welfare, although if you technically count Oli as an animal it could be his welfare, as he has to share a bed with me.

'And I am definitely not a baby boomer,' I say. 'Baby boomer isn't some generic term for anyone you consider to be old. If I was a baby boomer we'd live in a much bigger house and have pensions we could actually live on. And where's your sister?'

'She's trying to get that dog to do tricks,' he says, nodding over to where Lily is waving her hands about in front of an excited-looking spaniel. 'It's called Frank.'

Frank's owner looks like they might rather Frank wasn't being wound up by an eager seven-year-old, so

I go over to stage an intervention. Lily is shouting 'sit'. Frank is already sitting.

'Look, Mum!' she says as I approach. 'I told you I was good at dog training! Can we get a dog please? I promise I will take it out for all of its walks.' I think about Tommy and Tuppence and how often Lily feeds them or changes the litter tray or takes them to the vets. Okay, perhaps the vets one is a bit harsh as she's seven, but the other things. I would say at a rough estimate that she has fed them approximately zero times in the last six months.

'No, we cannot get a dog,' I say, my body giving an involuntary shudder at the thought. I still remember all too vividly the week we looked after my brother Toby's labradoodle, Bianca.

'She'll be fine!' Toby had said. 'She'll be super chill as soon as she's had a good look around!' He and Sav had been positively chuckling as they scampered out the door and off on their Ibiza holiday. Super chill my arse. The only time she was chill was for about two hours after her period of induced vomiting at the vets, after she'd eaten an entire carrot cake. Not a *slice* – an entire cake. With frosting.

The worst bit was when the vet emerged into the waiting room with what was clearly a pair of my pants in a clear plastic bag. He made a loud comment about how it had probably been a good thing that she'd eaten the carrot cake, and perhaps I shouldn't leave my pants on the floor, and everyone in the waiting room had turned and looked at me. A woman with a pug, who was a painful example of pets looking like their owners, had the audacity to tut. I'd tried to pretend that she must have got them out of the ironing basket but no one was buying it.

'Did you decide what you want?' I ask Lily.

'Not yet,' she says. 'I've been busy with Frank.'

Frank's owner gives a tight smile and I smile back in a way that I hope conveys a sense of adult camaraderie in the face of children and animals. My reflection in the glass of the cake display is more 'deranged asylum escapee'.

'Well choose now,' I say, 'and I'll send Ben over with the money.'

I go back to the table, get my bank card out of my wallet and hand it to Ben. 'You go and get whatever you and Lily want,' I say. 'Just tap the card.'

'Can I get a motorbike?' he asks, his voice dripping with teenage sarcasm.

'You'll be lucky if they get your ridiculous drink right,' I say, 'but sure, if they sell motorbikes, you go for it.'

Once he's gone I turn back to Oli. 'I did not kill Colin,' I reiterate, 'but somebody did. He's been stabbed with one of the Sabatiers.'

'Fucking hell,' he says. 'Stabbed?'

'Yep, in the stomach,' I explain. 'It's a right mess. There's blood and flour everywhere.'

There's a cough from the next table. I look up and see an elderly couple staring at us. They each have a black coffee and have cut a single croissant neatly in half. How depressing. Why on earth would you come to Starbucks and have black coffee? Surely you could do that at home, or at Morrisons café at least. Half the price, splash out on a croissant each?

'We're rehearsing for a play,' I say and stare at them until they have the decency to look away.

I look back at Oli and he's sitting with his head in his hand. I imagine him reflecting on the tragedy of death, perhaps wondering if he should review our life insurance policies, but I realise he's on his phone.

'Are you calling the police?' I ask.

He looks guilty and puts his phone on the table. I sneak a look and see the John Lewis website.

'You can't buy individual replacements,' he mutters sadly. 'Wait, have you *not* called the police?'

'Not yet,' I admit. It's my turn to look guilty now. 'I panicked. He's dressed as Father Christmas and I didn't want Lily to find out and then Jennie started talking about Agatha Raisin and I didn't know what to do.'

'Anna, come on, you've got to call the police. What were you thinking? You can't leave him there for fuck's sake. And where the hell does Jennie come into this?'

'I called her,' I say, 'from the kitchen.' He's looking at me in a way that makes me feel like I'm Lily's age. 'I was PANICKING,' I remind him.

'Right, well,' says Oli, 'you've panicked us all the way to Starbucks now, so when the police arrive and we say we casually left a dead body in the house to pop out for Frappuccinos that's going to look completely fine and we're definitely not going to seem suspicious at all. Seriously, what the fuck, Anna?'

'I'm very sorry for wanting to remove our children from the scene of a crime,' I say, in a voice that says I am not at all sorry and how could Oli be so callous as to not be thinking of the welfare of our precious children?

'I'm sorry,' he says, 'you're right. Shit. Are *you* okay? When did you find him?'

'I went into the larder for bin bags and coffee,' I say, 'and there he was, sort of slumped there, covered in blood.'

'And he's definitely dead? He's not just hungover and sleeping it off?'

'Sleeping it off? With a very expensive knife in his stomach, sat in a pool of blood? No, he's not *sleeping it off*.'

'Okay, okay.' Oli holds his hands up in mock surrender. 'Not that then.'

'He's definitely dead,' I say, remembering his cold skin under my fingers. 'I did check; I didn't just leave him there to slowly bleed out.'

'Shit,' says Oli again. 'You should have come and got me, Anna! You shouldn't have been doing that by yourself.'

'I was panicking remember? And also I wasn't sure if maybe you'd done it?' I let the thought settle. 'It wasn't you, was it, Oli? Because you should tell me if it is, if you've got a good reason I mean, and you're not a maniac pea salesman.'

'It wasn't me, Anna,' he says seriously. 'You know how much I love those knives. And if I was going to do it I'd hardly do it in our own home. I'd lure him somewhere quiet, with a fake telegram, or make it one of those elaborate slow poisonings, inject his eggs or something. Are telegrams a thing anymore?'

'The queen sends them, doesn't she?' I say. 'For birthdays?'

'Not anymore,' he points out.

'The king then – you know what I mean. So they must be a thing, unless it's just the royal family?'

He reaches for his phone, probably to google telegrams, and then clearly remembers about Colin and puts it back down. 'Who the fuck would want to stab Colin? I mean plenty of people probably – the guy's a dick, *was* a dick rather – but still.'

'So what now?' I ask.

'We call the police,' he says, 'but we try to keep the kids out of it. You stay here with them and I'll sort it out.'

'I found the body though, Oli, surely they're going to want to speak to me? It's going to have to be me who talks to them.'

Before we can make a plan, Ben and Lily arrive back at the table. Before anyone can say anything I stand up. The time has come to be decisive.

'Right,' I say, 'you guys hang out here for a bit. I've just remembered something very important I have to do with some cranberries and a roll of sausage meat.' Oli looks like he might be going to interrupt so I press on quickly. 'I'll take the car home and when you're done here perhaps you could do the holly foraging for me?'

Groans from my precious offspring.

'Where am I meant to forage holly from on Christmas Eve?' protests Oli as I head to the door.

'Dawn and Steve are in Swansea with their daughter for Christmas,' I call over my shoulder. 'There's a bush in their front garden!'

Back in the car I text Oli. 'Keep them out until I send

you the all clear,' I type. 'I saw Dawn cutting mistletoe out of the tree in the garden of number 17 on Tuesday evening. In the dark. So she's hardly in a position to judge.'

It's not theft that worries me though, it's murder. I hit send on the message to Oli and then I call the police.

CHAPTER 4

I pull up in the drive at home having spoken to the police and been told to sit tight, that someone is on their way. I sit in the car for a minute. I feel suddenly scared. When I found Colin this morning I was shocked, surprised, upset . . . but not scared. It's only now that it's beginning to hit home.

Somebody murdered my boss last night. In my home. Somebody I know, one of my friends, stabbed a man to death right there, under all our noses, and we have no idea who or why or whether or not they might come back. Maybe they didn't even leave? Maybe they are right now hiding out in the downstairs toilet or holed up in the shed?

I think about sitting in the car until the police arrive and can search the house, but my mind keeps going back to the footprint and that little buzz of excitement I got taking the picture of it. I know I can't actually solve the murder – this isn't a cosy crime novel – but is there any harm in having a quick look around before the police get here?

I pick up my phone from the passenger seat and see I have a missed call from Jennie and a string of messages, progressing quickly from 'how's it going?' to a more panicked 'have they murdered you too?!'

I call her back and she answers straight away.

'Oh thank God!' she cries. 'I thought they'd got you!'

'No,' I say, 'I'm still here. I made everyone get up and go to Starbucks with me.'

'Hardly the time for a latte, is it?' she says. 'Or were you looking for clues?'

'I don't know what I was doing honestly, Jen,' I admit, 'freaking out I think, but I couldn't bear the thought of Ben and Lily in the house with a dead body. I had to get everyone away from it before I did anything else.'

'Are you still there now?' she asks.

'They are,' I say, 'but I've just got back home. The police are on their way.'

'Oh,' she says, sounding disappointed, 'I guess you did have to call them. Do you want me to come over for moral support?' she asks, brightening.

'I'm okay thanks,' I say, 'but you could help me with something else.'

'Anything!' she says. 'Background checks on the guests? Dark web shit? Not that I know how you see the dark web. Is it a separate web for creeps? How do you get to it?'

'I've no idea,' I say, 'but I don't need you to find out, I just need you to stay on the phone. I'm too scared to go inside on my own, so you can keep me company while I check the downstairs toilet. If the phone goes dead, call the police.' I think about it. 'Actually, no need to do that I suppose as they're on their way. Maybe just come and tell them?'

'Got it,' says Jennie. 'I'll stay on the phone while you investigate. Let me get a pen.'

'A pen?' I ask.

'For notes!' she says. 'I've taken all the motivational quotes down from the corkboard in the study and I'm making a murder board. I didn't have any red string but I found some garden twine in the shed. It's a bit damp but you can't smell it unless you're close up.'

'Christ, Jennie,' I say, 'a murder board?! You're not Poirot.'

'Of course I'm not Poirot! He doesn't need a murder board, he just arranges the facts neatly in his brain and waits for the solution to come to him while he sips at a *sirop de banane*. I'm not that smart. Hence the board. Come on, Anna, you know how hard this Christmas is for me. I need this. Let me be distracted, please.'

I can see I'm going to have to let the murder board go because Jennie is right – I do know how hard this Christmas is for her. It's her second Christmas since she and her husband Michael split up, which means this year it's Michael's turn to have the children. He picked them up yesterday afternoon and took them up to his parents' in Keswick. They're not coming back until the 28th.

Jennie is being stoic about it but she's going to be lost without them; of course she is. Matty and Jake are six and nine and such balls of energy, you miss them when they leave a room for five minutes, let alone the house for five days. Christmas is chaos with them.

I invited Jennie to come and stay with us instead but she snorted and called Oli's mum a 'stuck-up cunt who looks like she's got a sprig of holly up her fanny' so I took that as a no. I don't blame her. Pamela has very strong feelings about divorce. One of her good friends divorced about twenty years ago after she discovered her husband had been shagging his secretary (I mean come on, man, use your imagination), and she still refers to her as 'Irene who *got the divorce*' in a stage whisper whenever she talks about her.

'Okay fine,' I concede, 'but could we call it something else? Something less murdery?'

'We *could*, but it is a murder. I'm just being factual when you think about it, and it's nicer than "brutal stabbing board" or "creepy bastard gets his comeuppance board".'

'Jeez, Jennie, he was a bit handsy for sure, but comeuppance is a bit strong.'

'Women don't stand for it anymore, remember, Anna? Look at Rolf Harris. He's dead now.'

'I think Rolf Harris had cancer?'

'Well there you go then. Anyway, are you inside yet?'

I'm not inside; I'm still in the car. I'm building up to it. I thought the time away from the house might make everything feel better but being in the real world has only made the whole situation feel more unreal. My boss Colin is dead in my larder and we don't know who did it.

'I'm going to check the garage first,' I say, clenching and unclenching my fists a few times before getting out of the car and locking it behind me.

'The garage?' asks Jennie. 'Do you think anyone is in there? Isn't it locked?'

'Yes,' I say, 'but, well, I don't know. I thought it was worth checking. Someone might have got in somehow.'

This is a lie. It seems highly unlikely to me that a murderer would flee the scene of the crime only to seek refuge in our garage. You'd have to be desperate to think that your only option was to jam yourself in between the kids' bikes and scooters, the countless half-empty tins of paint and all of the cardboard boxes that were too big for the recycling.

It's humbling to be honest, going into our garage. You see the giant box that your last vacuum cleaner came in, which you put there just until you could take it to the tip, and then you realise that you got the vacuum cleaner seven years ago and you feel your life slipping away from you a bit. It can't be just me who has felt a creeping sense of mortality since turning forty? A couple of weeks ago I was looking at the brochure for the arts centre near us and quite fancied learning watercolours (for the post-motherhood studio fantasy obviously), but I swear a little voice in my head said, *No point starting now, Anna, you'll be dead soon.* I mean seriously, brain? Way to make a woman feel good about herself.

I wrestle with the garage lock and feel a jolt of guilt. It's been playing up for months now and I haven't done anything about it. Every time I unlock it I tell myself to organise a locksmith and every time I get back into the house I've already forgotten. It's one of life's fun little ways of reminding me how shit I am.

I roll the door up and take a look around. There's

no one here, but then I never expected to find anyone. I'm not here for that. I shove a bag of compost to one side, brace myself and open the emergency batch-cooking freezer.

No heads.

I have a rummage, just to make sure, but it's only grim-looking bags full of what the labels assure me is bolognese. Made in 2018. There aren't even any peas. I didn't expect to find anything, but it's a relief nonetheless.

'Anna! Anna!' I realise Jennie is shouting at me from where I put my phone down on top of a portable barbecue. (Why? We never even have a regular static barbecue, why would I think that we'd suddenly want to barbecue things if only we could take our barbecue somewhere in the car first, to the middle of nowhere, without the benefit of being able to finish off suspect sausages in the oven?)

'Oh sorry,' I say, picking the phone back up. 'I'm here. You were on the barbecue.'

'Charming,' she says. 'I thought I was here to support you? Have you found anything?'

'No, no heads, no peas, nothing.'

'You didn't go into the garage to check the freezer, did you?' she asks suspiciously. 'We talked about this – Oli's not a serial killer. I bet he'll have ordered a Frappuccino at Starbucks. Serial killers don't drink Frappuccinos.'

She's right. I need to get a grip or the police are going to arrive and find me standing over a freezer of what claims to be bolognese but could easily be chopped and cooked human offal. I lock up the garage (note to

41

self: remember lock) and head for the front door of the house.

I take some momentary comfort from the sight of everyone's wellies, upturned on the welly rack tucked under a corner of the porch. I try to ignore the fact that mine look positively dusty. Once this is over with, I will definitely make more of an effort to go on wholesome walks in the countryside to appreciate nature and live in the moment. I just wish mindfulness didn't seem to involve so much *stretching* and getting up at the bloody crack of dawn. It's really too depressing in the winter to get up an hour before everyone else just to write a sodding gratitude journal when all you want is to be grateful to be still in bed. I know what it will say from now on though – '*grateful today to not find anyone stabbed to death in the house*'.

I unlock the front door and step inside, through the hallway, into the living room. Everything is silent, even Jennie, which makes a change. All of the mess is still there of course, which makes my chest tighten with anxiety, but otherwise everything looks normal.

'What should I do first?' I ask Jennie. 'The police are on their way so I don't have much time. I kind of want to look for clues but what if someone is still in the house? I don't want them to jump out and stab me too.'

'True,' she says, 'you can't afford to lose another knife from that set. Maybe just have a quick whizz-round to check obvious hiding places, but keep your eyes peeled too for stray buttons or the charred remains of a last will and testament in a fireplace.'

'I don't think clues are that obvious in real life,' I

42

say, 'and the will is unlikely as I don't have any real fires. I can see if anyone has left anything on top of the fake electric wood burner but doubt it will be charred.'

'Shame,' says Jennie, 'but you never know. Just be *alert*.'

I start with the downstairs toilet. I don't know why I'm so fixated on the downstairs toilet. I guess it's the practicality? If I was going to hide out somewhere then I'd definitely want there to be a toilet. It's always my first thought watching anything on TV where people get trapped somewhere. Where do they pee?

The downstairs toilet is empty. I check the obvious places in the living room – behind the sofa and the curtains – and give the dining room a cursory sweep. Nothing. There's nowhere to hide in the kitchen other than the larder and we know what's in there.

'Nothing downstairs,' I report. 'No murderers, no charred wills or blackmail letters or anything useful like that. I'm going outside.'

I unlock the back door. There's an ashtray on the patio table with a few cigarette butts, but not many people we know are smokers nowadays. I take a picture, but I'm not sure there's anything incriminating. I'd been thinking of the shed but I can see from here that the padlock is still on the door. I even slip some trainers on and traipse across the muddy lawn to check the back gate. It's shut and the bolt is drawn, nothing to see here. Definitely not worth getting my trainers mucky for.

'What about that footprint in the larder?' says Jennie.

'You could get another look at that before the police arrive. Can you measure it?'

'I don't know if I have a ruler,' I say. I must have a ruler surely? Ben will have one in his school bag I expect. I find it in the cupboard under the stairs, but all it contains are a load of crumpled bits of paper and a lunchbox that must have been there since the end of term. I leave it where it is so as not to contaminate the crime scene. I have better luck with Lily's bag, where I find a neatly organised Hello Kitty pencil tin complete with a pink plastic six-inch ruler. It feels a bit grubby to be about to use it to measure the footprint of a Santa killer, but I'll give it a rub-down with Dettol afterwards. She'll never know.

'I've got a ruler,' I tell Jennie. 'I'm going back in.'

When I open the door it's worse than I remember – a distinct metallic smell from the blood and an eerie silence that feels palpable. I move quickly, not wanting to be in here any longer than I have to be.

'Seven inches long and four inches at the widest part,' I tell Jennie, imagining her writing it down and pinning it to the murder board. 'I've not got the whole length though, so I'm not sure how long the full print would be. I'll send you a picture.'

'Ace,' she says, 'now check his pockets.'

'What the fuck? No, I'm not checking his pockets! Don't be ridiculous! I'm not touching him.'

'Come on, Anna, if we're going to figure out who did this then we've got to be prepared to make ourselves uncomfortable.'

'That's easy for you to say,' I point out. 'I'm the one here, surrounded by DEATH. And I don't WANT to

44

figure it out, I want for this to never have happened and to be arranging my holly into a casually chic table centrepiece. This might seem like light entertainment for you but it's scary in person.'

'No need to be dramatic,' she says. 'I'm not asking you to perform the autopsy; I'm just saying have a quick look in the man's pockets. Put rubber gloves on if it makes you feel better.'

'No amount of rubber gloves is going to make me feel better about this. And what on earth would the police think if they find me bending over Colin's body in a pair of rubber gloves with one hand rummaging in his groin? I'd never be allowed back on the PTA if that got out.'

'Even better,' says Jennie, 'you're obsessed with the stupid PTA. You need to be barred, honestly, for your own sanity. The police aren't going to find you anyway. They'll have to knock on the door, and when they do, take off the gloves, shut the larder and pretend to look upset.'

'I AM upset, Jennie, I don't have to pretend,' I say. 'Not about Colin admittedly, but I don't think most people who come across a body in their own kitchen would be unscathed.'

'Fine, fine, I hear you, but get the gloves. You know you want to.'

I sigh and get a clean pair of pink rubber gloves out from under the kitchen sink, because Jennie is right of course – I do want to. Yes it's horrific and a man has lost his life et cetera, et cetera but you don't grow up reading mystery stories every night without feeling a tingle of excitement at the prospect of a crime to solve. The hours Jennie and I spent as kids outside, roaming around the garages and the playground and behind the SPAR, desperate to stumble upon a ring of smugglers. My ten-year-old self would never forgive me for not at least having a quick look at the body.

Gloves on, I put my phone on speaker, prop it against a tin of spaghetti hoops and recreate the lean I did earlier to check his pulse, careful not to disturb anything on the floor. I can just about reach him, but not enough to reach his pockets.

'Hang on,' I say to Jennie, 'I can't reach. I need something to help.' Back in the kitchen I look through the utensils drawer and find some barbecue tongs (seriously, who am I kidding with this barbecue thing?) and take them back to the larder.

'Okay,' I say, 'I have tongs. I'm going in.'

'Atta girl,' says Jennie, 'I knew you wouldn't let me down. Tell me what you've got.'

I prod around his torso first. I'm assuming he's wearing the Father Christmas suit over his original clothes – please God don't let him be going commando – so he may have shirt or jacket pockets. I run the tongs over his body, the least sexy thing anyone has ever done, but I can't feel anything. I move down to the trouser pockets.

'I can't find anything,' I say. 'I don't think he's carrying anything? Oh wait, hang on, this pocket has keys in it.'

'Okay,' says Jennie, 'that makes sense. But what about a phone?'

'There's no phone here,' I say, 'not unless it's in a back pocket and I can't move him. Wait, there's

46

something in his left pocket, let me see if I can fish it out. I've got it. Hang on.' I stand upright and take a scrap of paper from the grip of the tongs.

'What is it?' says Jennie, but before I have a chance to look at it I hear the doorbell ring and shove the paper into my pocket.

CHAPTER 5

I'm not sure what I expected when I was told a team would be on their way, but it definitely wasn't the practically pubescent duo that are currently standing on my doorstep.

'Mrs Johnson?' says the man, if you can call someone who doesn't look like they can grow a beard a man. 'I'm Detective Sergeant Bacon.'

I laugh. Detective Sergeant Bacon does not.

'Oh right,' I say, 'I see.'

'This is Police Constable Simons,' he says, turning towards the young woman standing next to him, her eyes gleaming with excitement. 'We understand there has been an incident?'

'Yes,' I say, stepping back into the hallway, 'you'd better come in.'

They both step into the house. PC Simons smiles at me. 'It's my first murder,' she whispers.

'That enough, Simons,' says Bacon. 'Can you show us the body please, Mrs Johnson?'

I point them through to the kitchen and as they go ahead I quickly drop the rubber gloves I've been holding behind my back into the plant pot in the hall. I take them both to the larder and open the door. 'I didn't touch anything,' I say quickly.

'You haven't touched the body at all?' asks Bacon.

'Oh well yes,' I admit, 'I touched the *body*, but only to check he was dead. And I did a careful lean so as not to disturb . . .' I'm about to say 'the footprint', but as I do, Detective Sergeant Bacon steps into the larder, standing right on top of it, seemingly oblivious.

'He's been stabbed,' says Simons proudly. She holds her hands behind her back, chin held high.

'I can see that thank you, Simons,' says Bacon. He pivots on the spot, taking in the scene, obliterating the footprint as he does. I should probably tell him about it, show him my measurements and photograph, but I don't want him to know I didn't immediately call the police or to think I've been tampering with evidence so I keep quiet.

'Well this all seems fairly straightforward,' says Bacon, taking a phone-sized gadget from his pocket and tapping at the screen. I'm a bit disappointed that he doesn't have a little police notebook and a pencil. I think I might feel more reassured by a pencil. As it is he could be on TikTok for all I know.

'We'll notify the coroner and they'll come and collect the body,' he says, 'then we'll need to take a statement from you and process the scene. It shouldn't take long.' He looks at his watch and lowers his voice slightly. 'What time did you say the Christmas drinks were, Simons?'

'At 2 p.m., sir,' she says. So enthusiastic is she that I think for a moment that she might salute or possibly click her heels together. 'And the food's coming out at 2.30 p.m.'

'Right, well,' he says, looking back at me, 'we'll get out of your hair as quickly as possible, let you get back to your Christmas preparations.'

I'm surprised. I'd imagined spools of police tape being unravelled and us having to fall on the mercy of my brother for Christmas. He'd have been horrified of course. They'll be coming for lunch tomorrow but he and Sav like spending as much of Christmas as possible with just the two of them and the dog. As much as he loves his niece and nephew, they don't really fit with their Christmas aesthetic. Last year they bought matching designer Christmas pyjamas from Selfridges, just to wear on Christmas Eve.

'Nice tree jammies,' I'd said, when he'd sent me a selfie.

'They're Eberjey,' he'd replied, as if I knew what that meant, which I didn't. 'It's *winterpine forest stretch jersey* thank you.' Winterpine forest. I love my brother but he can be a tad pretentious.

Bacon is taking pictures now, with the energy of a teenage boy who's putting in the bare minimum on his GCSE photography homework, just so that he can make out like he 'did his best' when the teacher questions the shocking lack of effort.

'Are you sure you don't need us to move out of the house so you can get a team in or something?' I ask. 'Forensics, that sort of thing?'

'How about you leave the police work to the experts,' he says, slipping a little in the blood as he reaches down to feel in Colin's pockets. He grabs a shelf to steady himself and knocks two onions into Colin's lap.

After an inelegant ransacking of the body, Bacon seems satisfied that there's nothing else to be found. He instructs Simons to go and phone the coroner and taps some more on his device. Please let it be useful insights and not Candy Crush.

'He doesn't have a phone on him,' he says. 'You haven't come across it anywhere else in the house?'

'No,' I answer, truthfully. 'I'll keep an eye out though, and of course let you know straight away if I do.' This is less truthful. My faith in DS Bacon's detective abilities is not high.

Simons comes back into the kitchen and tells us that the coroner is on her way. Bacon looks at his watch. 'Right, well it's nearly 11 a.m., so let's get your statement while we wait for the coroner and with any luck we can get back to the station and have the paperwork sorted by 2 p.m.'

'For the Christmas drinks?' I ask sarcastically. 'Are you sure the murder isn't a bit more important?'

'Oh of course,' says Bacon, pulling himself up to his very tallest, 'I can assure you, madam, that we are taking this very seriously. Very seriously indeed.'

'It's the pies though,' interjects Simons. Bacon shoots her a look.

'The pies?'

'Oh yes,' says Simons, oblivious to Bacon's furrowed brow. If they were sitting at a table she'd be getting a sharp kick in the ankle right about now. 'The inspector makes these Christmas pies, with turkey and cranberry . . .'

51

'What Simons means to say,' interrupts Bacon, 'is that we'll be doing everything we can to discover the culprit, taking into account that it is Christmas. We don't want to interrupt your festivities any more than we have to.'

'How very considerate of you,' I say. Any remaining faith I had in Bacon is now completely gone, as it's clear that the inspector's pies are the priority of the day. My phone rings. It's Oli.

'It's my husband,' I say. 'Do you mind if I get it?'

'Go ahead,' says Bacon. 'We'll finish up here and if you could wait in the living room we'll come and take a statement from you shortly.'

I answer as I walk into the living room, pulling the door closed behind me so I won't be overheard.

'How's it going?' asks Oli.

'It's fine,' I say, 'except I've been sent a couple of schoolkids who seem more interested in getting back to the station in time for turkey pie than solving the murder. Honestly, Oli, they're a joke. I know on TV shows everyone is in and out in ten minutes but I thought in real life it would be a bit more thorough. The PC looks barely older than Ben. I half expected her to take a selfie with the body for Facebook.'

'I'm not sure kids use Facebook,' says Oli. 'I'm pretty sure Facebook is just for middle-aged people like us who want to stalk old school friends to see if they got fat and to complain about the bins.'

'Well whatever, Snapchat then. That's not my point; I'm just saying they're shit. I can't see how on earth they're going to find out who did it.'

'How long do I need to keep the kids out for?

They're getting a bit twitchy. Ben's phone is nearly out of battery.'

'Are you still in Starbucks?'

'Yes, but I don't know how much longer I can make it last. I've finished my Frappuccino.'

I smile to myself and wonder how I could have ever suspected Oli. 'The coroner is on her way,' I say, 'so hopefully not long. Keep them busy pinching some holly and I'll keep you posted.'

'I'll do my best,' he says, and then pauses. 'I love you, Anna.'

'I love you too, darling. See you soon.'

Bacon comes into the room as I hang up and I wonder how much he heard. I'm going to assume nothing based on his detection skills so far. He gets his gadget back out and we spend the next ten minutes going through the events of the party and my discovery of the body. While I give him as much information as I can remember (it gets a little hazy post-amaretto), Simons does her best to investigate the living room. This seems mainly to involve staring quite closely at the floor and lifting the cushions on the armchairs.

'Did you buy these olives?' she asks, picking up a half-empty bowl and giving them a knowing sniff.

'Um, yes?' I say, wondering what she could be getting at. Perhaps they've been drugged so that someone could use them to lure Colin into the larder in a weakened state. Perhaps she can tell that they're out of date and suspects me of attempting to give Colin diarrhoea. (She'd be right.) 'Do you think it's important?'

'For the murder?' asks Simons. 'No, I've been trying

to find somewhere that sells them with the garlic stuffed inside. These are just what I've been looking for.'

'Waitrose,' I tell her. 'I've got another packet in the fridge if you want them?'

'Oh well if you're sure you don't want them?'

'Simons, *please*,' says Bacon. 'We've talked about this before. No bribes.' He gives me a stern look.

'Oh I wasn't trying to bribe her,' I explain. 'I was just . . .'

'Let's say no more about it, Mrs Johnson,' interrupts Bacon. 'I understand that in desperate times it might feel like your only way out, but don't believe what you read about corruption in the police force. We are not here to be bought.'

'It was just olives though. I didn't mean it as a bribe, honestly.'

'Today maybe it's just olives. Tomorrow it could be cash or stolen guns. It's a slippery slope, Mrs Johnson, so let's nip it in the bud, shall we?'

'Yes, good idea,' I say, suitably chastised. 'Nip it in the bud, absolutely.' Murder he's seemingly unbothered by, olive bribes are clearly a different matter. Fortunately at that moment the doorbell rings and I'm saved from any further interrogation.

'Simons, get the door. That will be the coroner. Show her in and brief her while I finish up here.'

Simons looks beside herself with this new responsibility and trots off to answer the door, letting out an excited squeal as she goes. I hear her let in the coroner and show her to the scene of the crime. There's a loud clatter and a shout and Bacon and I both jump up and run out to the kitchen.

Simons is on the floor of the larder. The mop I'd earlier propped up outside to deter the kids is on the floor next to her. One hand is in the pool of blood. The coroner stands just outside the larder looking appalled.

'I tripped,' says Simons, sheepishly.

'Jesus Christ, Simons,' says Bacon, shaking his head. He leans over to help her up but she reaches out with the bloodied hand and immediately slips from his grip, knocking an open packet of pasta off the shelf and into the mix. Shells spill everywhere. With all the blood and the onions it's pretty much a bolognese down there now.

The coroner, clearly sensing that someone needs to take control, steps in. 'How about if you all take a moment,' she says, '*somewhere else?*'

Simons has just about managed to stand up without spreading her mess and she and Bacon go over to the kitchen sink to wash their hands. I look at the barbecue tongs hastily thrown onto the draining board on my way to let them in earlier, but neither of them bat an eyelid.

I retreat to the other side of the kitchen island while they get themselves cleaned up. Bacon is admonishing Simons in hushed tones, her head low as she takes the telling-off. I can't hear what they're saying – I just catch the odd word. I think I hear 'sausage rolls'.

I check my phone. It's 11.22 a.m. The house is even more of a mess than it was half an hour ago, Father Christmas has yet to be removed from the larder and Oli's family are going to be here in just over twenty-four hours. I've got the party to clean up, Christmas lunch to prep and let's not even talk about the tablescaping. And now to top it all off, thanks to Laurel and Hardy over there, it looks like I'm adding 'solve Colin's murder' to the list of things I need to do before I can even think about enjoying Christmas.

My phone pings with a WhatsApp. It's Jennie.

'How's it going at Homicide House? That's my new name for your house btw.'

'Nice,' I type, 'I probably won't get a sign made just yet, if it's all the same to you, and not well. The Chuckle Brothers are here and it's a fucking farce. Sharpen your pencil. We're going to need that murder board.'

CHAPTER 6

Half an hour later, the coroner has finished and Colin's body is being loaded in the back of a plain van. I'm on the doorstep, saying my goodbyes to Bacon and Simons. Bacon has given me his direct number and I've promised to call them if anything else comes to light, particularly if it's Colin's phone, and they've assured me that it will only be a matter of time before the murderer is brought to justice. I've not been less convinced of anything since Lily came home from school when she was in reception class, with a piece of cheese stuck in her left ear, and told me that 'the wind blew it in'.

As the van and the police car pull away I notice a figure darting out of sight behind the hedge that separates our drive from next door's. I have a flash of panic but then notice the sheepskin slippers just visible under the laurel.

'Hello, Margaret,' I call out. The slippers are still for a second or two, and then the figure of an elderly woman appears from behind the hedge.

'Oh hello, Anna!' she says, her voice strained and high-pitched in an effort to sound casual. 'I was just thinking about mowing the lawn!' We both look down at her slippers.

'On Christmas Eve, Margaret? It's a bit wet for the mower, isn't it?'

'Oh maybe you're right, dear,' she says, doing her best helpless old lady impersonation. We both know she is anything but. Margaret is eighty-three and one of the feistiest women I know. If she was up against Jennie in an arm wrestle then I honestly don't know who I would put my money on. Jennie is tough but Margaret does seniors body combat twice a week at the community centre and can cycle up the hill to Morrisons without getting off. We are the end two houses in the cul-de-sac, with adjoining driveways and gardens.

She's the sort of person that my mum would have said 'doesn't suffer fools gladly'. Her favourite pastime, apart from watching *Richard Osman's House of Games*, is trawling Facebook for local posts that she can leave abusive comments on. She has a very low tolerance threshold for badly parked cars and irresponsible dog owners.

I decide to let her off the hook.

'I'm guessing you saw the police car,' I say.

'The police have been here?' she says, feigning surprise but unable to hide the gleam in her eyes. 'I hope everything's okay?'

'There has been an incident,' I say, 'but I'm afraid I can't say any more at the moment. The police have given me very strict instructions.'

Margaret positively beams. She loves any hint of a conspiracy. When the local council started cutting back on street lighting in a bid to cut costs last year she led the protests, claiming it was all a ploy to induce falls in the elderly, have them moved into care homes, and buy up their houses to use for construction workers on the new factory by the motorway junction.

She taps her nose. 'Say no more,' she says, 'we all know what the police are like nowadays, Anna. I expect they'll have planted listening devices. Whenever you're ready, you come over to me. We can talk in the shed.'

I'm trying to formulate a reply when I see Oli, Ben and Lily walking up the road. I have to get Margaret out of the way before the kids are within earshot but the trouble is the minute she gets a whiff of someone wanting her gone she digs her sheepskin slippers in. The only thing I can think to do is to run up the road to greet them and somehow steer them clear. Margaret is nosy and interfering but I don't think she'll go as far as to run up the road after me.

'Oh look, the children!' I say, my voice shrill. 'I'd better go and say hello!' I trot away before she can protest.

'Darlings!' I say, as I approach my family, aware that I look and sound a little on the maniacal side, running to meet them halfway up the road. 'So lovely to see you all! Did you get some holly?'

Ben laughs. 'No,' he says, 'Dad got bullied and we ran away.'

'I did not get bullied,' Oli protests. 'It turns out Dawn and Steve are not in Swansea after all and they weren't thrilled at us trying to snap branches off their holly bush.'

'Steve shouted!' says Lily, looking like she's not sure whether to be thrilled or terrified.

'And Dad ran away,' adds Ben.

'I did not run away,' says Oli. 'I just wanted to get you and your sister out of danger, which is the sensible thing to do. He had a bat and was being very threatening.'

'It was a baguette,' clarifies Ben. 'He came out into the drive and told us we were interrupting his lunch and to get the fuck off his lawn.'

'Well it looked like a bat,' says Oli.

'Maybe when you're running away and can only see it blurred out of the corner of your eye,' says Ben.

'He was wearing Crocs,' says Lily helpfully.

'Yeah, Dad ran away from a man in Crocs waving a baguette. It's okay, Dad, it's good to be a pacifist.'

'Didn't you say anything about Dawn and the mistletoe?' I ask.

'No I didn't, funnily enough,' says Oli, 'not when I thought he had a bat.'

'A baguette,' I correct him.

'It *could* have been a bat, Anna, the man has LIFE and DETH tattooed on his knuckles. So we haven't got any holly, sorry. You'll have to use something else in the tablescape. How's the, er, sausage-meat thing coming along?'

'The sausage meat?'

'Yes remember, you had to rush home to do something with sausage meat?'

'Oh yes, the sausage meat. It's all taken care of. Probably just don't go in the larder until I clear it up as I got quite a lot of stuff on the floor. Got that, kids? If you want anything from the larder ask me and I'll get it. Because of the sausage meat.'

'Whatever, Mum,' says Ben, giving me a look that implies I'm a weirdo, but no more of a weirdo than usual.

I check over my shoulder and it looks like Margaret has given up and gone inside, probably to post something on the South Medling Matters Facebook group. Looks like the coast is clear for us to all get inside without her spilling the beans to the kids about the police presence. I'm not sure how long I'll be able to keep it from Ben, but at least I can do my best to preserve the magic of Christmas for Lily.

Back inside, Ben is quick to head off upstairs, shouting something over his shoulder about having said he'd FaceTime Sasha and Jaz. I'm about to shout after him to get himself back downstairs and help with the clearing up, but it occurs to me that having him out of the way for now is probably the best thing that could happen.

'I can help you, Mum,' says Lily. 'Can I do the carpet cleaner?'

I think back to the last time she asked to help clean the carpets. It had felt like a very good idea at the time, an excellent opportunity to be the kind of parent who prepares their children for adult life rather than the sort who sends them off to university unable to even load a washing machine. That type of parent (almost always mums sadly) seems to take a perverse pleasure in their children being utterly helpless without them – poor babies who can't survive a minute without their precious mother. 'He can't even boil pasta!' they laugh proudly. 'I don't know how he's going to cope without me!'

Wake-up call, Karen – he's going to cope just fine on pizza and vodka, and six months from now you'll be crying every night into your Chardonnay because your helpless son has not only managed perfectly fine without you, he's basically forgotten who you are.

I never want to be that woman. I want to be the mum who sends their kids off with proper knife skills. (Not the stabbing kind.) I want mine to be able to cook a lasagne and know how to change a lightbulb and all of those other tedious things that comprise adulting.

So I agreed that yes, Lily could definitely help clean the carpets. I showed her how to fill the tank of the Vax with water and together we topped up the cleaning solution. I popped into the kitchen to put the kettle on, ready for our tea break.

The Vax was heavy for her – she was only six – but she got the hang of it quickly and it was all going well. My first sign of trouble was a vague sensation of being at swimming lessons. I couldn't put my finger on it. For some reason I found myself having flashbacks to sweaty Tuesday afternoons sat poolside, pretending to watch Lily bob around enthusiastically in the kids' pool.

She was about halfway across the living room when I realised I could smell chlorine.

'Lily,' I said slowly, switching off the Vax at the plug, 'you didn't do anything while I was in the kitchen did you?'

She beamed at me proudly. 'Yes I did!'

'What did you do?' I asked, feeling a rising panic in my chest.

'I added a secret potion to get the carpets cleaner than ever!'

'Was it the secret potion in the downstairs toilet that Mummy uses to clean the toilet that I've told you not to touch?'

'Yes!' she replied, triumphant. 'I put lots of it in with the water to get all the germs out of the carpet.'

I looked at the half of the room left to be 'cleaned' – a beautiful dark grey – and then at the bleached half. It was an absolute shitshow. I immediately drained the Vax and tried to go over it to get out the toilet bleach but the damage was done. What a fucking mess.

'I think perhaps I'll do the carpet cleaning,' I say now, 'but I do have a very important job for you if you'd like to help? It's polishing all of the windowsills in the bedrooms and the bannisters. Could you do that for me?'

Polishing is always a winner – she'll take about ten minutes to do one windowsill, using half a can of polish in the process, and then she'll get bored and sneak off to play on the iPad, hoping I won't notice. Absolutely perfect.

She trots off to get the polish and cloth from under the sink and Oli and I are left contemplating our next move.

'Well,' he says, once Lily is out of earshot, 'where shall we start? Shall I look in the larder?'

I sigh. 'I guess so, if you want to? I mean it's not FUN, but we are going to need to clean it up at some point and I don't know if I can face that on my own.'

'How about if I just take a look, see what we're dealing with, and then we ease ourselves into it by getting the living room and kitchen sorted? You start collecting glasses and bowls – I'll get the dishwasher loaded and wash up the fragile bits.'

'Thank you, darling,' I say, giving him a hug. It's only now, having him here to share the problem, that I realise how much I had hated doing it by myself.

'What for?' he asks, hugging me back.

'Just for being here. It's a bit shit, isn't it?'

'It's not the best start I've ever had to a Christmas,' he admits, 'although the year we went to stay at my mum and dad's and they didn't tell us they were doing charity donations instead of gifts is a strong contender.'

'Oh God,' I say, remembering all too clearly, 'I swear your mum did that on purpose. Your sister-in-law handed out those toilet twinning certificates to everyone and we got your mum a cashmere scarf. Fucking cashmere! I've never seen anyone look so disgusted at the prospect of cashmere.'

'And don't forget Glenn,' adds Oli, raising his eyebrows.

'Glenn! How could I forget Glenn. No offence to Glenn but fucking hell. Fancy your mum not telling us he was an alcoholic and that everybody had agreed on a dry Christmas. Your mum watched me put that crémant in the fridge when we got there. She let me take it out on Christmas Day at lunchtime and I swear blind she waited until the moment after I'd popped the cork to say anything.'

'I'm sure she wasn't quite that calculated,' says Oli.

'She bloody was! Come off it, Oli, I know she's your mother but she's a sour old bitch and you know it. She'll do anything to make me look bad and she pulled it off in style that Christmas.'

'You're right, I know. I shouldn't make excuses for her.'

'She didn't stab anyone though. I guess. Or have a larder full of the congealed blood of a work colleague.'

'Also very true,' says Oli. He lets go of the hug. 'I'm going to go and have a quick look, then we'll get cracking.'

I wait in the kitchen. I've seen enough for now.

'What did you think?' I ask when he comes back, looking a little pale.

'It's grim, isn't it?'

'Yes, it's pretty grim. It was worse though honestly with the corpse in the middle of everything.'

'What are the pasta shells about?' he asks. 'Some kind of calling card? I've heard about those.'

'Don't ask,' I say. 'Let's just say that we were not blessed with the finest police minds. Anyway, the cleaning. We'd better start hadn't we?'

Oli checks his phone. 'Yep, we better had. It's quarter past twelve, which gives us not very long at all until Mum and Dad arrive.' I grimace. He starts running hot water into the sink and I head into the living room to pick up glasses.

'You know,' says Oli, a few minutes later as I come back in with the final armful of crockery. 'I was thinking about everything and it has to be someone who was at the party, doesn't it? *Criminal Crossroads* is always

65

saying how the majority of murder victims are killed by someone they know, so it makes sense.'

Criminal Crossroads is the true crime podcast that Oli is obsessed with, a rip-off of the *Serial* podcasts by a woman who talks in a weird American accent even though we've googled her and she lives in Kettering.

'It must have been,' I agree, reworking Oli's attempts at the dishwasher into some semblance of order. 'We would have noticed a stranger, surely? And how would anyone else know he was here? If you weren't a party guest you'd have to be pretty ballsy to break into a house full of friends and murder someone right in the middle of it without anyone wondering who the fuck you were?'

'Although someone *did* kill Colin right in the middle of the party and we *didn't* notice, which is a bit scary.'

'More than a bit,' I say, 'but I think you're right – it had to have been someone at the party, someone we knew. It's just too far-fetched otherwise.'

'Come to think of it,' says Oli, rewashing the guacamole bowl I had snuck back on the dirty pile after examining it, 'I think I saw Bruce coming out of the larder at one point, although I couldn't have said when.'

'You mean Colin's son Bruce? Well, that would be a bit of a stab in the back – or the stomach even – for his dad, wouldn't it? His golden boy turning rogue and doing him in?' I finish loading the dishwasher, add a tablet and close the door.

'It could make sense though,' says Oli, 'if he stood to inherit the business? Or maybe they'd had a fight and Colin was going to cut him out of the will?'

'Do people actually cut family members out of their wills in real life, or is that just something that happens in Agatha Christie novels? It feels like a bit of a faff admin wise. We still haven't redone our wills since Lily was born.'

'Maybe he just threatened it and Bruce got scared? Although on second thoughts, it probably wasn't him. He came out carrying a tube of Pringles.'

'So?' I ask.

'Well I hardly think you'd stab your own father to death in cold blood in the middle of a Christmas party and then immediately think to yourself, *Ooh I really fancy some sour cream Pringles now.* It feels a bit casual, doesn't it?'

'It does a bit. Did he look stressed at all? On edge?' I pick up a tea towel and start drying the dishes on the draining board while Oli wipes down the worktops.

'Not really, he looked kind of smug if anything. A bit cocky. He did a Tom Cruise-style toss of the Pringles, like he was mixing a cocktail. He didn't catch them though. That's why I noticed him, because of the noise.'

'I see what you mean, not exactly the actions of a killer. Unless he dropped the Pringles through nerves.'

'I guess we just have to leave it to the police; that's their job, isn't it? And we concentrate on Christmas and hopefully not traumatising the kids.'

'But that's just it, Oli,' I say, putting down the tea towel decisively, 'the police are never going to figure it out. You should have seen them; it was a mess. They're never going to catch the killer.'

'Give them some credit, Anna, they probably have a lot going on behind the scenes.'

I laugh out loud at the idea of Bacon or Simons having anything at all going on 'behind the scenes'. They barely had anything going on in *front* of the scenes. 'I'm not joking, Oli, you should have seen them. All they were worried about was getting back to the station as soon as possible so they didn't miss the Christmas buffet. The guy in charge properly destroyed evidence while I watched and he *didn't even notice.*'

'Seriously? What did he do when you told him?'

'Well,' I pause here, feeling a little guilty. 'I didn't tell him.'

'You didn't tell him?!'

'It was a footprint, and he trod in it, but I couldn't tell him without incriminating myself!'

'What do you mean by incriminating yourself? Was it your footprint?'

'No, but I had sort of taken a photograph and some measurements.' I'm avoiding eye contact and feeling decidedly shifty.

'Sort of?' Oli raises his eyebrows at me.

'Completely then. But isn't it a good job I did?!'

'Only if you then had handed that information over to the police!' says Oli, quite reasonably really, if you think about it too much.

'But if I had done that, then they'd have known I had been poking about and I'd have been in trouble. You can't just go around interfering with a crime scene before the police get there,' I say, as though Oli is an idiot for not knowing that.

'I'm glad you understand that in principle at least,' he says. 'So what are you saying, is that we'll just have to live forever wondering who amongst our friends is a murderer?'

'I'm saying the opposite. I'm saying if we want to know who killed Colin then we have to take matters into our own hands. We're going to have to solve the murder ourselves.'

CHAPTER 7

Five minutes later, we're sitting at the kitchen table with a pad of paper, pens, Post-its and highlighters. It wasn't a hard sell to be honest. I knew if I slipped in a nod to *Criminal Crossroads* then I could win him over.

'Plus,' I'd said, 'imagine how impressed your mum might finally be if we could turn this around, solve a serious crime and still get Christmas dinner on the table?'

This was a blatant lie, of course. Pamela was going to be horrified by the whole sordid affair and was very likely going to refuse to even stay in the house once she knew what had gone on less than forty-eight hours beforehand. And not unreasonably, to be fair. I don't know how happy I'd be to turn up to what I thought was going to be a festive holiday getaway, only to discover the wheelie bin was full of the results of a murder clean-up. It doesn't scream 'Christmas cheer', does it?

Sweet, naive Oli chose to believe, however, that this could be his opportunity to resolve the ongoing feud between his wife and mother and see everyone enjoying Christmas Day as a happily ever after, laughing merrily about murder over the sprouts and congratulating each other on a job well done.

'The first thing they do on *Criminal Crossroads* is to establish a timeline,' he says, writing 'TIMELINE' at the top of a sheet of paper in capital letters and underlining it in red felt tip, 'and a list of suspects.' (Note to self: replace Lily's full stationery set before school goes back.)

'Okay, that sounds like a good idea. Let's start from the beginning. Toby and Sav came over about 5 p.m. to help with the drinks and nibbles, then everyone else started arriving from 6 p.m.' We always start our Christmas party early as a lot of our friends are parents too and they're all quite keen to have their dose of being a grown-up and then be at home with the kids in bed in time for a solid hour of Netflix.

Oli writes this down.

'Colin, his wife Miranda and Bruce didn't get here until after 9 p.m. because that's when I told them the party started.' My plan had been to minimise the crossover with as many of our friends as possible. I hadn't wanted to invite him at all to be honest; I'd been cornered into it.

I'd been talking about the party to Cathy at work – Cathy with the guinea pigs. She wasn't coming because she always goes on a singles Christmas cruise and this year she was going to the Caribbean. I cannot think of anything worse honestly, but each to their own. She loves it, even after the year she got scammed into marrying the Puerto Rican magician.

She was telling me about a cocktail recipe she'd seen

71

on TikTok for a Christmas pudding martini. Apparently you put actual pudding in the cocktail shaker. Cathy said it does give you a bit of a greasy film on the drink, a sort of lardy scum, but that it's very nice if you can look past that.

It was just as she was saying 'these would be perfect for your Christmas party' that Colin and Bruce walked past on their way to what Colin likes to call the 'refreshment hub'. The 'refreshment hub' is just a corner of the office where Colin has installed an old coffee vending machine that used to be in the spectators' area of the old swimming pool. One of the buttons says 'tomato soup', but as far as I know nobody has ever pressed it.

There's also a basket of biscuits that Colin replenishes every time he comes back from a stay at a Travelodge, plus two beanbags. We're a marketing agency and Colin is obsessed with beanbags, even though most of us struggle getting in and out of them at team meetings. Colin himself sits on a normal office chair, which means we look and feel extra stupid and he gets to look down on us. The beanbags in the refreshment hub are never used. If I can't get down to a beanbag without a coffee I'm certainly not doing it with a flimsy plastic cup of 'chocomilk' in one hand.

Colin likes to imagine he is the life and soul of any gathering, so on hearing the word 'party' he stopped in his tracks, putting one arm out to stop Bruce too, and swivelled on the heel of one over-polished brown brogue to face me.

'Having a party are we, Anna?' he'd asked, clapping his hands together. 'Just tell us where and when and we'll bring the entertainment! Who am I kidding? We *are* the entertainment!' He'd laughed heartily at what he must have assumed was a joke.

'Oh,' I'd said, 'it's nothing, just a few friends for drinks, no biggie.'

'You know what they say, Anna, it's not the size of your boat . . .' He'd winked at me and I'd tried not to visibly grimace.

'It's really just close friends and family,' I'd said again.

'In that case I'm touched,' he said, 'that you would think of me and Bruce as family. I do always say that here at Buzz Wize Media we are one happy family, and this just shows how right I am.'

It had all been very awkward and I'd ended up inviting both him and Bruce, and Colin's wife Miranda, but telling them it was starting at 9 p.m. to try and spare some of the kids and their parents at least. Oli was not happy, but what could I do? I could hardly say no, could I? The joke was on him in the end anyway.

'Right then,' says Oli, 'let's think about the timeline. Do you remember the last time you saw him?'

I really didn't. I'd tried to avoid him as much as possible.

'I don't know, Oli. I don't think I saw him later on. He wasn't playing Twister, that's for sure. I wouldn't have gone anywhere near it if he had been. But then I don't know what time that was really either. I know that it was 2.10 a.m. when I got into bed?'

Oli writes some more notes and then shows me our timeline so far:

5 p.m.: Toby and Sav arrive at house

6 p.m.: Guests start to arrive
9 p.m.: Colin, Miranda and Bruce arrive no earlier than this
2.10 a.m.: Everyone has left.

'It's not very good is it?' I say, feeling a bit disappointed. Miss Marple makes it seem much easier than this.

'Not really,' admits Oli. 'I think we're going to need to narrow down the time of death and try to figure out who exactly was here and what they were doing. Did you not get anything from the coroner about when he died?'

'No, I was having my statement taken in the living room while the coroner was doing her thing.' I think for a minute. 'Oooh I know!' I say, leaping up to get my phone. 'Maybe we can work it out for ourselves! I touched his wrist remember, to check he was dead? That was before 10 a.m. and he was cold by then. We can google it!'

'Whoa!' says Oli, holding up a hand. 'Wait a minute! You know the police can access all of your phone records don't you? If they start to get suspicious of us, they could look at your messages, call logs AND browsing history. It's going to look dodgy as hell if you've started looking up how long it takes bodies to go cold.'

I look at Oli doubtfully. 'I don't know,' I say. 'You didn't meet the police officers. I really don't think they're going to be doing any deep background checks anytime soon. Besides, wouldn't it be more suspicious if I'd been googling things like that *before* the murder? Things like "best place to stab a man for instant death", that sort of thing?'

'Well, I guess so,' Oli concedes. 'Look it up then, see what it says.'

I unlock my phone, open Chrome and type 'how long before a body goes cold uk' into Google. I find myself in a Reddit thread.

'Jesus Christ,' I say, 'listen to this.' I read out the post I've found. 'My husband died in bed next to me. He was alive at 1 a.m. when I went to sleep but when I woke up to go to the toilet at 3.30 a.m. he was dead and already cold.'

'Fuck me,' says Oli, 'that's a bit much, isn't it?'

'Shit, it really is. Imagine that, you just get up for a wee and your husband's body is cold next to you. Fucking hell.'

'That means he was cold after only a couple of hours though, which isn't very helpful for us. It doesn't narrow it down at all.'

'Hold on, let me see what Florida State University says. That might be more reliable.' I scroll down the page to the rigor mortis section. 'Okay, if the body is warm and stiff, death occurred three to eight hours ago. If it's cold and stiff it's eight to thirty-six hours. Does that help?'

Oli looks at the ceiling and I see his mouth moving as he counts backwards. 'No,' he says. 'If he was cold and stiff that means he died sometime before about 2 a.m., and we already know that because everyone had gone home by then. I guess at least it rules out Colin hiding in the larder while we went to bed and an intruder sneaking in and stabbing him while we were asleep.'

'I guess,' I say, reluctantly, 'although that wasn't exactly high on my list of possible scenarios.' I scroll a bit further down the page. 'What about this – livor mortis. It's about how the blood pools and whether the skin goes white when you press it. Colin's did that. Let's see, no, that's no use. It stays blanchable for up to eight to twelve hours after death, which means he died between 10 p.m. and 2 a.m. It means he probably didn't get *instantly* stabbed at least. He got to enjoy *some* of the party?'

Oli sighs and adds, *9–10 p.m.: Colin probably not stabbed yet*, to his timeline.

'If only cats could talk,' I say sadly.

Oli looks at me like the stress of the day might be taking its toll.

'Because then they could help us solve the murder?' asks Oli, slowly. 'Their names don't actually mean they're detectives. You do know that, don't you?'

'I do know that yes, thank you, *darling*. I'm not completely mad yet. I just mean Tommy might actually have seen who did it.'

'Tommy?' says Oli, looking baffled. 'How on earth would he do that?'

'Because he was in the larder,' I explain. 'When I opened the door this morning he came dashing out, so presuming that nobody went into the larder, saw Colin, chose to ignore him, and came out again, trapping the cat as they left, Tommy must have been in there when it happened and got shut in.'

I smile smugly. I'm feeling pretty pleased with my deductions.

'Hang on a minute,' says Oli, picking up his pen excitedly, 'that's a really good point. You might not remember seeing Colin, but did you go in the larder for anything during the evening? We could narrow it down that way instead!'

'The amaretto!' I shout. 'I went in there looking for

fun festive drinks and came out with the amaretto. That was later in the evening, wasn't it? And there's Bruce and the Pringles too! Yes, come on, Oli, we're rolling now! Let's do suspects.'

'Okay,' says Oli, 'so quite a lot of people are off the hook already if we're saying Colin was still alive when you got out the amaretto. Everyone with young kids had gone home by then. And most of the neighbours. Your book club had left by then too, hadn't they?'

'Yes definitely,' I agree. 'They all came together in one car so they all had to leave when Sandra wanted to go home and let the dog out. And your work people had gone by then too – I was holding off the shots until they'd left.'

'Perfect, so let's think about who was left.' Oli writes SUSPECTS on his sheet of paper and underlines it. Then he draws out a table with four columns – *name, means, opportunity, motive.*

'That's very professional-looking,' I say. 'Have you done this before?'

'No, but it's what they always do on the podcast. It helps to see things clearly. It's all just a process of elimination really, like playing Cluedo.'

'Who do you think Colin would be if he was in Cluedo? I'm thinking Colonel Mustard. I've never liked him – he's got a smarmy moustache.'

'I don't think any of the six characters are actually the ones murdered – they're the suspects. Isn't there someone else, like Mr Black or something?'

'Oh is there? Maybe. Anyway, let's think about our suspects. We've got you and me, Ben and Lily for starters.' Oli looks up at me.

'Seriously?'

'Well maybe not Lily, but I don't know, darling – I do love you but you could be a pea salesman for all I know.'

'What is this obsession with peas?' he asks. 'I think if we're going to get anywhere we need to put ourselves in the clear at least.'

'Fine,' I say, adding his name to my own top-secret mental list just in case. 'Then there's Bruce for sure.' Oli writes down *Bruce* and then in the opportunity column he writes *Pringles?* I'm not entirely sure he's getting the point but he seems to be enjoying himself.

'And Colin's wife Miranda,' I add. 'She came with Colin, although I don't remember seeing her much so I'm not sure if she left earlier? Come to think of it, she *must* have left earlier, or surely she'd have wondered where Colin was? I wonder why she didn't call this morning though and ask why he hadn't come home? That's a bit suspicious – make a note of that on the list.' Oli writes it all down diligently.

'There's your brother and his boyfriend,' says Oli, 'they were some of the last to leave. They started the Twister, didn't they?'

'Yep, Toby and Sav were here, but I don't honestly know what their motive might be. Put them down though. Margaret was here quite late, keeping an eye on things, ready to report back to Neighbourhood Watch no doubt.'

'If we're doing neighbours, what about Marcus? I seem to remember him in a rather compromising position with Jennie on the Twister board?'

'Oh yes! He was there – I'd forgotten him. I had to

reach over him for a blue at one point. What about his girlfriend though, Georgie? I feel like maybe she'd gone home by then. Didn't she say something about having a headache? I'm not entirely sure though, so let's keep her as a maybe.'

'There's Jennie?' says Oli, hesitantly.

'Jennie didn't do it,' I say. 'I know Jennie. She's not a murderer. She's too public. Plus it was her idea to investigate. She wouldn't want us to do that if she'd done it, would she?'

'Of course she would!' objects Oli. 'That's classic killer – injecting yourself in the investigation, having the power to lead people in the wrong direction.'

'Still, I just don't believe it's her,' I say. 'I don't want her on the list.'

'I see,' says Oli, 'so you were happy to add me and your own children, but not your best friend? No way, Jennie's on the list.'

'What about Sasha and Jaz?' I ask.

'Ben's mates?' says Oli. He looks doubtful. 'They're only sixteen, love, and Sasha is vegan. Can you really see them as killers?'

'I can't see *any* of these people as killers, Oli, that's the problem! I think we need to write them down, even if we discount them later, just to be thorough.'

Oli concedes reluctantly and we look at the list:

Bruce
Miranda
Toby
Sav
Margaret
Marcus

Georgie
Jennie
Sasha
Jaz

'So we've got ten suspects,' I say, looking pointedly at Oli, 'not including us. We need to find out what time Miranda and Georgie left, and we do have two sixteen-year-olds on there, so we might be able to narrow it down even further. It's better than the timeline at least. Is there anyone we've missed?'

While Oli thinks, I get out a large packet of smoked salmon from the fridge.

'What are you doing?' asks Oli.

'I'm making the Christmas starter,' I say, getting out the old chopping board we keep just for smoked salmon because I can't bear the smell on our everyday boards. 'Do you think it would be weird to use one of the other knives from the set?'

'One of the murder knives?' asks Oli. 'I don't know, maybe a bit. It might be too soon.'

'You're probably right,' I agree, rummaging in the drawer for one of the old knives I keep for doing things like unscrewing the covers for the batteries in the kids' toys. I take a large melon and three avocados from the fruit bowl and a large mixing bowl from the cupboard.

'Is this really the time to be thinking about the Christmas starter?' says Oli.

I put the bowl down a little too loudly. 'It's Christmas Eve, Oli. When exactly *is* a good time to think about the Christmas starter? Boxing Day maybe? New Year's? Or maybe *you* had it on your list of things to do later today?'

80

'Well no, I didn't,' he admits.

'No, I didn't think so. In which case I'm doing it now.' I slice the melon through the middle in what I hope is a vaguely threatening way. I cut open the smoked salmon too.

Before Oli can react, my phone rings. 'Hang on, it's Jennie.'

'Anna!' she says when I answer, knife still in hand. I notice and put it down quickly. 'How's it going? Have the police gone?'

'Yes, they're gone, the you-know-what has been taken away and Oli and the kids are home. The kids are upstairs. Oli and I are doing a timeline and suspect list and I'm making the Christmas starter.'

'Oh lovely,' she says, 'the smoked salmon and melon thing? Which knife are you using?'

'One of the battery knives,' I say. 'I can't face one of the others yet.'

'Yeah,' she agrees, 'too soon. So how's the timeline shaping up? Anything I can put on the murder board?'

'So far we've managed to narrow down the time of death to between 10 p.m. and 2 a.m., which is pretty much the whole time Colin was here so it's not much help. Oh and Oli saw Bruce coming out of the larder with some Pringles.'

'Bruce?' says Jennie sharply. 'What was he doing in there?'

'Getting some Pringles I'm assuming,' I say. 'Oli says he looked pretty pleased with himself, but not in a murdery way, more of a "just scored some Pringles" way.'

'When was that?' asks Jennie. 'Did Oli see anyone else?'

'I don't think so. Oli, you didn't see anyone else with Bruce did you?'

He shakes his head. 'No, just Bruce.'

'Fine,' says Jennie. 'I can print out a Pringles logo, put that up. But you don't know what time?'

'No, we were just thinking about it when you called. Apart from that we've not got very far, honestly. We've not found Colin's phone anywhere either, so if we find that we might get somewhere. We have a suspect list though, so that's something.'

'Brilliant! Send it over and I'll do some background checks, bit of googling, see if I can find anything incriminating. We need to establish a motive that isn't just that Colin is a prick, sorry, *was* a prick. He's always been a prick – if that was enough to get him killed it would have happened years ago.'

'I'll get Oli to send you a picture,' I say, 'and let me know what you find out. I'd better get back to the starter.'

'Sure thing, Batman,' she says, and hangs up.

I look over at Oli, who is taking a picture of the suspect list ready to send. 'Not that one!' I say, snatching it away. 'We can't send that. Jennie's on it! Write it out again without her and send that. We can't have it looking like we suspect her. She's my oldest friend.'

Oli looks like he's about to argue but he doesn't get the chance.

'Mum,' says a voice from behind us and Oli and I both turn with a start to see Ben standing in the kitchen doorway.

'Ben!' I squeal. I look at Oli. He looks as guilty as I feel. I have a flashback to the time Oli's dad caught us sharing a Silk Cut Menthol behind his shed when we were nineteen years old. Fortunately Ben is too preoccupied (or maybe just too fifteen years old) to notice.

'Mum, I was just talking to Sasha and Jaz and we were wondering, have you heard from Colin today?'

'Colin?' I ask, my heart suddenly very loud in my ears. 'Not heard from him, as such. Why?'

'Well,' begins Ben. He kicks at the doorframe. He's wearing his filthy black trainers. The number of times I've told him to take those off in the house . . . It's a good job Lily bleached the carpets honestly. 'Well, we were just wondering because, well, don't be mad, Mum, will you?'

'I won't be mad,' I say, as calmly as possible, given that I can feel my pulse in my whole body now and my hands and feet are tingling.

'Something happened last night at the party, with Colin, and you should probably know about it.'

CHAPTER 8

'Oh, Ben,' I say in a low voice, 'how could you? Is it my fault? I knew I should have been stricter with screen time.' I grab at the kitchen side to steady myself and knock the salmon knife onto the floor with a loud clatter. I pick it up and then quickly put it down.

'Steady on, Anna,' says Oli, reaching out to put an arm around me. 'Give the boy a chance to speak.'

'It wasn't even me!' says Ben. 'It was Jaz and Sasha really. I know he's your boss; I didn't want to get you in too much trouble, even though he was being a massive dick.'

'Too much trouble?!' I shout. 'What the fuck were you all thinking? I've had one of the worst mornings of my life and now it turns out I have you to thank?!'

'I'm so sorry, Mum, really. It just got a bit out of hand; we didn't mean anything to come of it.'

'A bit out of hand? A BIT OUT OF HAND?!' This can't be happening. This must be an actual nightmare, the whole thing. If I concentrate really hard I'll wake up and Oli will be snoring next to me.

'Shit, Mum, he's not fired you has he? I can get Sasha and Jaz to apologise. We can fix it.'

'It's a bit past fixing, Ben. And how the hell could he fire me when . . .' I stop, realising what he's said. 'Wait, what do you mean? How would he have fired me?'

'We thought he might have been so angry that he'd take it out on you, get revenge you know? Teach us a lesson.'

I'm confused. What exactly has happened here? Thankfully Oli steps in.

'Ben, why don't you tell us exactly what happened? Nobody has been sacked, we're not angry, Mum is just a bit fraught trying to get everything ready for Christmas.'

A strangled cry escapes my body and Oli shoots me a look. Normally I hate this sort of comment. It's very much in the same ballpark as when Oli does something infuriating, like washing one of my wool jumpers on hot, and I get angry and call him an incompetent bastard and he asks gently if I have my period.

In this instance though, 'fraught' is the understatement of the year. I am more than a *bit fraught*, I am on the brink of having to make a citizen's arrest on my own son for murder. I am FREAKING THE FUCK OUT.

'Yes, Ben, nobody is mad,' I say through clenched teeth. 'Whatever has happened we love you. We'll make sure you get the best legal advice. We won't let you go down for this, Ben.'

Ben looks genuinely terrified now. 'Go down?! Dad,

what does Mum mean? I can't go to prison for this can I? It honestly wasn't me; I was really just watching.'

Another noise comes out of my mouth, a sort of wail. I think I might be having a breakdown.

'Just start at the beginning, Ben,' says Oli calmly. 'Anna, why don't you make us all a cup of tea?'

A cup of tea? Oh yes, that will make everything better, a nice cup of tea while my only son, my precious firstborn, tells us how he stood and watched his best friends stab a man to death in our own home. Tea is going to make that all better. For fuck's sake. What has my life become? When I woke up all I had to worry about was a hangover. Come to think of it, I don't feel hungover anymore. Perhaps I've discovered a cure for alcohol poisoning – all you have to do is discover your eldest child is a psychopath.

'It kicked off when we were sat outside, avoiding having to watch you all play Twister – no offence, Mum – and Colin came over and started smarming all over Sasha. He made some comments about her dress. It was seriously fucked up. Sorry, Mum, but it was. She's sixteen and he's what? Seventy-odd?'

'Fifty-four I think,' I say.

'Exactly,' says Ben. 'Hell old. He said he was just having a laugh, that we shouldn't take ourselves so seriously, but Sasha wasn't having any of it. You know what she's like, she was brilliant, Mum.'

He's got an odd gleam in his eye now that takes me a few seconds to process. Bloody hell, he *likes* Sasha. I thought they were just friends but that is the look of a boy in love. I knew I shouldn't have let them in Ben's room unsupervised. This is what happens – he's swept up in love and can't see she's a cold-blooded killer. I blame myself of course.

'She started going on about #MeToo and how paedos can't get away with it anymore and Jaz joined in and told Colin he needed to educate himself. Colin laughed then. Properly laughed. He said what did Jaz need to know about education? All he had to do was wait to inherit the family newsagent and worry about keeping the shelves stocked. The man is a fucking racist, Mum. Just because Jaz's parents are from India. Jaz's dad is a dentist and his mum works at fucking Google. Jaz went nuts.'

Can you even go to prison when you're fifteen? Maybe you get one of those special centres for juvenile delinquents. How has my boy become a delinquent? He had trumpet lessons for four years, for God's sake. He uses Duolingo!

'So Colin stands up and his chair falls over behind him and he shouts at us that we're a bunch of latte-drinking millennials and we need to pull ourselves out of our own arses and show him some respect. The man's a joke. We're not even millennials and no one drinks lattes anymore.'

'I drink lattes,' I offer feebly.

'There you go then, Mum. That proves it.'

I decide now is not the moment to bring up Ben's casual ageism as being no better than Colin's sexism and racism. 'What happened next?' I ask instead. 'How did you end up in the larder?'

It's Ben's turn to look confused. 'In the larder? We were in the garden.'

'But afterwards?' I prompt.

'Afterwards what? That was it – he stormed off. We stayed in the garden for a bit because Sasha was crying and she said she didn't want the bastard to think he had upset her. She was only crying because she was so angry. No one went near the larder. What are you on about?'

'You didn't see him again after that?' I ask. 'You didn't go after him?'

'God no,' says Ben, 'we wanted to steer well clear of him. We stayed in the garden for a bit, then it was half eleven so Jaz's dad came to pick him up, and me and Sasha went upstairs so we didn't have to see that creep again.'

There's an awkward few seconds where Ben looks from me to Oli and back again and realises this isn't quite going as he expected it to.

'Dad,' he says, rightly homing in on Oli as the most rational adult in the room. 'What's going on? Has Mum been fired or what? Why are you both being so weird?'

'It's okay, Ben,' Oli reassures him. 'Mum hasn't been fired.'

'Why's she acting like someone died then?' asks Ben. I make a guttural sound. Oli grimaces. 'And why did she say she's had the worst morning of her life?'

If this were before the internet, we'd be able to cover the whole thing up and Ben would only find out about Colin's death from a chance remark twenty years later. Sure, he'd then probably need therapy, and never trust us again, or maybe turn to a life of crime or become a Buddhist or something, but we wouldn't have to tell him the truth straight away at least. Nowadays though, you can't keep anything a secret for long. Someone will

88

tweet something or Snapchat something and there'll be a hashtag and then everyone will know. My instinct is that this is something that Ben needs to find out from us rather than from #santasdead.

I look at Oli and I can see that he feels the same. 'I think you'd better sit down, Ben,' I say, pulling out a chair for him at the kitchen table. I'm pleased to see that Oli has casually put an arm over the timeline and suspect list. Ben sits down and I sit down next to him.

'Seriously,' says Ben, 'you guys are freaking me out now.'

'We've got something we need to tell you, Ben,' I say, reaching out my hand and putting it on top of one of his, 'and it's not going to be very nice. We want you to know that your dad and I are here for you and we will do our best to answer any questions you have.'

Is this sounding supportive? I've no idea. I've never read a Mumsnet thread for 'how to tell your teenage son a man was killed in his house last night. Or possibly this morning because we've not as yet been able to determine the time of death. For some reason I find myself picturing Lorraine Kelly and wondering what she'd do. I've always found Lorraine very comforting and she's always so nicely turned out, but in a non-threatening way, like she doesn't want to make you feel bad about yourself. It's very clever.

'Are you and Mum getting a divorce?' Ben asks, looking suddenly much younger than fifteen.

'God no,' says Oli, 'definitely not. Everything is tickety-boo with us Ben, don't worry.'

Tickety-boo? Ben might not need to worry but Oli will if he tries to make *tickety-boo* a thing.

'Something serious happened last night,' says Oli, taking over while I wrestle with my internal monologue. 'There isn't a nice way to say this, but someone died.'

'Someone *died?*' says Ben, wide-eyed. 'At our party? That's so cool!' We both look at him quickly and he catches himself. 'I mean not cool obviously, I mean sad. That's so sad. Was it Mrs Rooney next door?'

'No!' I say. 'It wasn't Mrs Rooney. Why would you think that?'

'Oh just because she's old I guess.' Ben shrugs. 'Too much excitement.' There's a minute or so then when we're all quiet. Oli and I watch Ben as he processes the last five minutes and begins to put things together.

'Wait,' he says slowly, 'is COLIN dead?'

'Yes,' I say sadly, giving his hand a squeeze, 'I'm afraid Colin is dead.'

More thinking from Ben. He looks at me and takes his hand out from under mine. 'Mum, did you think I had something to do with it? Did you think us having a go at him gave him a heart attack or something?'

'What? No!' I recoil. I reach out for his hand again but he avoids me. 'I know it wasn't your fault, Ben, I swear.'

Oli steps in. 'Ben, we know you didn't have anything to do with it. Colin didn't have a heart attack. Somebody killed him.'

Ben looks horrified and I think perhaps Oli went in a bit hard there.

'Mum!' says Ben, his voice raised now. 'Did you think I KILLED Colin?!'

'Of course not, darling! I love you!' Fuck, this has backfired a bit. 'I would never think that! Also though, could you keep your voice down a little bit? We don't want Lily to hear. Colin was dressed as Santa and we don't want to spoil Christmas.'

Ben actually laughs. 'It's okay, Mum, it's kind of funny if you did, tbh. I wondered why you looked so freaked out. So when I came in to do my big confessional, you thought we'd got mad at Colin in the garden and hit him with a spade or something?'

'Of course I didn't think for a minute you could have killed him!' I lie. 'I was upset that's all, and shocked. It's been a long day, and it's Christmas. I was just a bit overwrought.'

'Sure, whatever.' Ben laughs. 'So what happened? He's not still here is he? You've not buried him under the patio?'

'Ben, this is serious,' I say. 'A man has been killed in our house. It's okay to be shocked and scared. You don't have to pretend in front of us.'

'I'm not pretending, Mum, honestly, and I know, of course it's awful and I feel bad for his family or whatever, but I can't pretend like I'm really cut up about it. He was not a nice person, Mum.'

Ben has a point, but I can't help feeling like I should be insisting on a little more respect for the dead.

'So what happened? Who did it?' he asks, almost gleefully.

'This isn't a TV show, Ben,' Oli says. 'This is real life, in our house.'

'I get it, I get it!' He holds up his hands in a gesture of surrender. 'You're always saying you wish I'd show more of an interest in family life though, so here I am, showing an interest.'

It's not quite what I had in mind but also there is something lovely about sitting around the table with him actively talking to us. That doesn't happen that often anymore. Perhaps this could be an opportunity for quality family time? Okay, so maybe not *quality* exactly, not in the same vein as mini golf, but *time* at least.

'He was stabbed,' I say impetuously, ready for the bonding to begin. Oli frowns. 'And we don't know who did it. We have a list of suspects though.' I gesture at Oli for him to share our deductions so far.

'Anna,' says Oli gently, 'I'm not sure this is really okay. I don't think it's a good idea for us to be dragging Ben into a murder investigation.'

'Oh don't worry, Dad,' Ben says, animated now. 'It's really okay. We've done emotional resilience in PSHE so I'm cool. Anyway, you're going to need someone on the tech side aren't you?'

'What do you mean the tech side?' I say. 'You're not to do anything illegal, Ben, no hacking or anything on the Black Web.'

'I think you mean the dark web, Mum, and no, that wasn't what I meant. I was thinking stuff like going through the footage on the Ring doorbell to check what time people got here, that sort of thing? I've got the app on my phone.'

I hadn't thought of the Ring doorbell. Maybe Ben has a point. I look at Oli plaintively. 'We could do with his help,' I say. 'Neither of us are great at that sort of thing and there is always a tech guy on the podcast isn't there? Someone behind the scenes?'

'Okay fine,' says Oli, 'but *just* stuff like that. I don't want you in any danger and you have to promise not to post or tweet or anything about it. You can't even talk to Sasha and Jaz about it, do you understand?'

'Got it, Dad, from now on I'm undercover. I can go and change if you want?'

'Why do you need to change?' I ask.

'Into something black, to blend in. Tech guys in films always wear black. Maybe I could wear the suit I wore for Grandad's funeral?'

'I don't think you need a suit, Ben,' I reassure him, 'especially not for the first very important job I've got in mind for you.'

'What is it?' asks Ben, cracking his knuckles and looking keen.

'It's getting your sister out of the house while your dad and I clean up the larder.'

'Wait what? No way! I'm not doing that! That's not tech work!'

'Maybe not, but it's a vital part of the team investigation, Ben.' I shrug as though it's out of my hands. 'We need Lily out of the house so we can get it cleared up – you don't want your little sister accidentally walking in on a blood bath do you?' A bit graphic maybe, but I need to make the point.

'No, but can't you take her out, Mum? I'll stay here and help Dad?'

'Absolutely no way,' I say. 'Tech man is one thing but there's no way you're getting literal blood on your hands.' I fetch my bag from the hallway, come back in and hand him my credit card. 'Take her to McDonald's,' I say, 'and get whatever you want.'

'Anything?' says Ben.

'Anything,' I say reluctantly, knowing that Ben can

inhale a sharing box of nuggets in about three minutes. 'If you sit her at one of those interactive tables you might be able to keep her quiet while you go through the doorbell footage. We'll message when we're done here.'

'Okay fine,' Ben agrees, 'but I'd better get to do something more fun later.'

He heads out of the kitchen and I hear him thumping up the stairs, shouting for Lily as he goes.

'I'll just do the starter quickly and get that in the fridge, and then we'll clear up, shall we? And copy out the list without Jennie and send her a photo – she can start checking people out. I'm guessing if Jaz's dad came to pick him up right after the altercation in the garden that we can cross Jaz off the list?'

'Yes,' agrees Oli, 'that seems pretty conclusive, plus we've narrowed down our time of death if Jaz's lift was 11.30 p.m. and Colin was alive and well just before that. We do potentially have a motive for Sasha now though, if she was still angry and Colin tried something on later maybe?'

I don't like the idea of it, but I have to admit he has a point.

Just then my phone pings. I guess that it's Jennie wondering where the suspect list is, but I'm wrong, it's my brother Toby. I read the message.

'It's Toby,' I tell Oli, 'he says they found a phone last night. They're just taking the dog out and then they're dropping it round.'

CHAPTER 9

Once Ben and Lily are out of the house we spend a frantic half an hour doing our best to clean up the larder before Toby and Sav arrive. The larder somehow manages to feel worse every time I look at it. When we open the door, old towels and buckets of soapy water in hand, I start to retch.

Oli gallantly offers to be head cleaner and puts me in charge of holding bin bags for him to fill with bloodstained towels, cloths and pasta shells. We're liberal with the bleach, but I can't shake from my mind the police crime shows where they go over crime scenes with those special lights that show up bloodstains, even after they've been bleached.

Overall it's not a bad job – fortunately the pool of blood was fairly contained. I dread to think what we'd have done if it had been something like a shot to the head. I think we'd have just had to burn the house down and start again. The tricky bit is the grout between the floor tiles. The blood has seeped into those and doesn't want to shift.

'Can you have a rug in a larder?' Oli suggests.

'Not traditionally,' I say, 'but I guess you could have some kind of hessian mat? I don't think I'd feel great about it, though, to be honest. There must be something we can do.'

Reluctant to give too much away in a Google search, I try 'Mrs Hinch bloodstains' and find a lot of results for women whose husbands suffer with nosebleeds. Really when you come to think about it, a very *suspicious* number of nosebleeds. Perhaps they're all doing the same as me. A lot of people are recommending Elbow Grease, which feels a bit patronising, but then I realise that it's an actual product called Elbow Grease – they're not just suggesting I try harder.

'You don't have any "grout and tile deep cleaner" do you?' I ask Oli, hopefully, 'Tucked away in the garage somewhere?'

'Funnily enough no,' says Oli. 'I use the garage in exactly the same way that you do. I don't have a secret man corner where I tuck away important chemicals.'

'I might try baking soda,' I say, having read through all the helpful comments from people like Sheila in Lancaster who seems to have a very complex five-step strategy for her husband's pillowcases. 'Or maybe vinegar. Are you meant to choose or use them at the same time?' I shake my head in confusion.

I know these natural cleaning methods are something I should probably know, but I'm a supermarket own brand multi-surface cleaner girl really. I just decant it into the nice brown glass bottle so that people will think I'm wholesome and care about the planet and probably steep my own cleaning sprays with home-grown lavender. Not that I *don't* care about the planet of course, it's just that it all takes up such a lot of time, doesn't it? And when you've got a full-time job, two children, two cats and a husband who doesn't even own any grout and tile deep cleaner, there isn't a lot of time left for steeping things.

'I think if you mix them you get a mess,' says Oli. 'Remember we did that volcano homework with Ben? I reckon stick to one. Maybe not vinegar as the larder will smell like a chip shop.'

I rummage through the baking shelf. I have baking *powder,* but is that the same as baking *soda*? I'm never sure. 'Oli, will you go and grab me your toothpaste?'

'What do you want my toothpaste for?' he asks.

'It's the whitening one with the baking soda in, isn't it? I'm going to use it on the grout. Maybe it will whiten things. Plus it will smell better than vinegar.'

'I'm really not sure toothpaste is for cleaning floors, Anna,' he says, but I give him a look that says, 'I've just cleaned a man's blood off the floor, humour me,' and he goes off upstairs to get it.

I've just about finished smearing toothpaste along all of the affected lines of grout when the doorbell rings. It reminds me of Ben and Lily and I hope they're getting on okay. I haven't heard from them at least. I wonder what Ben will find if he's able to keep Lily busy and check the footage.

'Toby and Sav are here!' Oli shouts from the hallway, adding, 'And Bianca,' just as their labradoodle bounds enthusiastically through the kitchen. I quickly step out of the larder and close the door behind me. The last thing I want is for her to come back out with toothpaste on her paws. Oli and I have agreed that we're not going to mention Colin's death for now, we're going to see how Toby and Sav are acting, see if we can gather any intel. Not that either of us think they'd be capable and they don't have a motive, but you never know. We're playing it cool.

'Darlings!' I squeal, with a distinct lack of cool. 'Come in come in! Can we get you a drink? Happy Christmas Eve! How was your walk?' I kiss them both in turn and try to act chill.

'Happy Christmas Eve, Anna!' squeals Sav in return, looking around the kitchen at the distinct lack of festivities. 'How's everything going? I thought you'd be knee-deep in stuffing balls by now! How's the glorious tablescape coming together?'

'I've made the Christmas starter,' I say, trying not to sound defensive, 'and the tablescape is next, definitely! Absolutely! We've just been a bit distracted this morning, getting cleaned up after last night.'

'How are you feeling today?' asks Toby, giving me a knowing look. 'You seemed to be enjoying yourself last night!'

'God yes, the amaretto? I'm getting there. There's nothing like the reality of the morning after a party to sober you up, is there?'

'Any good goss?' asks Sav conspiratorially. 'Any bust-ups? Anyone get off with anyone they shouldn't have?' Sav absolutely loves gossip. It's one of my favourite things about him usually, but today I'm on my guard.

'I don't think there's anything too juicy to report, is there, Oli?' I say, turning to my husband for some moral support. 'Nothing scandalous?'

'Not unless you count Margaret from next door lecturing Marcus about leaving his recycling boxes on the pavement,' agrees Oli.

'What about Miranda and Colin though?' says Toby. 'We saw them having what looked like a massive barney in the kitchen. Something about how Colin had only come dressed as Father Christmas to lure women onto his lap. Not that anyone was falling for it, mind.'

'Oooh yes she was furious!' Sav agrees. 'She actually slapped him! Can you imagine? It was like watching a live soap opera!'

Oli and I exchange a look.

'I didn't know about that,' I say. 'When was that? What happened afterwards?'

'Oh I don't know,' says Toby. 'It wasn't massively late I don't think, but she'd clearly had a few. Nothing else happened. She shouted that she was "calling Don straight after Christmas" and then stormed off. I don't know if she *left* left.'

'It was terribly exciting,' says Sav. 'We were desperate to know who Don was. My money's on a lover.'

'Miranda?' I say. 'I don't know. I wouldn't put it past Colin but Miranda, I'm not sure.'

'Oh Colin for sure,' agrees Sav. 'The man's scum. We were delighted to see him get slapped.' I look more closely at Sav, as he almost spits out the word 'scum'. His light-hearted, gossipy demeanour has definitely taken a turn.

'I didn't know you knew him?' I ask, cautiously. 'Other than from me bitching about him of course, which is probably reason enough to dislike him.'

Sav looks uncomfortable and I notice Toby discreetly place a supportive hand on his arm.

'It's a bit embarrassing really,' says Sav. He looks like he would rather be anywhere else. Toby gives his arm a squeeze.

'It's not embarrassing at all,' says Toby, his voice angry. 'You've got nothing to be embarrassed about. It's Colin who should be ashamed of himself. Or maybe the town council for letting him on that panel in the first place.'

Sav flashes Toby a grateful smile. 'I didn't realise who he was,' he explains. 'He just introduced himself as a local entrepreneur. He called himself a venture capitalist!' Sav laughs bitterly. 'What a joke.'

'Sorry,' says Oli, 'catch me up here. What are you talking about?'

'A few months ago I applied to attend a business event that was being run by the local council, a *Dragons' Den* style thing where half a dozen local start-up businesses got to go and present to a panel of local experts and potential investors.'

'Oh that's awesome, Sav, I didn't know that!' Sav works full-time as a teacher at Lily's school – it's how he and Toby met in fact, when Ben was there – but a while ago he started making his own treats for Bianca, just for fun. Dog-friendly biscuits and dried fruit and vegetable chews. He started making them for people he knew at school, and they told their friends and before he knew it he was going along to markets at weekends. It turns out that dedicated dog owners are prepared to spend a lot of money on dried-up bits of sweet potato.

'I got chosen, possibly because they get to tick the gay box *and* the ethnic minority box with me,' he adds cynically, 'and I pitched Pup's Pantry to the panel. They all loved the idea, but it was Colin – or Col as he called himself for the event – who wanted to invest. He made me an offer and I accepted.'

'And that's when we started to figure out that Colin's investment might not be all it was cracked up to be. He'd been quick to transfer the initial first part of the investment, and Sav started looking at new branding and packaging options, but then Colin started throwing his weight around.'

'He told me he wanted to have his business logo on every bit of packaging, and as part of the logo – he even talked about changing the name Pup's Pantry to something that incorporated his company name, Buzz Wize Media. I knew that was the company you worked for, Anna, so that was when I realised who he was. He got aggressive, saying I wouldn't see the rest of the money and that he was going to take all of my ideas and recipes and launch his own rival business unless I agreed to his terms. It was awful, Anna. I didn't know what to do.'

Sav looks so dejected, I want to throw my arms around him. 'Oh, Sav,' I say instead. 'I'm so sorry! What a dickish thing for him to do. You should have told us!'

'I couldn't,' says Sav. 'The whole thing was so horrible and I didn't want to put you in an awkward position with your boss. I just felt such a fool for not realising sooner or for not being more professional about the whole thing. I should have taken legal advice from the start, drawn up proper terms, but I was just so excited and thrilled that someone like Colin, or what I *thought* Colin was at least, believed in me! I've been a right idiot.'

'Mate, you haven't at all,' says Oli, giving him an awkward pat on the back. 'Of course you were excited. This is all new stuff – you weren't to know he was out to swindle you. There's no shame in trusting people.'

'But I shouldn't have rushed into it,' protests Sav. 'I should have researched him at least, found out more about my potential business partner before I got carried away designing packaging. I just loved the idea of creating a legacy for Bianca.'

At the sound of her name her ears prick up and she goes to stand by Sav, leaning herself against his legs and gazing up at him adoringly.

'It's been a bit of a shit couple of months really,' says Toby, his hand still on Sav's arm in a gesture of solidarity.

'And then when he showed up at your party last night,' says Sav, 'we didn't know what to do. Toby was all for having it out with him then and there.'

'I was fuming,' says Toby. 'He came over to say hello and was so obnoxious, it was all I could do not to throttle him.'

'But we didn't want to cause a scene,' says Sav, casting a sideways glance at Toby, 'or I didn't at least, so I took Toby off into the kitchen until he calmed down. We agreed that for the sake of Christmas harmony we would do our best to stay out of his way and not ruin the evening for everyone.'

'It was hard, believe me,' admits Toby. 'I've seen how it's taken its toll on Sav. With that and the end of the Christmas term at school, well, we've had some dark days.' Toby moves his arm around Sav's shoulder and pulls him into a side hug.

I look at Oli for a cue and he has his arms clasped across his chest and is nodding vigorously, which I know means: 'I don't have a fucking clue what to do or say here.'

'I'm so sorry you've had to go through this,' I say to both of them, and then remember and add, 'are still going through this,' because although it's Toby and Sav and I hate lying to them, I don't want them to know that Colin is dead, not quite yet. 'I'd have never let him come to the party if I'd known, guys. I'm so sorry.'

'It's not your fault,' says Sav kindly, 'and it's okay, because we've taken steps to sort it out.'

I hear Oli draw a quick intake of breath next to me and I force my face to not look horrified. 'Taken steps?' I say casually. 'What have you done?'

'We're keeping our cards close to our chest for now,' says Toby, 'because he is your boss after all and we don't want to put you in a difficult situation, but let's just say he shouldn't be bothering us too much from now on.'

Fuck. What have they done? What do they mean by taking steps?! Does taking steps mean stabbing him to death amongst the tins of sweetcorn and half-empty packets of Fruit and Fibre? Surely leaving my boss dead in my larder would fall under 'putting me in a difficult situation'? It's definitely not an EASY situation. But would they be so blasé about it if they'd killed him?

'Anyway,' says Sav, clearly wanting to change the subject, 'we brought the phone over – we found it on the driveway as we were leaving last night. Hopefully you can rehome it.'

'Oh yes,' I say, reminded of why they came over in the first place, 'Colin's phone.'

'It's not Colin's,' says Toby, looking confused. 'I would have run over it if it was. Why did you think it was Colin's?'

'No reason,' I say. 'I didn't think really – we'd just been talking about Colin I suppose and my brain made a jump.'

'If it is Colin's then it's a pretty weird picture to have,' says Sav. He takes the phone out of his pocket and taps it. The lock screen lights up. The picture is taken on a beautiful day. The sky is a deep blue and in the background you can see Stonehenge. In the foreground, smiling happily into the camera, are Marcus and Georgie.

CHAPTER 10

Sav and Toby left once they'd handed over the phone – they were going home to watch *The Search for Santa Paws* with Bianca and some Pup's Pantry doggy popcorn. (Liver flavour.)

Oli and I stand in the hall for a minute, trying to process everything that just happened.

'Well,' I say eventually.

'Well indeed,' says Oli. 'That was a lot of new information, wasn't it?'

'It really was. Shall we have a sandwich?' I saw the time when we all looked at the mystery phone – nearly two o'clock – and realised I haven't had anything to eat yet today.

'Good idea,' says Oli. 'There was some smoked salmon left, wasn't there? We could have that.'

We go into the kitchen and Oli looks for the salmon in the fridge while I put the kettle on and put teabags into mugs. 'I can't see it,' says Oli, his head in the fridge. 'You didn't use it all, did you?'

I sigh. One of my pet hates is my entire family's inability to see things that are right under their noses. They all do it and it drives me nuts. I don't know if they genuinely have something wrong with their eyes or if it's just easier to whine until I come and find things for them.

'Let me find it,' I say, gently shoving him out of the way. 'You do the tea.' He grabs the milk and retreats.

It is actually quite hard to see anything in the fridge because it's so full of the random food that you only ever buy at Christmas, like that cheese in a ring, rolled in nuts. What's that about? Oli insists he loves it and that we absolutely have to have it for Christmas, but I secretly think that if he loved it that much he'd buy it at other times surely? I'm not even sure what kind of cheese it is, or what nuts, come to think of it.

I start pulling out jars of pickled cabbage and tubs of taramasalata but I only just had the salmon – it wouldn't be right at the back would it? But where is it? I don't specifically remember putting it away, but then I often don't *specifically* remember driving to Tesco, but I always seem to get there.

And then I remember the cats rubbing around my legs while I made the starter and the fact that in all the confusion, they haven't eaten yet today either.

'For fuck's sake,' I say, closing the fridge. 'The cats have got it.'

'The whole lot?' says Oli, looking sad.

'Packet and all I'm assuming. It's not in the fridge and they were hanging around while I was making the starter.' Marvellous. The last thing we need is for them to have dragged it off somewhere, only to be discovered tomorrow when Oli's Mum sits down on the sofa, checks under the cushions (she does do this) and comes out with a handful of fish.

'I'm too hungry to look for it now,' I whine. 'Let's just have something else and look for it afterwards, otherwise I'm going to get grumpy.' We switch back roles and Oli takes over the fridge.

'Ooh!' he says, bringing out the nut cheese. 'Let's have this! I love this – we should really get it more often.'

'You really should,' I say. 'What type of cheese even is it?'

'I don't know,' says Oli, shrugging. 'Soft?'

'Is *soft* an actual type of cheese?' I ask, picking up the packet and examining the ingredients. 'Wow, okay, sixty-nine per cent soft cheese it says, so maybe it is a type.'

Oli sniggers. I give him an enquiring look.

'You said sixty-nine,' he explains and sniggers again. I roll my eyes.

'And it's eight per cent candied papaya,' I add. 'Who knew?'

Oli has gone to the larder for crackers. 'It smells very minty in here,' he shouts back into the kitchen.

'That'll be the toothpaste,' I shout back.

While we eat our weird tropical nut cheese and crackers we discuss the lost phone.

'It could just be that someone lost their phone,' I say, 'and it has nothing at all to do with the murder, but I don't know. It's the afternoon already. If you'd left your phone at a party you'd have noticed by now and said

107

something, wouldn't you? Unless you knew that you dropped it in suspicious circumstances.'

'Maybe,' says Oli, 'although maybe you just haven't noticed yet? Especially if you're hungover. I've definitely been there before. . .'

'I don't buy it. You'd notice straight away. Who doesn't check their phone every five minutes?' As I speak the mystery phone lights up with a WhatsApp message and we both jump guiltily, not so guiltily though that we both don't immediately crane to see what it says.

'It's from someone called Alex,' says Oli, 'but the preview is switched off. We don't even know if that's a man or a woman.'

I have another cracker and cheese. It is actually pretty good. Maybe I will buy it more often.

'Well it must belong to either Marcus or Georgie,' I say, 'otherwise it's super creepy. I have Marcus's number. I'll just call it and see.'

I get my own phone and see that there's a message from Ben. 'Can we come home yet?' it says. I'd sort of forgotten about them, to be honest.

I type back quickly, hoping Ben can't tell. 'Yep, coast is clear.' I add a magnifying-glass emoji, press send, and immediately regret it. Is that too flippant? Probably. Oh well.

I call Marcus. The mystery phone stays silent and instead Marcus answers my call. I don't know why, but I hadn't been prepared for that as a scenario, so I feel rather put on the spot.

'Oh hi!' I say, as though I'm surprised to hear from him. 'How are you?'

'Fine,' says Marcus. 'Everything okay?'

'Oh yes, sorry,' I mumble, 'we found a phone, left behind last night, and I think it's Georgie's. Is she with you?'

'No, she wasn't feeling great last night so she left early and went back to her place. I haven't heard from her today but if you've got her phone then that makes sense. How's the house looking this morning? It was a bit of a crime scene by the time we all left,' he jokes.

'A crime scene?' I say sharply. 'What do you mean?'

'Oh just that we'd made a bit of a mess, you know. It looked like you'd had burglars and they'd ransacked the place! I think we got everyone home in one piece though – no one passed out on the sofa when you came down this morning?'

'Ha-ha no!' I joke back. My laugh is too long and shrill. 'No, nothing like that, no dead bodies in the larder or anything!' Oli stares at me in horror.

'I should hope not.' Marcus laughs. 'Not after all that work – that larder is a thing of beauty! I'd say I'd let Georgie know about her phone, but I can drop it round to her if you want to bring it over?' Marcus lives a few doors away from us, so this would be the easiest thing to do.

'I actually wanted to ask Georgie's advice about something,' I bluster, 'you know, *women's things*, so I could pop it round if you let me know where she lives. I have to go out anyway for something.' I'm hoping the stage-whispered 'women's things' is enough to put off any further questioning.

'Oh sure,' says Marcus, 'if you don't mind? And ask her to give me a call maybe? We were going to go out this evening, if she's feeling better.' He gives me her address, we say our goodbyes and I hang up.

'What the fuck was that?' asks Oli as soon as Marcus has definitely gone. 'What was all that dead body in the larder shit?'

'I was testing him,' I say, feeling rather pleased with myself. 'I thought it was a bit much him saying about the house looking like a crime scene, so I was looking for a reaction.'

'And?' says Oli.

'Nothing,' I say. 'He just laughed and said something about how lovely our larder is. He didn't skip a beat, Oli. I don't think it's him.'

'I don't know if it's as easy as that,' cautions Oli. 'I don't know if you know this about murderers but they can lie, especially on the phone when you can't see their facial expressions or body language.'

'Murderers can lie?' I say, in mock horror. 'Yes thank you, genius, I do know that as it happens. I just think it's unlikely that he wouldn't even flinch a teeny bit – he was so relaxed about the whole thing. I'm not saying we cross him off the list; I'm just saying we make a note.'

'And the women's things,' says Oli. 'I'm guessing this is just a ruse to go round and test Georgie too?'

'A good detective speaks to every suspect, Oli, you know that, and this is the perfect excuse given that we barely know her. I know she probably left the party before it happened, but we don't know for sure, and the chance to talk to her in person is too good an opportunity to miss.'

'Before you go though, we need to find the smoked salmon.'

110

God. I'd forgotten about the smoked salmon. We start our search in the kitchen but with no success, so move on to the living room. I check all of the cats' favourite hiding spots – behind the curtains and the sofa and under the sideboard – but still no luck.

'You know,' I say to Oli as I get down onto all fours to check underneath the armchairs, 'if this was an Agatha Christie novel, this would be the point at which I would find a loose button. Then I'd go round to see Georgie and notice she was wearing an unusual blazer that had a single button missing and I'd have a lightbulb moment where I'd stare off into the distance, all the pieces clicking together, and she'd break down and confess. Before the police arrived, though, she'd tell me exactly how and why she did it. I've never understood why they do that.'

'She was at the party,' Oli points out, spoiling my fun. 'She could just have lost a button. Anyone can lose a button. Unless we find the button clutched in the closed fist of the dead man then I don't think it necessarily proves anything.'

'Or a hatpin,' I say, 'a lot more things came down to hatpins in the 1940s.'

'Here's something!' says Oli. 'It's torn in half, so I'm not sure. Let me see.' He's examining a scrap of paper. 'Wait, I think it's a ticket. It says, "The Orient Express".'

'Ha bloody ha,' I say, throwing a cushion at him. 'Point taken. You just feel like there should be some *clues*, you know? Something a bit more obvious. But I guess that's only in books. Where the hell have the cats put this salmon?'

There's a noise from the hallway. The front door opens and we hear Ben and Lily explode into the house, arguing about something, as usual. The front door slams.

'Shoes off!' I shout, but they are already both in the living room, still wearing them.

'Mum!' Lily runs over to me, waving a Happy Meal box. 'I didn't get the toy I wanted and Ben wouldn't go and ask them if I could swap. He said I was being an "ungrateful swine" and should just be glad I had food to eat.'

'She wouldn't shut up about it, Mum, but no way was I going up to the counter again. I'd already had to go and ask for more ketchup *and* another straw because Lily said hers was a funny shape.' Ben stops and takes in the fact of me on the floor on my knees. 'What are you doing, Mum?'

'I'm looking for some smoked salmon,' I say.

'Have you tried the fridge?' he says.

'Everyone's a joker today aren't they?' I reply. 'I have tried the fridge, thank you, but the cats got it. They've taken it somewhere and we are trying to find it so it doesn't stink the place out.'

'Can't you just look at their trackers?' calls Ben over his shoulder as he goes back out into the hallway and kicks his shoes off.

'What do you mean their trackers?' I say.

'You know, the stupid GPS things you make them wear so that you can find them if they go missing and not have a breakdown like you did when Tuppence got stuck in Mrs Rooney's shed. Just go on the app and see where they are.'

'Have I even got the app?' I ask. I get easily overwhelmed by apps. At last count I have SIX different apps just for paying for car parks and yet somehow I still never have the one I need. How can there even *be* six car parking apps? Why can we not just keep 20p coins in the car like the good old days?

'You set them up,' he says, 'or I did at least, so you must have. You know you pay a monthly subscription for those, Mum. Do you not even look at them?'

I'm pretty sure I have never once looked at the cat tracking app. 'It's just for emergencies,' I explain. 'Like the shed. Show me how to do it then, Ben. My phone is on the side in the kitchen.'

Ben goes off to get it and when he comes back he already has the app open and a little map showing on screen. 'There's an icon for each cat, see? You can get a pretty accurate location, so we should be able to find them. Let's see.' He looks at the screen and then heads off into the dining room.

Thirty seconds later and he's back, holding a mauled packet of smoked salmon. Tommy and Tuppence are trotting after him, looking annoyed that their lunch has been interrupted.

'Ben, you're a genius!' I say. 'That's so clever! I'd never have thought to do that.' I give him a kiss on the shoulder (he's too tall now for me to kiss him on the head unless he's sitting down), and he returns the sign of affection by giving me the smoked salmon packet.

'It's not hard,' he says. 'It's a pretty decent app. You can see how far they're going from the house, look back at where they've been, all sorts.'

113

I stop in my tracks on the way to the bin.

'See where they've been?' I ask, turning back around and coming to look at the screen. 'Does it store stuff then?'

'Yeah look, in this tab,' Ben taps the screen a couple of times and I can suddenly see exactly where each cat has been for the last twenty-four hours.

'Oli!' I shout, grabbing the phone from Ben and brandishing it at him. 'This is it! There *are* clues!'

'Have you found a hatpin?' asks Oli. I hit him on the arm.

'No,' I say, 'better!' I remember that Lily is in the room. 'Lily,' I say, 'do you fancy picking out an outfit for Christmas Day tomorrow? You should choose something extra lovely as Grandma and Grandpa are going to be here!'

She looks unsure. It's something she wants to do I know, but there's the undertone of being *asked* to do something that's putting her off.

'I was thinking you could plan out a selection of outfits and then do a fashion show!' She loves anything performative, so I know this will swing it for her. 'And make us tickets?'

'Can I use your jewellery?' she bargains.

'Absolutely,' I say, 'you can use anything in the special red jewellery box on my dressing table.' The special red jewellery box is the box I keep all of my crappy costume jewellery in, knowing it's the faux velvet inside that Lily loves as much as anything. All of my decent stuff, not that there's much of it, is in an old Oxo stock cube tin in one of my drawers.

Lily runs off upstairs and I start waving the phone at Oli again. 'I've not found any buttons,' I say, 'but

114

remember what I was saying earlier about how I wished Tommy could tell us who did it? It's all here!'

Oli looks confused. 'You know who did it? Are there cameras in the trackers?'

'God no, nothing as good as that, but this is almost as good! Our timeline just got a glow-up – Tommy's going to tell us the exact time of death!'

CHAPTER 11

'I don't get it,' says Oli. 'How does knowing where the cats were help us?'

'Don't you remember? When I first opened the larder this morning and found Colin, Tommy was stuck in there. He ran straight out and went out through the cat flap.'

'Colin was killed in the larder?' asks Ben. 'That's gross. Is it a mess in there now? What about the Pop-Tarts? Are they okay?'

'It's all fine, Ben,' I reassure him. 'We've cleaned it all up and the Pop-Tarts were fine. There was just a little bit of blood on the floor but it's all okay now, I promise.'

'Eww, Mum, a little bit of blood? That's grim.'

'It was grim, Ben, I'm sorry, but look, take my phone and show me how we get at the history. If we assume that no one opened the larder after Colin was killed until I came down this morning, then that means that Tommy was shut in there *when* it happened. If we can see how long he was in there for, we can see exactly what time Colin died!' I look at Oli and Ben triumphantly.

'Oh yeah, Mum, you're right! Look.' He scrolls down the page. 'This is for Tuppence – she went outside a bit after 9 p.m. and didn't come in for the rest of the night, but Tommy was in the house and moving around.'

I'm leaning over Ben's shoulder, trying to make sense of it. 'Here we are,' says Ben, 'this is where he stops moving. He's in the same spot in the house here from 11.57 p.m. last night to 9.53 a.m. this morning.' He looks up at me and he's beaming. Who knew it would take a murder to bring us together?

'That's it!' I say, clapping my hands together. 'We've got it! 9.53 a.m. is when I opened the door this morning and he ran out, so he must have been in there since 11.57 p.m., meaning Colin was killed just before midnight!'

'Maybe,' says Oli, 'but let's not get ahead of ourselves. There could be another explanation. What if the cat went in earlier when someone was getting something, and then just stayed in there when Colin went in later.'

I sag. He's right of course. It's unlikely, but possible. 'I guess,' I say reluctantly, 'but I feel like Tommy would have run out if he'd been stuck in there for a while already and someone opened the door. And it fits with what we have so far, doesn't it? The kids saw him outside around 11.30 p.m. but none of us can remember seeing him afterwards, and he definitely wasn't there when we finally kicked everyone out and went to bed, was he?'

'No, he wasn't,' admits Oli. 'I just don't want us to jump to conclusions, that's all.'

Damn Oli for being so reasonable. I was so excited; it felt like such a neat answer. 'Can we have it as a working hypothesis at least?' I ask.

'Fine,' Oli relents, 'working hypothesis.'

'I think it's spot on, Mum,' says Ben, and he holds up a fist for me to bump. It's almost as good a feeling as fixing the time of death.

'Let's just say that it's right for now,' I say, hoping Oli will forget about the hypothesis aspect if I throw myself into it enough, 'where does that leave our timeline and suspect list?'

We decamp to the kitchen table with Ben and re-examine our earlier list making. Ben looks over the suspect list.

'Hang on,' he says, 'how come Sasha is on here? She didn't do it!'

'We're just being thorough,' says Oli in a placatory tone. 'We discounted Jaz because you said that his dad picked him up just after you guys all saw Colin in the garden, but Sasha stayed on and we don't know for now where she was. We're just being sensible, mate.'

'It definitely wasn't her,' says Ben in a low voice. I can understand he doesn't want to think that the girl he fancies would ever do anything wrong so we need to tread carefully.

'I'm sure it's not her,' I say. 'We just need to include her until we can cross her off.'

'Well, cross her off now,' says Ben firmly. 'It wasn't her.'

'You can't know where she was every minute though,

Ben,' says Oli. 'I'm not saying she snuck off and killed Colin, I'm just saying we need to be sure before we discount people. She could have gone to the toilet anytime, gone to get a drink.'

'It wasn't her,' says Ben, the colour rising in his cheeks. 'Not if it was at 11.57 p.m. Definitely not.'

'Why?' I ask, sensing there's more to this than we think. 'What was happening at 11.57 p.m.?'

'Nothing,' says Ben quickly. 'I just know it wasn't her. Can't you just take my word for it?'

'Of course we can, Ben,' Oli says. He looks at me over Ben's head and shakes his. I give a little nod of agreement.

'Maybe we can eliminate her another way,' I say brightly, remembering that we still have the footprint clue. I get my phone out and open the photos app to show Oli and Ben the photograph I took before the police arrived and Bacon trod in it. Unfortunately I open the camera by mistake and it's in front view, meaning I get a sudden and unwelcome look at my face from below – it resembles a sort of skin landslide.

What is it that happens to your face once you turn forty? I've always looked young for my age and remember finding it annoying when I was in my early twenties, how I could never get served anywhere. Older people would laugh and tell me I'd be grateful for it in my forties, but it's not worked out like that. One minute I was thirty-nine and listening to people tell me how great I looked for my age and then BAM, I turned forty and aged at least seven years seemingly overnight.

Where once I had a jawline and a smooth, tight

neck, now I have a sort of soft crêpey fold that runs down my chin and onto my chest. And the jowls! Dear Lord, let's not even talk about the jowls. Sometimes I'll experiment in the mirror, pulling my skin back just a little bit on each side from my cheekbones to the top of my ear and I get a flash of me a few years ago. And then I let go and it's horrific, the way my face *falls* back into its new, relaxed state. I know it shouldn't matter, that it's normal and natural and it's just the patriarchy, and I should be grateful to experience the privilege of ageing, blah de blah, but I do miss my old neck.

I close the camera as quickly as possible and vow never EVER to go on top again.

I open photos and find the footprint. The flour was a good base for it, and the part of the print we have is very clear. Unfortunately there isn't a complete print – only about the front two-thirds of it were in the flour. The part that we do have is a right foot and has a pattern of wide chevrons, pointing towards the toe end. The toe is round and wide.

'Well that's not Sasha,' says Ben, looking relieved. 'She was wearing Converse and there're diamonds on the bottom.' He looks again. 'It's pretty chunky,' he says. 'It looks like it might be a boot? It's definitely not a heel or anything like those shoes you were wearing last night, Mum.'

I'm touched that Ben even noticed my shoes. He barely seems to notice me entering a room normally.

'I remember them because they looked like the ones Granny wore to Grandad's funeral. Bit grim, Mum. No offence.'

Wow. I make a mental note to put the shoes on the charity shop pile as soon as we're done with the whole *solving the murder* thing. I'd been in two minds about them last night, to be honest, but I thought with the sparkly dress that I could get away with them. Now I feel ancient. I love how teenagers seem to think that adding 'no offence' to the end of a sentence makes everything okay.

I open the notes app on the phone and have a look at the measurements I made. I have the width and the length, but without the full print it's not very helpful. We try scaling it up based on some estimates, but the difference between sizes is too small to be able to say for sure. There's no logo or anything distinctive to help us either.

'There was an episode of *Criminal Crossroads* a while ago where they caught the killer based on a shoe print,' says Oli. 'They were able to look at the pattern and see that the shoe was worn down on one particular edge, and they matched that to someone based on how they walk. Is there anything like that on these?'

I zoom in on the photograph and we all look closely for anything that might help us narrow down our suspect list. The only thing we can come up with is that there's a small circle, about half a centimetre across, that doesn't seem to fit with the rest of the pattern – a stone maybe, stuck in the tread? It's not exactly conclusive.

'Can we even say for sure that the print belongs to the murderer?' Oli asks.

'If not then are we saying that someone else, someone who didn't kill Colin, went into the larder, got close enough to stand in the flour, but chose to just ignore the presence of a dead body?'

'No,' says Oli, patiently, 'I'm not saying that, but what if it belongs to Colin? What if it's his shoe print?'

'Maybe,' I say, 'but it's facing the opposite way – towards him. Surely if he'd stumbled backwards it would be toe towards the door?'

'Not necessarily. There could have been a struggle. Maybe someone walks in on him when he has his back turned – he's looking for something on one of the shelves maybe. There's a scuffle, the flour gets knocked over, and *then* he turns around and gets stabbed.'

'It feels a bit far-fetched Dad,' says Ben.

'I agree,' says Oli, 'but we can't go leaping to conclusions. It's like the cat GPS – we can't assume that it gives us the time of death. We need some more evidence that corroborates it to be sure. We can easily disprove the theory though; we just compare it to Colin's print.'

They both look at me expectantly.

'Did you take a picture of that?' ask Oli, hopefully.

I am forced to admit that no, I didn't. They are disappointed, but seriously, I doubt that they would have thought to do it in my position.

'Guys,' I protest, 'I'd just found my boss dead in our larder. I wasn't working through a crime scene analysis checklist, I was *panicking*. It's what you're meant to do in situations like that. I wasn't calmly thinking about evidence gathering, I was freaking out about how I was going to cater Christmas dinner for a large group of people with a corpse in the kitchen.'

Oli puts his hand on my arm and assures me that

what I've got is amazing, that most people would never have thought to even photograph the shoe print, and that if I hadn't done that then it would have been lost forever.

'It could be the deal-breaker,' he says, 'you never know. Anyway, parking the print for now, let's go back to the timeline and our suspects.'

We all agree that if we are working with 11.57 p.m. as the time of death then we can discount Margaret next door. Ben clearly remembers her leaving at about 11.45 p.m. and I've heard her say before that she makes it a point always to get up and go to bed again on the same day. She says she doesn't trust people who don't, that it's unnatural. Fine – whatever, Margaret. I don't think she even knows Colin, and she is in her eighties, so we give her the benefit of the doubt and cross her off.

That leaves us with Toby, Sav, Marcus, Jennie, Bruce and Sasha as people who were definitely here and Georgie and Miranda as maybes.

'I can help with the maybes,' says Ben. 'I went through the Ring doorbell footage at Maccies. Georgie left at 11.15 p.m.'

'You're sure?' I ask.

'Positive,' says Ben. 'She looks right at the camera, so you can see her really clearly. Miranda though doesn't leave until 12.10 a.m., so she's still in the running if she made a quick getaway, which I guess you would really, wouldn't you? She doesn't turn back and look at the camera and she's got a coat on but you can tell it's her from the hair.'

'Well I'm going round to Georgie's with her phone

so I can do a little bit of digging,' I say, 'just in case, but I don't know about Miranda. How are we going to talk to her? Her husband has just died after all. You'd need to have a distinct lack of tact to just turn up and start asking her questions.'

'Well it's obvious then, isn't it?' says Oli.

I pick up my phone and call Jennie.

'Anna! I'm so glad it's you,' says Jennie excitedly as soon as she answers. 'Guess what?'

'Hang on,' I say, 'Oli and Ben are here so I'm putting you on speaker.' There's an awkward few seconds as I try to figure out how to do that without cutting her off and Ben rolls his eyes a lot. 'Right, what have you found out?'

'Susannah Mortimer blocked me on Facebook! Can you believe it?'

I'm not sure what to make of this information or how it's relevant. Susannah is one of the mums from Lily, Matty and Jake's primary school but she wasn't at the party last night. I'm pretty sure they've gone to Lapland for Christmas. She and her husband own a chain of nail salons, which they make a surprising amount of money from. Money laundering Oli says, but I'm not sure – I know they're National Trust members.

'Of course I'm not really surprised,' continues Jennie. 'She's had it in for me since I was the editor of the PTA newsletter and I switched out her piece about littering on the infant playground for a raisin flapjack recipe. It was three thousand words, Anna! No one wants to read three thousand words of sanctimonious preaching about crisp packets.'

'Sorry, Jennie, I don't get it – what has Susannah got to do with Colin?'

'With Colin?' Jennie says, surprised. 'Nothing! I just thought it was a bit of a cheek of her to block me after I gave her darling Jemima lifts to gymnastics every Tuesday for like *six months*.'

'Right,' I say, 'so nothing to do with the murder investigation at all?'

'Well no,' says Jennie, 'except I was only on Instagram in the first place to see if other people had posted party pictures and to do a bit of snooping, and then I remembered they were in Lapland and thought I'd have a look and see what smug photos she had up – all that crap about being so fucking blessed and how much she loves her family – and there I was, blocked! I've never bought how fucking grateful she claims to be to spend all those precious school holidays with Jemima anyway; she's a whiny little shit. She was always stealing Matty's Haribo on the way to gymnastics.

'I do have some other good dirt on our suspect line-up though, which I have added to the murder board. I don't have any photos though – I was going to print some out from Facebook but I'm out of ink. It's okay though because I've assigned everyone a Pokémon.'

'A Pokémon?' I ask, bemused.

'Yes, I dug out Jake's Pokémon cards and I'm using them on the board. It looks very colourful. I'll send you a picture. You're Mimikyu.'

Ben gets his phone out. He taps for a few seconds and then laughs. 'It says Mimikyu is raggedy, Mum, and desperate to be loved.'

'It's cute!' protests Jennie. 'Although kind of hungover-looking, but I thought that was a good shout for you, Anna.'

Ben holds up a picture. Jeez. Raggedy is right, although to be fair it's about how I feel right now.

Before we get too sidetracked I catch Jennie up with everything we've found out so far – the footprint, Georgie's phone and the revelations from Sav and Toby, plus the information from the cat GPS tracker.

'That's so cool,' she says. 'Nice work, Ben. I always knew you were the brains of the family. And how about the note?'

'The note?' I ask. 'What note?'

'You know, the bit of paper you found in Colin's pocket just as the police got there. What did it say? Anything useful or was it something boring like a receipt for laxatives or something? I've always pictured Colin as the constipated type. Not enough roughage.'

I can't believe I'd forgotten about the bit of paper! I'd just shoved it in my jeans pocket when the police knocked, and I'd been in such a state trying to get rid of the tongs and the rubber gloves and then focused on everything that has happened since. I fish it out of my pocket and spread it out on the table.

It's not a receipt for laxatives, or a receipt of any kind in fact. On one side it's printed with a date and a quote: *'Be grateful for slow internet, let it be an opportunity to practise the art of patience.'*

It's from the daily gratitude calendar that I got in the PTA Secret Santa last year that I keep in the kitchen. The date on this one says March 29th, which is a good indication of how grateful I am on a daily basis, but they're useful for shopping lists.

I turn it over. On the back is a note, written in blue pen.

MEET ME IN THE LARDER AT MIDNIGHT.

CHAPTER 12

I switch Jennie to video call so that she can see the note and we all agree that this is an excellent clue. Oli seems happy to accept it as corroborating the time of death, agreeing that it would be too much of a coincidence otherwise. We also agree that it means the murderer was definitely one of our shortlisted guests – nobody else would have had access to the gratitude calendar to be able to write the note.

The note tells me something else – my brother did not write it. When you grow up with someone you know their handwriting as well as you know their face and their voice and Toby did not write that note. Oli points out to me that he could have disguised his handwriting, but even so, I don't believe it.

I also don't believe that someone dashing off a quick note like that in the middle of the kitchen at someone else's party would be *thinking* about trying to change their handwriting. It's all in capitals and so it's harder to tell than if it was more natural writing, but it's not Toby's.

Of course there's still the possibility that the person who wrote the note isn't the same person who murdered Colin, but that feels like a remote possibility right now.

While she's on video Jennie gives us a tour of the murder board. It's pretty much all Pokémon cards, joined together with pins and garden twine and a few handwritten notes.

'It would look more professional if the printer was working,' says Jennie, 'but I'm going to copy out the note and draw the shoe print, that will help, plus I've not written up all of my background checks yet!'

It's the least professional-looking murder board I've ever seen but I haven't the heart to tell her as she's beaming, clearly very proud of her hard work. I can tell that this has given her a much-needed distraction from being without the kids at Christmas, so I'm not about to take that away from her.

'It's brilliant!' I say in a show of support. 'And how about these background checks – have you found anything useful?'

'It's hard to know what's useful or not,' Jennie admits, 'but I've definitely found out *stuff*. I'm not done yet though, so how about I talk you through what I've got so far and we can see if anything stands out?'

We watch as she shuffles various scraps of paper on the table in front of her, before settling on a place to start.

'Right,' Jennie begins, 'let's get the awkward one out of the way first – we've got Toby and Sav. I didn't do much digging on Toby, because I thought we both knew his background already, but I had a bit of a nose around for anything more recent that might connect him to Colin. The company that he works for is mentioned on Buzz Wize Media's website as a client – so there could be a connection there.'

'There's nothing in that,' I reassure her, 'that was basically me writing a couple of press releases for them in work time and Colin made me ask for permission to call them a client as he said it added gravitas because they're a well-known name locally. It wasn't a big deal though and it definitely wouldn't be a motive for murder – they were pretty decent press releases.'

'Okay, that's cool, makes sense. Then we've got Sav. This is where it gets a bit more interesting. Did you know that Colin was an investor in Sav's dog treat business?' Jennie leans back in her chair and taps her pen against her teeth. I have to admit that I do and Jennie looks a little deflated.

'Not until a couple of hours ago though, and it sounds like there's some beef there for sure.'

'And not just in the dog biscuits,' quips Oli, smiling. Ben groans. Jennie and I both look at him and then back to the phone.

'It looks like they first met at a local *Dragons' Den* type event,' continues Jennie, 'and there's a bit of local press coverage about the deal, but then I found a few tweets from Sav that gave the distinct impression that the partnership wasn't turning out quite as expected.'

'It's not called Twitter anymore,' chips in Ben. 'It's X.'

'So what do we call tweets now then?' asks Jennie. 'Xeets maybe?'

'You just call them posts,' says Ben.

'Whatever,' says Jennie, waving one hand, 'tweets, xeets, whatever they are now, Sav wrote some and they were shady AF.' We watch her scroll through something on her laptop.

'Here, listen to this that he *posted* a few weeks ago: *"I'm a positive person who only ever wanted to create a legacy for my dog Bianca that I could feel proud of. I can't go into details here but let's just say that I feel I've been taken further and further from that dream. #corporategreed #snakeinthegrass"* – those are feisty hashtags, aren't they?'

'Snake in the grass?' says Oli. 'That's a bit much, isn't it? Sav is so sweet normally. I can't imagine him saying that in real life. It's bizarre, isn't it, how people will say shit on Twitter that they'd never say in the real world.'

'It's X, Dad,' says Ben.

'X then. X-rated it should be, the amount of bile people spew. What is X even meant to mean? That's not a name, is it?'

'It's Elon Musk, Dad,' says Ben, as though that explains everything, which it does really.

'Anyway,' says Jennie loudly, trying to get us back on track, 'safe to say Sav has been pretty pissed off. A few days ago though he tweets again.' Ben looks set to speak but Jennie interrupts. 'He *posts* again: *"Thank you so much to everyone who has been supporting me through this difficult period with Pup's Pantry. I'm pleased to tell you that a plan is in place to take things into the New Year on a more positive note. #DavidandGoliath #standuptobullies".'*

We all agree that it's suspicious and unfortunate timing for Sav.

'David did kill Goliath, didn't he?' asks Jennie. 'In which case you could argue it's a death threat.'

'I don't know about that, Jen. Isn't it a bit more metaphorical than that? I'm not sure Sav is saying he's off to shoot Colin down with a catapult or anything.'

'Maybe not,' says Jennie, 'but he clearly had something planned, and we don't know what that was. We can't discount him for sure.'

'You're right,' Oli says. 'I feel like it's a pretty strong motive if things had gotten out of hand and Sav couldn't see a way out.'

'Honestly, you two,' I say, looking between Oli and Jennie, 'we've known Sav for years. Can you really see him planning to kill a man over a few dog biscuits?'

'It's not just dog biscuits though, Anna, it's Bianca's legacy! You know how much he loves that dog – it would be like someone coming after Ben.' She nods at Ben and Ben looks at me.

'Yeah, Mum,' says Ben, looking at me all wide-eyed and innocent, 'you'd stab a man to stop him coming after my legacy, right?'

'I love you very much, Ben,' I say, 'but I don't think I'd murder someone just because they wanted a piece of my biscuit-making business, even if it was meant to be about *creating a legacy*.'

'Plus we're not saying he *planned* it,' adds Oli, 'he could have been so taken aback by seeing Colin at the party that he lost his cool. Maybe he just wanted to have it out with him once and for all, tell him to back off. He reached for the knife in a moment of passion and BOOM, there he is, dead on the floor.'

I sigh. 'Fine,' I say, 'fine, it's not impossible. But it's unlikely.'

'Somebody did it, Anna,' says Jennie, 'and let's face it, nobody seems *likely*. Somebody did it though, no matter how unlikely it might appear to us right now. Somebody killed Colin.'

The thought sobers us all because she's right. I'm sure none of us could look at our list of what twenty-four hours ago were party guests and now are murder suspects and pick any one of them out as 'likely' killers. And yet one of them must be.

As harsh as it feels, I would rather someone like Bruce or Miranda were responsible than my brother's partner, someone who I've trusted with my children, so I quickly change the subject.

'What next?' I ask Jennie. 'Anything else that could be pertinent?'

'Marcus and Georgie have a lot of recent pictures on Facebook,' says Jennie, 'but nothing exciting to report there. They've only been together about a year and I couldn't find anything very incriminating on either of them. Marcus plays for the local cricket team so there were a few bits about that. He did a sponsored triathlon in the summer for Cancer Research, which hardly sets alarm bells ringing.'

'Not really,' I agree. 'Raising money for charity isn't a well-known red flag for a murderer.'

'Same with Georgie really,' says Jennie, 'nothing much of note, except that a couple of years ago there was a piece in the paper about her parents being killed in a car accident. Her adoptive parents actually. The reports I read didn't reference any suspicious circumstances; it was being talked about because it was on a stretch of road that people are always complaining about, but you never know, there could have been more to it. Colin's death could have been some kind of revenge? Although it was in Leeds – that's where they lived at the time.'

'Maybe,' I say, 'although if I was planning to avenge the death of my parents I think I might do it a bit more discreetly and with a bit more planning, or even make it look like a car accident, circle of life and all that.'

'Is that what you'd do when you were killing to protect my honour, Mum?' asks Ben. 'Make it look like an accident?'

'I am not killing to protect your honour, Ben, I'm just saying it's a bit public. Plus we know she'd already left the house at 11.15 p.m.'

'And how about Margaret?' asks Jennie.

'She's off the table too with our new timeline,' I confirm.

'That's good,' says Jennie, 'because all I have for her is endless Facebook complaints about recycling boxes and street lighting and people parking in your street to walk into town. She seems to think the street belongs to her and no one but her should be allowed to park in it.'

'Don't I know it,' I say, rolling my eyes. 'There's a Nissan Micra that parks outside her house on weekdays and it drives her absolutely batty. I never stop hearing about it. She goes on and on about how she wishes she didn't have to complain about all of these things, but I don't know what she'd do if she didn't – her whole life seems to be spent peering out of one window or another, checking that the postman is doing his job properly and none of the kids in the street are daring to enjoy themselves. You'd think she'd be glad to see children playing outside, but you should have seen the fuss she kicked up when they accidentally knocked over one of her gnomes with a football.'

'So now we get onto the family,' says Jennie, 'and first up we have Bruce Broadbent.'

Ah yes, Bruce, Colin's only child and sole heir to the Buzz Wize Media empire. Bruce is a suspect I could get behind. He's inherited all of his father's arrogance, although without the sleazy element thank God, but none of Colin's albeit limited business acumen.

Everyone at work resents Bruce because Colin made him COO, even though he can barely work the coffee machine. Buzz Wize doesn't even need a COO; it's just a title to make Bruce feel like he can swan around the office criticising people. The only thing he has in his favour is that he got his looks at least from his mother, so he's not unattractive, but that really only fuels the arrogant office swagger.

Bruce has worked for his dad since he left school, presumably because no one else will have him, and he's thirty-one now. Everyone in the office has noticed the tension growing between Colin and Bruce over the last year or so – from Bruce's side at least. Colin may well be oblivious to it but it's clear that Bruce thinks Colin is getting too old for the job. He makes a lot of comments about *trends* and the need to innovate and pivot and other wanky phrases that essentially mean 'change the way we do things for the sake of changing them when they work perfectly well already'.

With Colin out of the way Bruce would be the big boss man, but is that enough of a motive for murder?

'Oh it's not just that,' says Jennie, when I fill her in on all of this. 'I reckon there could be more to it than that. I've been doing some googling and pretty much every single image of him online is one of those naff society-page photos from that magazine you can get in Sainsbury's that pretends it's super glossy and chic but is mainly ads for kitchens and private schools – you know the one.'

I do know the one. Susannah Mortimer has a column in it that she calls 'The Good Life'. Just because she has a couple of chickens and once made jam for the PTA summer fair, she thinks she's Felicity fucking Kendal.

'Well when I started looking a bit more closely, I noticed that an awful lot of them were taken at things like the races, or at charity casino nights, and he's always holding a glass of something, without fail.'

'Isn't that just what these events are about though?' I ask. 'Local business owners get together somewhere suitably showy and drink cheap cava, pretending it's champagne, and compare where they went for their last skiing holiday?'

'Yes, there is that, but did you know that a little while ago Bruce got a temporary ban for driving under the influence? He was pulled over by police in the early hours of the morning and found to be significantly over the limit and, get this, was driving home from a *casino*.'

'How on earth did you find that out?' I asked, genuinely impressed. I'd not heard anything about it.

'I have my methods,' replied Jennie, smiling smugly. 'It's an interesting angle though, isn't it? What about if Bruce has addiction problems – gambling or drinking or even both? He's got in too deep, maybe he owes a few people money, things have got desperate. Could he have killed his dad for the money?'

'Colin dotes on Bruce though,' I point out. 'He's the child who can do no wrong. If Bruce were in trouble wouldn't Colin help him?'

'He doesn't dote on him that much, Mum,' interrupts Ben. 'That's not what it looked like when they were arguing last night anyway.'

We all look at Ben. When had they been arguing? What were they arguing about? Why hadn't Ben mentioned this before? Oli, Jennie and I start firing questions at him.

'Whoa, hang on,' says Ben, 'one at a time. I hadn't mentioned it because I'd forgotten about it. It didn't seem like a big deal at the time. I figured Colin was just a dick who would argue with anyone. And I don't know what it was about. I went through the kitchen to get Cokes from the fridge for Sasha and Jaz and they were in there. I was barely there any time. Bruce was looking mad and Colin said something like: "It's not all about you anymore, Bruce. You're going to have to get used to that." And then I left again.'

We spend five minutes or so thinking about what Colin could have meant by that. Perhaps Colin was planning on replacing him at work? Jennie suggests that Miranda could be pregnant and we all screw up our faces. Ben speaks for us all when he declares it gross. We agree that Bruce is looking like a strong suspect and that we're going to have to figure out some way to speak to him.

'I haven't got as far as Sasha and Miranda yet,' Jennie

says. 'I went on Instagram to look them up and that's when I got distracted by Susannah "stick-up-her-arse" Mortimer. I can do them next though.'

'It wasn't Sasha!' Ben interjects. 'For God's sake, Mum, how many times do I need to tell you it wasn't her?'

'I know you don't want to think it could be her,' I say gently, 'we're just being cautious, remember, Ben?'

'It's not that I'm being simple or naïve, Mum, I'm telling you for a fact, hands down, Scout's honour, IT'S NOT HER.' He shouts this last bit and we're all silent for a minute or so, even Jennie, who looks down at her notes, avoiding the screen.

'It doesn't matter that you've not done Miranda yet,' I say, hastily changing the subject, 'as we've had an idea and we've got a job for you, if you're up for it.'

'Hell yeah I'm up for it!' says Jennie, looking pleased with the prospect of being assigned a task. 'What is it exactly? I mean I'm sure I *will* be up for it regardless. It's either that or watching *The Snowman* on my own and drinking Baileys in a fit of self-pity, so fire away.'

'We thought you could go and see Miranda,' I say. 'I know she's only just found out her husband has died, and the situation is going to require a lot of tact and sensitivity, which is why we thought of you.'

Oli coughs. I give him a kick under the table, out of shot of the phone's camera.

'Oooh, I like it,' says Jennie, 'questioning the grieving widow, see what I can get out of her while she's raw and angry? Nice thinking.'

'I wasn't imagining it to be quite as exploitative as that makes it sound but yes, that's the gist. We know that she and Colin argued last night, and there have been all kinds of rumours over the years about his fidelity, so I imagine she's going to be feeling a mix of emotions right now. We also know from the Ring doorbell camera footage that she didn't leave here until about ten minutes after midnight last night, so we need to know what she was doing between having a stand-off with her husband and heading home.'

'Leave it with me,' says Jennie. 'Ping me the address. I'll go and change into something widowy and I'll get right round there.'

'Something widowy?' I ask, feeling slightly worried now on Miranda's behalf.

'Oh you know, just something suitable, something respectful,' explains Jennie, 'something in black probably, or maybe a hat. Do people wear hats for funerals or is it just weddings? I might have a hat with a lace veil on it from the 1980s hen do we went on a few years ago?'

'Isn't that hat neon pink?' I ask. 'Not very widowy, I don't think.'

'True, true, maybe not that then. Maybe just a nice blouse, keep it classy.'

'Just remember her husband did just die, Jennie, okay? So don't go in there all guns blazing, demanding to know her whereabouts. You're there as a concerned friend, making sure she's okay.'

'Except we're not friends are we? I don't actually know her very well at all – we've only met a couple of times maybe. Isn't it going to look odd?'

I think about it for a few seconds because Jennie's right of course: it *is* going to look odd. I try to come up with something that might be a plausible reason for her turning up unannounced.

'How about the missing phone?' I suggest. 'We know it's Georgie's but it wouldn't be lying to say that we found a phone. We don't have her number so couldn't call to check, and couldn't call Colin obviously, and as you live nearby, we asked if you'd pop round and check if it was hers.'

'Do I live nearby?' asks Jennie.

'No, not really,' I say, 'but she doesn't need to know that. And while you're talking about phones, see if you can find out if she knows where Colin's phone is. We haven't found it here and the police didn't find it on his body, so it could be important.'

'Got it,' says Jennie, 'concerned local acquaintance checking to see if she's lost her phone, but then casually get the subject around to her alibi and any potential motive. Leave it to me, team! I'll report back asap!'

She hangs up.

'Do you think she's gonna be okay, Mum?' asks Ben, grimacing.

'Jennie will be having the time of her life, Ben,' answers Oli. 'It's Miranda I'm worried about.'

CHAPTER 13

As nervous as I am about sending Jennie off to talk to Miranda, I am way more nervous about the fact that I still have to pay Georgie a visit and take back her phone. It feels silly – we know that she left the party while Colin was still alive – but all of the 'investigating' I've done so far has been from the comfort of my own home. If the police were to find our actions suspicious so far, then I feel like I could get away with it, but going to see suspects in their homes? On Christmas Eve? It could be seen as a bit much.

I'm just returning a phone, I remind myself, that's all. Georgie left her phone behind; I'm taking it back. But if it's really about returning a phone then why did I just not walk one hundred yards down the road and give it to Marcus? Why did I make up that excuse about having a *woman's problem* to ask Georgie about?

Oli does his best to reassure me but I don't know. I should be changing beds and making sure we have guest towels and arranging the stupid fucking tablescape, but instead I'm chasing around after footprints and phones. Perhaps we're being ridiculous even trying to figure it out ourselves. Bacon might have seemed like an absolute buffoon, but maybe that's all part of a clever act?

Shit, maybe he's a secret Columbo type and the whole time he was astutely watching me, taking it all in? Maybe he's going to turn up any minute in a trench coat and say, 'Just one more thing, Anna, I'm wondering why you didn't tell me about the note in Colin's pocket that you fished out with barbecue tongs when you thought we weren't looking?'

Fuck. Surely not?

I remember him standing in the footprint. Surely even Columbo wouldn't do that? There's bluffing and there's bluffing. Deep breaths, Anna, you've not done anything *really* wrong. You didn't bury the body or anything. Keep it together.

The beds though. I must remember to make up the beds. I remember the time Oli's parents came to stay just after Lily was born and the lecture I got about a new baby not being an excuse to 'let things go' in the house, and that just because I had a second child didn't mean I didn't need guest soap.

There's a shrill shout from the stairs.

'Muuu-umm-mm!'

How do children manage to turn the word into three syllables? It's very clever.

'Yes, Lily!' I shout back. 'What is it?'

'I'm nearly ready for the fashion show! I just wanted to check that it's okay for me to use your make-up?'

Christ.

'You'll need to go and supervise her, Ben,' I whisper. 'Don't let her use mascara or the Chanel lipstick.'

Ben groans. 'Why do I have to do it? Why can't you?'

'Because I have to take this phone to Georgie's and ask her casual yet probing questions about things she might have seen at the party, and unless you've recently learnt to drive and not mentioned it then you can't do that.'

'Dad could do it?'

'Dad is going to be busy changing all the bedding and finding guest soaps,' I say, gathering up my phone and Georgie's.

'Guest soaps?' asks Oli. 'Do we have guest soaps?'

'I've no idea,' I say. 'You'll have to improvise.'

'Which bedding do you want me to use where?'

'Just use your initiative, Oli,' I snap. 'Honestly, I can't be in charge of every single decision.'

I shout back up the stairs to Lily. 'Mummy just has to pop out for a few minutes, Lily. Ben is coming up to help you with make-up and then as soon as I'm back I'll watch the show!'

I head to the front door before anyone can ask me any more questions, grab my keys from the hall table and close the door behind me.

Georgie's flat is about a ten-minute drive away, across the other side of town towards the station. It's the first floor of a Victorian terrace with a yellow front door and a potted bay tree. I press the bell next to the 'flat 2' label and an intercom buzzes.

'Hello?' says a tinny voice.

'Oh hi,' I say, 'is that Georgie?'

'Yes,' says the voice.

'Right,' I say, put off a bit by the bluntness of her tone, 'it's Anna here, from the party last night.'

'I'm not well sorry,' says Georgie, and fearing she might be about to leave me on the doorstep I quickly interject.

'I have your phone!' I say quickly. 'You left it at the party? I'm just dropping it back, that's all.'

There's a pause. 'Oh, right. In that case you'd better come in. Push the door and it's up the stairs.' The door buzzes, I push it open and go into the hallway. It's a typical shared hall – scuffed woodchip painted white, a bike propped against the wall and a table for post and parcels.

At the top of the stairs Georgie is waiting for me in the doorway. She does look terrible.

'I'm really sorry to bother you,' I say, truthfully, 'but I thought you might be missing your phone.'

She remains in the doorway. I can see I'm going to have to work hard to get invited in here.

'Are you sure it's mine?' she asks.

'Pretty sure,' I say. 'It has a photo of you and Marcus at Stonehenge.'

'Oh yeah, that's mine. Thanks for bringing it over.' She holds out a hand expectantly. I have no choice but to hand it over. 'I really appreciate it,' she adds, waiting for me to leave.

I have to think fast. 'I couldn't use your toilet, could I?' I ask. It's not exactly genius-detective-level stuff but you can hardly refuse someone a quick wee. I do a little jiggle. 'Middle-aged mum bladder,' I say, cringing internally.

A look flashes across Georgie's face. What is it?

Annoyance? Not quite. It's more like fear, but what could she have to be scared of?

'Sure,' she says reluctantly, taking a step back into the flat and opening the door wide enough for me to come in. We're in the kitchen. She points to a door on the opposite side of the room. 'It's in there.'

I thank her and scuttle across the kitchen. I try to take the room in as I go without making it obvious. It's a small room, colourfully decorated. There's a big corkboard of pictures of her with friends and an older couple that I imagine were her parents. A large round table with an assortment of items on it – letters, a pen, laptop, phone and a large blue jug of twigs and holly.

In the bathroom I realise I actually do need to pee, which is useful as it means I don't have to worry about faking the noise. Sat on the toilet I take a few deep breaths. I need a way in, a conversation starter. Georgie is obviously not in the mood for a friendly chat, but I told Marcus I needed to ask her something – that's the whole reason I'm here after all. What can I ask? I really should have thought about this beforehand.

'Tampons!' I say, sounding only mildly hysterical as I burst out of the bathroom. Georgie is sitting at the table.

'Tampons?' She looks understandably confused.

'I saw you use organic cotton tampons,' I say. 'They were on top of the toilet – I wasn't going through your cupboards!' I add a forced laugh. Jesus Christ, woman. Pull yourself together.

'Yeah sometimes,' she says.

'Just sometimes?' I ask. *Just sometimes?* What am I

even thinking? This could be officially the creepiest I have ever sounded. 'I mean, that makes sense, I'm the same. I don't use tampons at night. Great for swimming though!' I haven't been swimming in about fifteen years.

We are both about as uncomfortable as it is possible for two acquaintances to be, so I go all in.

'What do you use the rest of the time?'

Please, ground, swallow me. Take me now.

'I use a Mooncup,' she says. She seems nervous. I don't blame her.

'Oh that's cool!' I say enthusiastically. 'What's that?'

She pulls one of the letters on the table towards her, picks up the pen and, to my horror, draws a picture of a Mooncup and writes something on the bottom of the page. She tears it off and hands it to me. 'I mean, it looks a bit like this . . .' She's looking at me as if I'm insane. It's possible that I might be. 'I've written down the website there for you as well,' she says.

I shove it in my pocket, embarrassed now. I look around desperately for something else to talk about but it's clear my time here is up. Something strikes me though about the scene around me, but I can't place it.

'Well thanks so much for coming to the party last night,' I say, admitting defeat, 'and I hope you feel better soon.'

'What do you mean?' she asks, eyes darting.

'You said you weren't feeling well, so just get well soon,' I smile.

'Oh yes of course,' she says, smiling back awkwardly. 'Thanks.'

She stands up and walks me to the door. As I turn to say goodbye I see the table top again and realise what looked odd – there had been a phone on the table when I went to the bathroom and it wasn't there now.

Back in the car I immediately call Oli.

'Hey, darling,' he answers. 'Where do I find pillowcases?'

'In the airing cupboard,' I say, 'with the rest of the bedding, where they've been since we moved into the house eight years ago.'

'Super, thanks!' he says, the sarcasm in my voice apparently lost on him.

'Have you actually made any of the beds yet then?' I ask.

'I've done the sheets and duvets,' he reassures me, 'just not the pillowcases.'

I want to ask him where on earth he thought the pillowcases would be other than in the airing cupboard. Did he think I had a special pillowcase storage area that I kept inconveniently separate from the rest of the bedding, just to make things difficult for myself? It's not worth it though.

'Georgie now officially hates me,' I say instead. 'It was horrendous.'

'Oh no,' says Oli, 'what happened?'

'It was just awful. I asked her about her Mooncup.'

'Jeez, what's that? It sounds sacrificial.'

'It's a menstrual cup,' I say, 'for periods.'

'Bloody hell,' says Oli, 'worse then. Why did you ask her about that?'

'I don't know – I panicked. She obviously didn't

want me there, so I asked to use the toilet, and I panicked, okay? I'm not good at this. She did seem oddly cold with me though. She was okay last night, wasn't she? I didn't do or say anything embarrassing, did I?'

'Well there was Twister. That was pretty embarrassing, especially when you were so adamant you could do a crab.'

'I don't mean *generally*,' I say, 'and I can actually do a crab. It's just difficult on a Twister mat because it's slippery.'

'Sure, sure,' says Oli, 'it *looked* difficult – you're right there. And I'm not sure how Marcus felt being underneath you at the time.'

'I *can* do it. I'll show you when I get home if you don't believe me. And I meant specifically with Georgie. I thought we were getting on well last night but she did *not* want me there. She said she didn't feel well but I don't know, the whole thing was excruciating.'

'Did you manage to find out anything useful though?' Oli asks.

'Not unless you want the Mooncup website details,' I say. 'There was one thing though that was weird. When I went to the toilet and walked through the kitchen, I'm sure there was a phone on the kitchen table but when I came out again it was gone.'

'What's so weird about there being a phone on the table?' Oli asks.

'Well I was taking her phone back, so why did she have one already?'

'Maybe she's a secret drug dealer or a sex trafficker

and it's her burner phone?' says Oli, excited. 'But probably just a work phone — a lot of people have separate phones for work. What does she do?'

'I think she works at a baby boutique in town,' I say. 'I'm not sure you need a special phone for working in a baby shop. And the weird thing was that it wasn't there afterwards. She must have hidden it when I was in the toilet.'

'We don't know that she hid it,' Oli points out, quite reasonably, 'she might have just checked it and then put it in her pocket.'

'I guess so,' I say. 'The whole situation was just so uncomfortable, maybe I'm reading too much into it, I don't know.'

'If she isn't well, then she probably just didn't want to see anyone, end of story. Or maybe she's a drug dealer *and* works in a baby shop — the perfect cover! Remember that mum from Ben's class when he was in year six?'

I did remember. It had been the scandal of the year. They'd moved into the area the year before and we'd all thought she was just a regular mum. She'd made an effort to fit in, helped out at a few PTA events and donated some great raffle prizes.

We'd invited her family to our Christmas party that year and there had been an awkward moment, for me at least, when she'd come over on the playground when the kids went back in January. She'd handed me my National Trust membership card, laughing, and said she'd taken it home with her by mistake after using it to do some coke in my bathroom at the party. I'd laughed, thinking perhaps that this was what all the cool mums were doing and I was just out of the loop, but I'd given it a good clean with an antiseptic wipe when I got back to the car.

I didn't think anything more about it until a couple of months later her son stopped showing up for school. She wasn't responding to messages in the class WhatsApp group and no one knew what had become of them until a couple of days later there she was on the front page of the local paper. It turns out she'd been arrested for dealing drugs. She'd been using her toddler's buggy as transport and had been dealing out of the changing bag on the school playground.

'But Colin found out about Georgie's exploits – maybe he caught her at the shop – and threatened to turn her in,' continued Oli, 'so she stabbed him in desperation.'

'How would he have found out? He doesn't seem like the baby shop type to me. He doesn't have grandchildren or anything. I think we might be pushing it a bit with the drug-dealing angle honestly, Oli. I expect she just felt shit and I was being super annoying and she has a work phone.'

'I'm just saying, you never know.'

'Plus we know Georgie left at 11.15 p.m.,' I remind him, 'and she's tiny – I don't think that footprint could have been hers even if she *was* there. I really just wanted to find out if she'd seen or heard anything suspicious during the party, before she left.'

I look at the car clock. It's 3 p.m. Shit shit shit. I keep forgetting it's Christmas Eve and there's still so much to do. I haven't wrapped any of the stocking presents yet. That was meant to be my thing to do this evening after I'd spent the day turning the house into a magical Christmas wonderland and had everything ready for Pamela. Fuck.

'How much Sellotape do we have?' I ask Oli.

'I've no idea,' he says. 'Where do we keep it?' The royal 'we' again. I sigh.

'Never mind,' I say, 'I'll stop in the Co-op on my way back and get some. Can you put the Buck's Fizz and white wine in the garage fridge to chill? There isn't room in the big fridge. And maybe check on the kids.'

In the Co-op I spot Margaret in the ready meal aisle. I've not asked her what she's doing for Christmas and when I see her pick up a chicken dinner for one I have a momentary pang of guilt and almost invite her for lunch tomorrow before reining myself in and ducking into the next aisle.

She catches up with me at the tills. 'Oh, Anna,' she says, 'I'm glad I ran into you. I've got something I need to talk to you about.'

The self-service checkout spews out my Sellotape receipt. I really don't have time for another lecture about my recycling storage so I pick up the Sellotape, grab the receipt and make my apologies.

'It's important!' she says, following me out of the door. The alarms sound and I turn to see her horrified face as a security guard approaches her, eyeing the chicken dinner for one still in her hand, unpaid for.

'Get your hands off me,' I hear her snap as the security guard tries to guide her back into the shop. 'I'm not a shoplifter, I'm chair of my Neighbourhood Watch!' She shakes off his hand on her arm and storms back into the shop. I suspect the store manager and several local Facebook groups will be hearing a lot more about this shocking mistreatment of an upstanding member of the community.

'I really do want to hear all about it,' I call back to her, getting in the car and chucking the Sellotape onto the passenger seat, 'I've just got to get home for a fashion show!'

CHAPTER 14

I arrive home at 3.15 p.m.

I sit in the car for a minute to gather my thoughts. I check my phone for any word from Jennie but there's nothing yet. I wonder how she's getting on with Miranda. Better than I did with Georgie hopefully. I feel my cheeks getting hot at the memory of it, my cry of *tampons!* and her look of horror.

I have a quick scroll through Facebook and start watching a ten-minute-long video of a woman making a lamp base from a plaster cast of her own leg. It's comforting initially, to be taken away from thoughts of murder, but it's the sort of video that leaves you questioning what it means to be human. Particularly when I get to the bit where she dresses the leg in a fishnet stocking and screws it into a stiletto. Am I missing something in my life without my own leg lamp? Or is this me and my tablescape, just going through the motions, killing time with ridiculous craft projects until we die or are killed in someone's larder?

I hear my own thoughts and quickly switch off the video just as she's drilling a hole into her thigh for the cabling. I need to get inside before Margaret catches up with me. Assuming she's talked herself out of any shoplifting charges. Margaret is not the sort of woman to stand for being arrested.

As I approach the front door I see there's a piece of paper stuck in the letterbox. I assume it will be junk, or another local tradesperson reminding me of one more maintenance job I am failing at – window cleaning, drain unblocking or the classic gutter clearing. *I'll be in your area on Tuesday cleaning your neighbours' fascias and soffits!* they say, implying that everyone else in the street appreciates the importance of home maintenance and that it's just me who had to google what a 'soffit' was.

I pull it out as I open the front door and find that it's a handwritten note. I get a whoosh of butterflies – could it be a clue? A confession from the killer?

Just a quick note, it begins, *to let you know that I shall be reporting your attempted theft from our garden this morning to the Neighbourhood Watch. Steve was shocked to see you on our lawn from the kitchen window, especially with the kids with you. It's a slippery slope you know – they'll be on drugs and in a gang before you know it. Steve was very distressed by the whole thing and his lunch did not sit right at all – he had a nasty bout of acid reflux thanks to your exploits, which we were both most upset about as he loves his baguettes normally.*

It's signed *Dawn at number 13.*

'Look at this!' I say, stomping into the living room where Oli is sitting eating a Wagon Wheel and watching *The Snowman* with Lily. I drop the note into his lap.

'The woman has a bloody cheek. I might go over there and tell her I saw her cutting down that mistletoe.'

'Mummy!' Lily jumps up and throws herself at my legs, giving me a long hug. 'You were ages!' She looks up at me and smiles. She's wearing a significant amount of blusher and bright pink lipstick.

'You look very lovely,' I say, smiling back down at her. I go to sit down next to Oli but she stops me.

'You can't sit down,' she explains. 'You need a ticket.'

'I need a ticket to sit on my own sofa?' I ask.

'Yes, it's for the fashion show. Here you are.' She hands me a small piece of torn paper that she's written 'TICKET' on. I take it. 'Now you can sit down. Here's your pen. You write the outfit scores on the back.'

I sit as instructed. Oli smiles at me and waves his own ticket. I look at his Wagon Wheel and he offers it up for a bite.

'Wait!' says Lily, shoving a small hand between Oli's Wagon Wheel and my mouth. 'I'll get you one if you want one. They're fashion show snacks.'

'Oh lovely,' I say, 'yes please.'

She runs off into the kitchen and returns with a Wagon Wheel. I hold out my hand and she places it in my palm before holding out her own hand. I look at her questioningly.

'They're 50p,' she says.

'But I already bought them once in Tesco, and I think they were cheaper than that.'

'They're 50p,' she says again.

'She takes cards,' says Oli, 'I recommend it.'

'I'll pay by card please,' I say to Lily and she duly produces a calculator and carefully types in '50'. I tap my phone, make a beeping noise and look at the calculator display.

'That's gone through,' I say and she hands over the Wagon Wheel. She snatches up the TV remote and turns off *The Snowman*.

'We're ready for the fashion show now,' she says. 'Everyone has to stay in their seats while I get changed into my first Christmas outfit. No talking.' Oli and I both nod silently.

'Don't worry about Dawn,' he says as soon as Lily is out of earshot, nodding to the note on his lap. 'I'll sort it.'

'What are you going to do? You can't just turn up there. What if Steve gets his baguette out again and you get scared?'

'Har bloody har,' he says, 'I would like to have seen you faced with Steve brandishing his French stick at you. The man's terrifying. But I won't go to the house, don't worry. I'll go and see her at work.'

'That's a bit full on, isn't it?' I ask. I'm not sure we want to be turning this into a *thing*. I don't want a neighbourhood feud. Steve seems like the type who might quickly escalate to posting a dog shit through your letterbox.

'She works in the bakery remember, by Tesco Express. I go in there quite often for a cheeky sausage roll when I'm getting bits from Tesco. We always have a chat so you know, I've got a rapport.'

'Oh do you now?' I say, raising my eyebrows and giving him a jab in the ribs. This is the first I've heard of any cheeky sausage roll action. 'You have a *rapport*? Should I be worried?'

'You should definitely be worried,' he says, nodding seriously. 'She does a great apple turnover and her baps are exquisite. I'll go in next time she's there and say something complimentary about her iced buns. She'll be putty in my hands.'

The door opens and Ben comes in looking fed up. A small voice shouts from the stairs, 'Start the music!' Ben taps his phone and 'Baby Got Back' starts playing.

'Don't blame me,' he says, anticipating my next question. 'This was her request.'

I don't have time to argue because at that moment Lily sashays into the living room, hands on hips. She's wearing one of her favourite dresses – the one I discouraged her from buying recently in Matalan because of the many, *many* layers of rainbow petticoat, but that she refused to change out of. I ended up having to get her scanned at the checkout, the clothes she'd arrived in bundled into my handbag.

She's paired the dress with a glittery belt, sequined tights and the hat I bought two summers ago for my cousin's wedding. It's a strong look. She walks to the fireplace, twirls, and walks back towards the door.

'Beautiful!' I cry from the stalls, writing *8/10 – very colourful!* on the back of my ticket.

'I said no talking,' she says sternly, not turning to look at me but keeping her eyes fixed on some point at the end of her catwalk.

She leaves, shouting after Ben who rolls his eyes at us and follows her. He's a good kid really. There aren't many teenage boys who would happily assist their seven-year-old sister in putting on a Christmas fashion show. Although 'happily' might be pushing it, and there is the small matter of him being allowed to help solve a murder if he agrees to play with her. As far as bribes go in the world of teenagers, it's a high-value one.

'Do you think I should text Georgie?' I say, turning to look at Oli. 'I'm worried I might have come off as weird.'

'I don't think there's any *might* about it,' he says, ever the supportive husband. 'Do you have her number?'

'No.'

'Well then.'

'I could text Marcus and ask him to pass on my apologies, or ask for her number?'

'I reckon just leave it, Anna. It's done now, and it's not like you're best friends or anything. It doesn't matter if she thinks you're a bit odd.'

I'm about to argue that actually it does matter to me, thank you very much, that despite the fact he might be perfectly happy being seen in public in his gardening Crocs, doesn't mean that I don't have *standards*, when Ben comes back into the room.

He presses a button and the music starts. I think I recognise it as Cardi B. Ben shrugs and shakes his head.

This time Lily has gone for what I'd say was a fairly summery Christmas look. She's wearing buttercup yellow shorts and a blue and yellow striped vest, and one of my scarves is draped over her shoulders. She's put her hair into bunches, badly, and is wearing a hairband with ladybirds on it.

Oli and I stay quiet as she does her fashion show walk to the fireplace and back. I write down, *6/10 (bit cold?)*.

They leave again. 'There's still three more!' Lily shouts

as she does, just in case we were thinking of going anywhere.

'I put a load of washing on,' says Oli, once the coast is clear to speak. 'Lily's basket is empty now, but I haven't ventured into Ben's yet.'

'Okay, I'll do that after the show. Ben was actually putting laundry in it this morning so I might as well seize the moment.' We're both quiet for a minute. I reach over and take hold of Oli's hand and he gives mine a squeeze.

'You doing okay, little one?' His voice is soft and full of fondness. It makes me want to bury my face into his chest but I imagine that sort of behaviour is not allowed at the fashion show.

I take a deep breath and smile at him. 'I'm okay,' I say. 'It's just a lot, isn't it?'

He nods. 'It is a lot.'

'And it's Christmas,' I add in a small voice. 'I'm not sure you can ever feel the same about Christmas once you've seen Santa with a knife in his stomach.'

'I'm not sure you feel the same about anything once you've seen *anyone* with a knife in their stomach,' he says. 'I'm so sorry it was you who found him.'

I'm doing my best to be brave, but there's something about having someone ask you if you're okay when you're feeling a bit wobbly that makes you immediately want to burst into tears. I purse my lips together tightly and look up at the ceiling to trick any tears into falling back into my eyes.

Oli gives my hand another squeeze just as the living room door opens and Lily bounds in to Kanye West singing 'Gold Digger'.

'It's the radio edit,' says Ben, looking at us, and Lily shoots him a silencing look.

She has really outdone herself with this one, wearing one of my black dresses – short on me but floor-length on her – and what might be *all* of my jewellery. She's also wearing a pair of my black heels. The effect is a little startling – an unbidden flash into the future of things to come.

I write, *5/10 – nice dress but maybe a little old for you.*

I look over at Oli's ticket and see that it's blank. 'Haven't you been writing your scores down?' I ask once Lily has left for the third time. 'You'll get in trouble.'

'Shit, I forgot that,' he says, looking genuinely worried. 'What have you put? Can I copy yours?'

'You can look,' I say, showing him my notes, 'but make yours different or she'll know and she'll tell us both off.'

He writes on his ticket.

'What do you make of the whole Ben and Sasha thing?' I ask him.

'What Ben and Sasha thing? *Is* there a thing?'

'I don't know if it's a Ben *and* Sasha thing,' I say, 'but it's definitely a Ben thing, don't you reckon? He goes all pink and angry when he talks about her, and the way he leapt to her defence – he definitely likes her.'

'I hadn't noticed,' admits Oli, which doesn't surprise me. He claims he had no idea I liked him for months until in the end I lost patience waiting for him to make his move and pounced on him at a house party after some medicinal shots of tequila.

160

'We don't actually believe Sasha could be the murderer though, do we?' he asks.

I picture her, the girl we've known since the first day in reception class when she and Ben came out at the end of the day holding hands. Do I think she's capable of stabbing a large man to death? No, I can't see it, either physically or emotionally.

'No,' I say, 'of course we don't. Ninety-nine point nine per cent no.' He raises his eyebrows very slightly. 'Never say never,' I add. 'Kids nowadays can get pretty passionate about stuff.'

'Outfit number four!' announces Lily to the sound of 'Barbie Girl' by Aqua. This is the full Barbie experience, head-to-toe pink including a pink dress, leggings, pink trainers and a knitted pink scarf. She does her walk, twirls, and retreats.

I write on the back of my ticket, 7/10 – very pink.

'And what about the stuff Jennie was saying about Bruce?' says Oli. 'The whole gambling, debts, wanting to take over the company vibe – does that ring true?'

I think about it for a minute. He would love to take over the business I'm sure – he thinks Colin is past it and is convinced that all it takes is good looks and beanbags to run a successful marketing company. His business strategy would be to install a foosball table, have us all work in breakout pods and let the work pour in. The gambling thing though, I'm not sure that fits with my idea of Bruce.

'I'm just not sure he's smart enough,' I say. 'Not that you have to be smart to get into gambling debt – that's kind of the point – but I just don't think he has that edge? Colin is, or was rather, an idiot in lots of ways,

161

but he was wily. He had his sleazy side, he was a risk taker, and he wasn't afraid to step on people. Bruce is a bit more, I don't know, innocent? He's really just an overgrown baby who's used to getting everything he wants and assumes that's all there is to life. I don't know, it's hard to explain.'

'I get it,' says Oli, 'but that naivety could be what has got him into trouble. He might have started gambling just assuming he'd win, because things always turn out okay for him, and he's been taken by surprise that they haven't?'

I picture Bruce standing at a roulette wheel, genuinely baffled that even though he put his money on red, the ball has landed on black. Perhaps he'd approach a member of staff, explain to them that their games seemed not to be working properly.

I laugh. 'Maybe I could see that,' I say.

We're interrupted by a blast of Mariah Carey's 'All I Want for Christmas'. Much more festive and appropriate. Lily enters the room smiling proudly in what she obviously considers her Christmas pièce de résistance and I can't help but say how beautiful she looks, before remembering the rules and covering my mouth with my hand. Lily doesn't seem to mind.

She's wearing the bottle green velvet Christmas dress we got her last week from Marks and Spencer. It has a white lacy collar and a wide green ribbon that ties into a bow at the back. She's brushed the messy bunches out of her hair and instead has a plain red hairband holding her fringe out of her face.

I write, *10/10 – Christmas perfection!*

'What do you think?' asks Lily, bouncing up and down on the spot.

'You look beautiful!' Oli exclaims. 'Like Father Christmas's chief helper ready for the annual North Pole Christmas ball. Grandma and Grandpa are going to absolutely love it.'

'That's the one!' I agree. 'You can check my scores, but that's the winner. You are going to look absolutely gorgeous for Christmas Day. Well done you!'

She runs over and gives us both hugs. 'I'm going to change back now,' she informs us, 'so I don't get my dress mucky, and then can we watch *Chicken Run*? We always watch *Chicken Run* on Christmas Eve!'

'We can definitely put *Chicken Run* on,' I say, technically answering a different question to the one she asked. 'Mummy and Daddy might have to do some jobs as well because we have to get everything ready for Christmas, but we will sit down with you whenever we can.'

'Can I have popcorn?' Lily asks. I say that she can and she seems happy that Mummy, Daddy *or* popcorn are all equally acceptable viewing companions. Oli gets up to get the popcorn and Lily runs upstairs to change while I find the film on one of the forty-seven different subscription channels we seem to be signed up for. Lily comes back and snuggles into me as the film begins with Mr Tweedy and his ferocious dog patrolling the chicken coops, prison camp style. The tension mounts as there's an escape attempt and just as the dogs have Ginger the chicken cornered, my phone rings and we both jump.

'Hi, Jennie,' I say, answering it.

'Sssh!' says Lily loudly, taking the popcorn that Oli has brought in.

'Hi, Jennie,' I whisper, extracting myself from Lily's snuggle and letting Oli replace me. He wastes no time getting settled and starting on the popcorn. He bloody loves *Chicken Run*.

'Everything okay?' asks Jennie as I walk through to the kitchen, closing the door behind me. 'You sound tense.'

'Just the opening scenes of *Chicken Run*,' I say. 'You always wonder if this time might be different. Anyway, have you seen Miranda? How did it go?'

'Hell yeah I've seen her,' says Jennie, 'and the woman is a fucking train wreck.'

'Oh no,' I say, 'is she really cut up about Colin?'

'Honestly,' says Jennie, 'I have no idea. I think she might just have lost the plot, full stop. I didn't even have to give her the line about the phone; she just seemed to vaguely recognise me and seized on the opportunity to rant at somebody for half an hour. I mean seriously, that woman has *so many thoughts*. I wouldn't be surprised at this point if Colin had stabbed himself just so he didn't have to listen to her anymore.'

'Unlikely,' I say, 'but sure, I see what you're saying. Did she tell you anything actually useful though?'

'Oh yeah,' says Jennie, 'I hit the fucking jackpot, Anna. I've got so much to tell you I had to take notes as soon as I got in the car so I didn't forget anything. Headline news first though . . .'

She pauses. I can tell it's deliberate.

164

'Come on Jennie, this isn't bloody *X Factor*.'

'Don't be a spoilsport,' she says. 'Okay, are you ready for this? Because I'm telling you, it's big.'

'I'm ready!'

'This could blow the case WIDE OPEN.'

'Get on with it!' I shout.

'Okay okay! So, you know how Bruce has always been the golden boy, only child, sole heir to the alleged family fortune?'

'Jennie,' I say, 'do I have to come round there and get the information out of you by force?'

'I'm getting there, I promise, I'm just having my moment.'

'Have it later.'

'Fine. Bruce isn't the sole heir,' she announces, triumphant.

'Wait what?' I say. 'Yes he is.'

'No he isn't,' she says, 'Colin has another child.'

CHAPTER 15

Jennie takes about fifteen minutes recounting her visit to Miranda and it's quite hard to follow. It's difficult to distinguish between things that Miranda said that are true, things Miranda said that might *not* be true and things that Jennie is adding for atmosphere. I love Jennie, but I wouldn't necessarily choose her to give a reliable witness account of anything. 'Colourful,' my mum calls her, 'and prone to excitements.'

From her colourful account of her talk with Miranda, a few important facts have definitely emerged though – firstly that Colin has recently been contacted by somebody claiming that he was their father.

This contact had initially been via email from a random Gmail account that didn't give any clue as to who this person might be. This could be seen as suspicious but it makes sense to me – I would be cautious if I was contacting a stranger out of the blue on the possibility that half of our DNA might match.

Colin had told Miranda about it – it was from before

they'd met, so he wasn't having to confess to an affair or anything sordid – but he'd dismissed it as a prank or spam. 'You know what spammers are like,' he'd apparently said to Miranda. 'It will be a Nigerian prince wanting me to send him his airfare so that we can be reunited.'

Some time had passed, though, and they'd got in touch again, this time with more details that had made Colin suspect that perhaps they weren't a Nigerian prince and might actually be telling the truth. There had been a few more emails exchanged and Colin's feelings about it had started to change. According to Miranda, he'd seemed almost excited about it.

It's a lot of new information to process. When she's finished and promised to keep in touch I text Oli. 'Can you get away from Chicken Run?'

A minute or two later he appears in the kitchen.

'What's up?'

'Plenty,' I say, and catch him up with the story of Colin's newly discovered illegitimate child.

'Wow,' says Oli, 'that IS a lot. So had Colin met them yet? How far had it got?'

'No, Miranda says they'd not met in person, or even spoken on the phone, just exchanged these emails, and they hadn't even told Colin their name yet, so it *could* still be a scam. Colin didn't seem to think so though, not based on the details they were giving about their mum and how she and Colin had met.'

'So why reach out after all this time? What are they hoping to get out of it, do you think?'

'Maybe they just wanted to get to know their father? They might have only just found out who he was,

167

perhaps discovered a stash of letters or photos or something like that, who knows. But it does throw in a new suspect, doesn't it?'

'I don't think so,' says Oli thoughtfully. 'Firstly because we've already agreed it had to be someone at the party who knew he was here and could have written the note about the larder and all of that, but also if you *were* reconnecting with your estranged father and were wanting to gain from it, you'd be shooting yourself in the foot by killing him.'

I think about it and Oli's right. Let's say this person was hoping to get some money out of it, possibly short-term or even to build a relationship and get written into the will, then they'd have no reason to kill off their gift horse before it started giving them gifts.

'I'll tell you who it *does* incriminate though,' says Oli.

'Who?'

'Bruce. If he knew about this then he could well have seen this new sibling as a huge threat, not just to his inheritance and his job but also to his position as much-loved only child. If you're used to swaggering around the family business, just having to lounge about in a beanbag and do the odd bit of blue-sky thinking, then you're not going to take kindly to having someone else come in and upset it all.'

I try to imagine Bruce doing anything remotely resembling blue-sky thinking but something else in my brain jangles, a connection that wants to be made, but I can't quite reach it. Oli starts to say something else and I shush him. 'Hang on,' I say, 'I'm trying to have a thought.'

'Be careful,' he says, rather rudely I feel.

And then there's a spark, a teeny neural pathway is forged and I've got it.

'You're right! Ben overheard Colin and Bruce arguing and Colin said something that didn't make sense at the time but now makes perfect sense! What was it exactly? Something like: "You're not the only person I have to think about anymore." He was talking about his *other child*, which means Bruce *did* know about them!'

I slap my hand down on the worktop. I'm triumphant. Finally it feels like we're having a breakthrough. Is this what it feels like to be Poirot? The little sparks firing in your brain, connecting the clues – it's very satisfying.

I haven't felt like this since the time we did that escape room in Swindon. We didn't actually *escape* exactly – a lot of things were said that day that shouldn't have been said – but there were moments when I did manage to solve a puzzle where I felt the same surge in brainpower. It's worrying really to actively *notice* your brain working like that, because it does make you wonder what it's doing the rest of the time.

Perhaps I should do more escape rooms? It could be our thing as a family – we could get really good at it and break records and the staff at every room we visited would be blown away by our skills. Maybe there are championships? Lily was crying by the end in the one we did, but that might not have been the room – we *were* in Swindon.

'That's it!' Oli cries, shattering the fantasy of us all on the podium of the World Escape Room Championships, me modestly accepting a giant cheque on behalf of the family. 'He must have known and that must have been what they were arguing about – Bruce was worried about what it would mean for him. He panicked, wanted to do something before Colin gave all of his money away, so he put a stop to it by stabbing him! Case solved!'

'Hang on a minute,' I say, 'it's a great motive but I'm not sure we can go as far as case solved. We've got evidence to check, means and opportunity. We can't go leaping to any conclusions remember? Besides,' I add, 'Colin's love child wasn't the only thing Miranda talked to Jennie about.'

'It wasn't?' Oli looks a little deflated.

'Nope, she also had a lot to say about Colin's affairs.'

Oli doesn't look as impressed with this as he did with the revelation of the mystery offspring. 'I think we could see that coming a mile off,' he says.

'True,' I say, acknowledging Colin's reputation for general sleaze and nastiness, 'but there's a big difference between being the sort of man who will brush up against you too closely reaching for some crisps at a party, hypothetically, and someone who actually has full-blown affairs. Plus you can never assume that the wife knows about them if they are happening.'

'That's a good point,' concedes Oli, 'plus you've got to find the women *willing* to have affairs with you when you're as awful as Colin. Take me for instance,' he says, brushing the popcorn crumbs from the front of his T-shirt and doing what he thinks is his sexy face but is actually a rather disconcerting snarl. 'I would have no problem charming any number of women, should I choose to.'

'Well obviously, darling,' I say, giving him a quick pat on the arm and then picking a loose kernel from his chin. 'You're a catch, any woman can see that. I'm grateful every day that you choose me out of all the women hammering at the door for you.'

He curls his lip at me and narrows his eyes and I smile at him and blow him a kiss. He drives me nuts in about a trillion tiny ways but, if I'm being honest, then I *am* grateful. He doesn't know where we keep the pillowcases, he thinks washing up means dunking things in soapy water and he snores like a congested walrus, but he lets me warm my cold feet on his hot legs in bed and he once booked the kids' appointments for dental check-ups completely unprompted, *just because he knew* that it had been a year since they last went. When I told some mums at school about that at the time, a few of them positively swooned. In the grand scheme of *men*, he's not bad at all.

I don't tell him that of course. He needs to think I'm the catch, which I am, naturally, because I am a woman and we're just *better*. It's nature – we can't help it. If Oli were ever to get stabbed in a larder I would definitely be looking to take a wife. There would be the issue of sexuality but perhaps I'd have a mid-life pivot into bisexuality, you never know. I've just repressed it until now because of the patriarchy and released from the shackles of straight marriage I might discover a whole new lease of life. I might open a llama farm.

'I'm assuming then that Miranda isn't cool with the affairs,' interrupts Oli, 'that they don't have an open marriage or anything like that?'

'Does *anyone* really have an open marriage?' I ask, cynically. 'I always thought that was just something people said when one of them wants to sleep with other people and the other one doesn't want it to look like they're a doormat. That's how it was with that couple at school remember – the ones who helped build the set for *Aladdin*. She was always glowing and wore a lot of purple silk and he looked like he wanted to cry every time they talked about it.'

'I think that was just them,' says Oli, frowning at me. 'I'm not sure that's how it works generally. I don't think you can make judgements like that, not nowadays. You could get cancelled.'

'Cancelled from what though?' I ask. 'I've never really understood that. I'm not anyone anyway. But fine, okay, I'm sure some couples have open marriages, but Miranda and Colin did not.'

I recount to him Jennie's description of Miranda pacing her kitchen, hands in the air, head thrown back, as she raved about how Colin didn't deserve her and how she must have been mad all of these years to put up with his philandering. The picture Jennie gave me was not of a woman happy to share her husband with other women.

'So perhaps it came to a head last night,' continues Oli, 'maybe Miranda witnesses the casual crisps molestation lean and it's the final straw. She's had enough and she snaps. I mean we *know* she snapped, because Toby and Sav saw them having a blow-up row. Miranda goes off somewhere seething, decides she can't take it anymore, and lures Colin into the larder with the note. She stabs him, sneaks out of the larder, grabs her coat and leaves. It fits with the timings.'

It does fit, but I'm not sure I buy it. A crime of passion I get, but that would surely be in the heat of a row. If they were already in the larder arguing, maybe I could see her reaching for a knife in fury, but to think about it and go to the trouble of writing a note? I'm just not sure I can imagine it.

'We have to come back to the footprint too,' I say. 'Miranda was wearing heels – I remember noticing them because they looked like they cost a fortune – she did not make that boot print in the flour, which would mean someone would have had to go in after her, unless we are going with it being Colin's print and we believe the weird "Colin pirouettes on the spot before collapsing dead" theory, which I don't.'

Oli sighs and runs his hand through his hair. He looks disappointed. 'This is hard, isn't it?' he says. 'It never sounds this hard on the podcast. They just find one piece of the puzzle and it leads to the next and before you know it they've got a complete picture. I feel like we've got lots of pieces but none of the edges, so no idea where anything goes.'

'At least we've got pieces,' I say. 'They're just a bit muddled. Let's get our lists back out and update our suspects and motives.' He brightens at the idea of the lists. We tackle clues first, the physical evidence that we've collected to help us narrow down the field:

Shoe print in the flour

Note in Colin's pocket but missing phone?

Arguments witnessed – Colin and Miranda, and Colin and Bruce

Ring doorbell camera footage showing people arriving/leaving

Cat GPS tracker for time of death

Then we work through our suspect table and it's

173

reassuring seeing that we've been able to eliminate quite a few people already – Jaz, Margaret and Georgie left the party while Colin was still alive and Toby didn't write the mysterious note I found in Colin's pocket. We decide to keep Miranda on the list for now despite the shoe print.

Our list of suspects and their motives now reads as follows, ordered with the most likely culprit at the top:

Bruce – new sibling could mean cut inheritance, potential gambling problems?

Miranda – revenge/anger for Colin's affairs

Sav – anger over doggy snack investment

Marcus – no obvious motive but he was there and we haven't eliminated him

Jennie – ditto (Anna says it's not Jennie)

Sasha – anger over sexist comments/possible self-defence? (Unlikely)

Ben comes into the kitchen. I wave the lists at him. 'Colin had a love child,' I tell him, 'so we're updating motives!'

I'm expecting him to get excited so that we can rekindle our earlier mother–son bond, but apparently the idea of solving a murder together has already lost interest for him.

'Can I get some Pringles?' he asks. 'Lily has popcorn.' Everything is always point-scoring with kids, isn't it? As though it's an unspoken rule of the universe that if one child has something, the other child has to have something of equal worth otherwise a butterfly somewhere might flap its wings and cause an earthquake.

'They're in the larder,' I say, 'if you don't mind going in there. Just mind the toothpaste.'

He goes in, clearly not minding in the slightest, and re-emerges with a tube of salted Pringles. Oli looks like he's seen a ghost.

'The Pringles!' he shouts.

'They're mine, Dad,' he says, hugging them to his chest. 'I need them for *Chicken Run*.'

'No, not those Pringles,' says Oli, 'the other Pringles!' Ben shakes his head at him and goes back into the living room, taking his Pringles to safety. 'Remember I saw Bruce coming out of the larder with a tube of Pringles? We'd forgotten about it! We've not got it on the clues list and it puts him very definitely *in the larder!*'

Oli's right – we had forgotten about the Pringles. I add it to the list. 'What time was it though? Could you pin it to the time of the murder?'

'I don't know,' says Oli, 'I just remember seeing him – I don't know when. Sorry, that's not much help, is it?'

'Oooh! Let's do the memory thing! I've seen it on *Criminal Minds* – they get you to close your eyes and walk you back through the scene and suddenly you can remember everything. It's very clever.'

Oli looks doubtful.

'Close your eyes! It will work – I've seen it!'

'On a fictional television show,' Oli reminds me, 'the same one where they identified one suspect by using the enlarged reflection in the victim's eyeball remember?' That episode really stuck with us both.

'Let's try it at least. Close your eyes.' Oli closes his eyes. 'Relax and breathe deeply,' I say, using my best spa voice. 'Let your mind feel free to drift through space and time.' Oli opens one eye and looks at me. I frown and he closes it again.

'We're drifting back to last night,' I say slowly, waving my hands gently to and fro. I'm not sure why, but it feels fitting. 'You've come into the kitchen and you hear a noise from near the back door. Somebody is in the larder. You look over and Bruce comes out. What else can you hear?'

'I can hear music,' he says, 'and some shrieking. I think it's you.'

'I don't shriek,' I clarify. 'I chuckle lightly at best. What else do you notice? Look around in your mind.'

'There are a lot of crisps about,' says Oli, 'which actually is a bit odd and makes me wonder why Bruce went into the larder for Pringles.'

'Excellent!' I say, clapping my hands and ruining the moment. 'Keep your eyes closed,' I say, back in spa mode, 'and tell me what else you see.'

Oli furrows his brow. 'I see Bruce try to flip the Pringles and drop them. I think he might have been distracted by your shrieking.'

I honestly do not shriek. Possibly there was a small amount of cheering during Twister but that's all. Shrieking makes me sound like an old hag who lives in the woods with a raven. Wait a minute . . .

'Listen to the shrieking,' I say, 'where is it coming from?'

'It's coming from the living room where you are showing off on the Twister mat,' he says, then snaps his eyes open. 'Twister!'

'You see? It worked! Oh ye of little faith. We know that we started Twister before the kids were in the

176

garden, so before Jaz got picked up at 11.30 p.m., but how long were we playing for? If it's more than half an hour then it could work?'

'It *felt* like a long time as a watcher,' says Oli, 'but I wouldn't like to say for sure. I'm not sure you could have stuck at it for half an hour without hurting yourself or someone else.'

I sigh. We're close, but not close enough. We need something more concrete, something incriminating. I get up and start unloading the dishwasher. I'll do this and then I'll get the washing from Ben's room and clean all the toothpaste off the larder floor, see how well it's worked on the bloodstains.

I'm putting clean spoons into the cutlery drawer when the doorbell rings and we hear Ben thumping his way to get it. There are voices in the hallway, getting closer as they approach the kitchen and then standing in the doorway is Bruce.

CHAPTER 16

'Hey, Anna,' he says cheerfully and then, nodding at Oli, 'Hey, Oscar good to see you, mate!'

We both stare. Bruce carries on, a little more hesitantly as neither of us have said a word.

'Sorry to barge in on you like this on Christmas Eve, but I don't suppose you've found any keys lying around, have you? I can't seem to find them and I think I must have left them here last night.'

We're still staring. One of us really needs to speak soon or it's going to get super weird. Bruce ploughs on.

'I walked home last night, you see, left the Beemer here, and then my flatmate let me in, so I didn't miss them until I thought I should come and get the car. I left my phone in it too, so I couldn't call. You haven't seen them, have you? The keys?'

Ben senses the awkwardness and uses his privileged status as 'child' to make a swift escape, mumbling something about not wanting to miss any more of *Chicken Run*.

Bruce looks from me to Oli and back again, and then down at the papers on the table. Before he can see that they name him as prime suspect in his father's murder, I spring round to stand between him and the table, still clutching a handful of spoons.

'Bruce!' I say. 'Lovely to see you! No bother at all coming round, although we haven't come across any keys sorry. We can look though. Why don't you have a sit-down? You must be feeling awful. Oli, make Bruce a cup of tea.'

I gesture with my head towards the crime paperwork and Oli takes the hint, sweeping it all up, dumping it in the cutlery drawer and flicking on the kettle in one swift motion.

'Must I?' says Bruce, looking a bit confused. 'I guess I did have quite a bit to drink last night, but I'm not really a hangover person, too much of a seasoned pro for that, all those years playing rugby!' He laughs heartily.

'Oh I meant because of your dad,' I say, putting a hand on his shoulder and giving him my best sympathetic look.

'My dad? What's he done now? He's not been up to mischief, has he?'

'I hardly think we can class it as mischief. There's still toothpaste on the floor but that's hardly his fault.'

'What on earth has he been doing with toothpaste? Sounds a bit odd, even by the old man's standards!'

And then it dawns on me. He doesn't know. Either that or he's doing a brilliant acting job. I look at Oli. There's an expression of panic on his face. He shrugs at me. I sit down at the table next to Bruce.

'Bruce,' I say gently, 'have you spoken to your mum today?'

'My mum? No, my phone's still locked in my car so I haven't spoken to anyone and no one would have been able to get hold of me. What's going on here, Anna? You're being weird.'

Does he really not know that his dad is dead? Surely if he did it he wouldn't be here now, so chipper. I know that sometimes killers like to revisit the scene of the crime but this would be a ballsy move.

The kettle boils and clicks off and Oli gets out three cups.

'Maybe it would be a good idea to speak to your mum,' I say, desperate not to have to be the one to tell him, especially not when we're sitting so close to the scene of the crime. I picture myself cocking my head towards the larder as I tell him his dad has been stabbed. 'Yeah just in there, mate,' I say in my imagination. My brain is really sick sometimes.

'I don't have my phone and I can't get it until I find my keys, so whatever the fuck is going on here, how about you just tell me?' His tone is sharp now; he's unsettled. Oli puts a mug of tea down in front of him.

'I've made it with two sugars,' he says.

'I don't take sugar,' says Bruce.

'You might in a minute.'

'Bruce,' I say, 'there's no good way to say this. I'm afraid we have bad news. It's your dad.'

Both Bruce and Oli are looking at me expectantly. Why is it always me that ends up doing these shitty jobs? Shouldn't Oli be having some sort of man-to-man chat with him, maybe at the pub? It was the same when

180

the hamster died, it was me who had to sit Ben down, aged six, and try to explain why Nibbles was now in an empty tampon box and that no, it wasn't going to be a good idea for Ben to get him out for one last cuddle. Not that we'd put Colin in a tampon box.

'I'm so sorry, Bruce,' I say, 'but your dad is dead.'

For a few seconds nobody says anything and then suddenly Bruce lets out a loud bark of laughter. I am horrified and slightly terrified. Is this what happens when a murderer snaps? Is he about to confess all and then murder us all as witnesses, laughing maniacally as he plunges each of my Sabatier knives into us in turn.

I hope that Ben hears the screams at least and can escape with Lily. I wonder what will happen to them? I silently curse Oli and myself for not having updated our wills in years to specify who we'd like to take the kids. My mum loves them but she's always on a cruise. She's obsessed with the river cruises they advertise on ITV2 during episodes of *Poirot*. Good God, what if they end up with Pamela? She'll make Ben wear chinos and Lily will probably have to learn Mandarin and take cello lessons. One of Pamela's friend's granddaughters learns Mandarin and she brings it up every fucking time we see them.

Bruce thumps the table and guffaws a bit more, snapping me back into the room. I've never thought of 'guffaw' as a word used in real life, outside of suitably grotesque occasions at least, like Tory party conferences, but it suits Bruce very well.

'Very good, very good!' he says, shaking his head and giving a slow round of applause. 'Brilliantly done! You almost had me for a minute.'

'It's not a joke, Bruce, your dad was killed last night, at the party.'

'You can let it go now, Anna! Top marks for your acting but you can tell my father it's not as easy as all that to get one over on Bruce. I saw through his prank in a second!'

'Bruce,' I say again, looking him dead in the eye this time and reaching out to hold one of his hands, 'it's not a prank. I'm really sorry. I don't want to be this blunt, but your dad was murdered here last night. He was stabbed. In the larder.'

He looks towards the larder door. All the humour has left his face now.

'Seriously?' he asks.

'Seriously,' I say. 'I'm so sorry for your loss, Bruce. I know how much you looked up to your dad.'

I watch, horrified, as his face betrays the journey that his brain is on – disbelief, shock, realisation; it appears to crumple before us and Bruce starts to sob. Huge sobs that shake his whole body. Oli and I look at each other. *Do something,* I mouth silently to Oli, but he looks stricken and takes a step back before sighing and coming forward to pat Bruce awkwardly on the back.

'Sorry, mate,' he says, 'can I get you anything? A brandy maybe, for the shock?'

Bruce doesn't seem to notice Oli is even there. His head is in his hands and he's rocking gently backwards and forwards in his seat.

'Why don't you go and look for his keys?' I whisper to Oli. 'We've searched most places already, so somewhere less obvious maybe.' I remember that this is the man who couldn't find pillowcases in the airing cupboard and I don't fancy his chances, but a couple of minutes later he comes back holding a bunch of keys.

'Bruce,' he says gently, laying a hand on his back. Bruce looks up, his face a mess of tears and snot. 'Are these your keys? You'd hung them on one of the key hooks in the hallway – very organised! – I can go and get your phone for you, if there's someone you want to call?'

Bruce looks at the keys and nods pitifully. Oli gives me a tight smile and leaves to retrieve the phone from Bruce's car.

'I'll get you some tissues,' I say. We don't have tissues of course because I'm not a pensioner or a therapist, so I bring him a couple of handfuls of toilet paper from the downstairs toilet and he blows his nose loudly and then wipes his face, smearing snot into his eyebrows.

I gag and then cough to hide it. I'm not good with snot. It's probably my least favourite bodily fluid. There was a boy in Ben's toddler group called Lucas who always had a runny nose. Not just a dribble that you could wipe discreetly with a sleeve – this was full-on *dangling* out of both nostrils. You know the massive dogs that have the lines of drool permanently dangling from the sides of their mouth? It was like that, but *mucus*. Sometimes if it dangled too low, Lucas would stick out his tongue to catch it.

It was possibly the most disgusting thing I have ever seen, and that's saying something now that I can add 'a man in a Santa outfit stabbed to death', and the very worst bit of it was that Lucas's mum didn't even seem to notice. I'm fairly certain I never saw her wipe it. I had to stop taking Ben to the group in the end as it was just too traumatising and I couldn't cope with the fear of it one day dangling *onto Ben* as they negotiated turns in the red and yellow Little Tikes Cosy Coupe. It was a shame as the coffee was decent and the biscuit selection was unrivalled on the toddler group circuit.

'I just can't believe it,' says Bruce, having composed himself a little. 'Someone *killed* him did you say? Who?'

'We don't know who yet,' I say, 'although the police have been, of course, and I'm sure they're doing everything they can to find out what happened.' I am absolutely not sure of this at all, but I don't feel it's the time for honesty.

'But who would want to kill him? He was such a cool guy, so generous and fun-loving.'

This time it's a snort that I turn into a cough.

'Of course sometimes not everyone appreciated his sense of humour,' Bruce goes on, 'but it was just banter! He was old-school you know?'

'Oh I know,' I agree, and an uninvited image of Benny Hill pops into my head.

'But he never meant anyone any harm; he was never malicious. Surely there must be some mistake?'

'It's not a mistake, Bruce, I found him myself. It was definitely Colin, I'm afraid.'

'But maybe whoever did this made a mistake? Maybe they thought it was someone else, in the darkness, and got the wrong person?'

'It's possible,' I say slowly, 'but your dad was dressed as Father Christmas, remember? It would be pretty hard to mistake Father Christmas for someone, well, for someone *not* dressed as Father Christmas.'

Bruce looks again at the larder, and I realise I haven't

actually told him where the larder is, having managed *not* to do the head cock.

'Did you go into the larder by any chance during the party, Bruce?' I ask, trying to sound as casual as possible.

'Did I go into the larder? No, why would I go into the larder? It's not my house.'

'Oh, no reason, I just saw you looking at the door and thought perhaps you'd been in there, and that's why you knew where it was.'

'Well I didn't,' says Bruce quickly. 'I just guessed that's all. It's an obvious place for a larder.'

'I wouldn't have minded if you had – plenty of people were going in for stuff, you know, drinks, snacks . . .' I pause, daring myself to say it '. . . Pringles.'

I watch Bruce carefully and there's a definite flinch. I don't know what to make of it all. He's adamant that he didn't go in the larder and I would have been sure that he hasn't been faking his reaction to his dad's death, but then why on earth would you lie about helping yourself to some Pringles? It doesn't make sense.

I can't think about it any longer as Oli comes back into the kitchen. He's now holding keys *and* a phone. He sits down at the table, puts them down in front of Bruce and as he does the screen lights up with a message. We can all see that he's had multiple missed calls, messages and voicemails, meaning he very likely wasn't lying about not having spoken to anyone yet today.

Bruce opens his phone and reads through all the notifications, resting his head on one hand as he does.

'Bruce,' I ask as he scrolls, 'I don't suppose you remember if your dad had his phone with him at the party, do you? He didn't have it with him when the police checked and we haven't found it in the house. I thought perhaps he might have left it at home, maybe given it to you for some reason?'

Bruce furrows his brow. 'He definitely had it with him, because he was showing me some emails at one point – I remember that.'

'Was that what you were arguing with him about?' I ask.

'What?' His voice is sharp. 'We didn't argue. Me and Dad don't argue! We're best mates . . . were best mates.'

'Oh my mistake. Ben, my son, said he'd seen you and Colin arguing about something in the kitchen, but he must have been mistaken. You know what kids are like.'

'We *talked*,' he admits, 'but I wouldn't call it an argument. A heated conversation at best, but it was nothing. I can't even remember what it was about now, so it can't have been important.'

'Well we'll keep an eye out for his phone then, or maybe your mum has it at home. I'm sure there's a simple explanation.'

He's back to scrolling now through his messages. He looks a lot older than when he arrived – that baby-faced innocence has gone from his face.

'I should call Mum,' he says, 'but I don't know if I can face it. She's going to be hysterical. I don't know how to cope with her when she's like that. What am I meant to say to her?' He looks at me as though being a woman qualifies me to answer.

'Perhaps you don't need to say very much at all if you don't want to, perhaps just being there and listening is enough?'

'Really?' He looks sceptical, as if the idea of simply listening to someone as a way of showing them support hasn't occurred to him before.

'Really,' I say. 'She needs you though, and I expect you need her really. Family is what's important at a time like this.'

This comment seems to upset him. 'That's what I always thought,' he says sadly. 'But after the last few weeks I'm not so sure.'

'What do you mean?' Oli asks.

Bruce's eyes dart from side to side. 'Nothing,' he says, 'it doesn't matter. Just that sometimes people surprise you and you wonder how well you really know them.' He sighs loudly and gives his nose another large blow. 'You're right though,' he says, standing up, 'Mum needs me. I'll go straight there now, rather than call her. Show her she has *someone* at least that she can rely on.'

'Are you sure you don't want your tea?' I say, standing up with him. 'Are you okay to drive? Oli or I could drive you home if you'd like us to?'

'I'm fine,' he says, 'thanks. I'm feeling okay. It was just a shock, out of the blue like that.'

'Of course,' I say. I open my arms to offer him a hug and he accepts, leaning in and resting his face on my shoulder. I try not to think about the snot.

Oli stands too and we both show him to the door. 'Nice shoes, mate,' says Oli, as Bruce is on the doorstep. 'You were wearing those last night, weren't you?'

Bruce looks down at his shoes. Shiny brown brogues. 'Yeah I was,' he says. 'Cheers, mate. Well, I'd better be going.'

'Where are they from?' blurts Oli. I give him a questioning look. 'I've been looking for something similar and I can't find quite what I want. Those are perfect though.'

'I don't know,' says Bruce. 'I've had them a while, sorry.' He turns to leave.

'Maybe they say on the bottom?' says Oli, a note of desperation in his voice.

Bruce turns back. 'Honestly, mate,' he says, 'I don't know where they're from and I don't think it says on them.' He lifts one foot up so that we can see the bottom. 'There, see? No idea. I really have to go now.'

'No worries,' says Oli, smiling and waving him off. 'Thanks anyway! Take care.'

He closes the door and I look at him like he's lost the plot.

'What the fuck was that? The guy has just found out his dad has been murdered and you're banging on about his shoes, getting him to check the bottoms of them in the street when he wants to be going home to his grieving mother? Have you lost it?'

He just looks at me, eyebrows raised and a half-smile on his face. What is he playing at? And then I realise what he was up to, asking Bruce to see the bottom of the shoes he was wearing last night.

'Ooh you're a genius!' I say.

'Right?' He holds up one hand and I high-five him. 'I'll have my own podcast before you know it – you just wait.'

CHAPTER 17

Unfortunately, despite Oli's quick thinking, we're not really any closer to finding out who killed Colin, as the sole of Bruce's shiny brown brogue was smooth – not a chevron in sight. If those were the shoes he was wearing last night then it wasn't Bruce who left the print in the flour.

What we can't decide though is whether or not that lets Bruce off the hook completely. Oli is ready to cross him off the list – he says Bruce just isn't smart enough to fake that kind of reaction – and although I'm inclined to agree with him, I can't help but feel like there's something Bruce isn't telling us.

'You're one hundred per cent sure it was him you saw coming out of the larder last night with the Pringles?' I ask Oli for about the fourteenth time.

'Absolutely completely sure. I can picture it clearly, him giving the Pringles a toss-up in the air and dropping them. I'm totally sure.'

'Well something just doesn't add up then,' I say,

'because he was adamant he'd not been in the larder at all. Even when I specifically mentioned Pringles – he flinched at that for sure – he stuck to his story.'

'Well he's lying then.' Oli shrugs.

'But why? If he isn't lying to cover up the fact that he was in there stabbing his dad then what is it? Surely there's nothing he could have been doing that would have been worth throwing such suspicion on himself?'

'Maybe he was having a wank,' says Oli. I stare at him, horrified. 'You know, for a dare or something?'

'For a dare?! Who on earth has a wank in someone else's larder at a Christmas party FOR A DARE? I worry about you sometimes.'

'I don't know,' says Oli, 'it was the first thing I thought of that might be bad enough to have to lie about. He did say he used to play a lot of rugby – rugby types are always doing weird stuff like that, aren't they?'

I grimace and point out that our party mainly consisted of neighbours and school friends, not a full rugby team.

'Who would have been daring him?' I ask. 'Can you picture Margaret being behind it? "Oh hey, Bruce, dare you to go and jack off into their Coco Pops"? Seriously, Oli, I don't think it's that.'

He concedes that it feels like an unlikely thing to come from Margaret. 'But he *is* lying, so we know he's hiding something.'

Oli gets our paperwork back out of the cutlery drawer and we take a fresh look at the evidence, weighing up what we can add following our visit from Bruce.

'Let's look at the for and against it being Bruce,' says

Oli, pencil poised. 'On the for side, we know he was at the party at the time and we know he went into the larder, even though he says he didn't. That gives him the opportunity.'

'We've also got the potential motive,' I add. 'He says that he and Colin didn't argue but we know that they did, and did you notice the comment he made about not even knowing what family is anymore? He *knew* about Colin's other child and we can be pretty sure that's what they were arguing about. Bruce sounded bitter about it and if he felt like this new sibling was going to be a threat to his future financial security, then that could have been reason enough to kill his dad before he did anything more about it.'

On the against side though, we both admit that if Bruce had known already that his dad was dead then turning up to the house and giving that performance of emotion was impressive. I don't think Bruce has the dramatic range or the subtlety to pull it off. Surely you can't produce that much snot at will?

And then of course we keep coming back to the footprint. It's the footprint that's so hard to explain. None of our suspects so far fit the evidence – Bruce's brogues, Miranda's heels; the footprint is making it hard to pin it on anyone at all. I'm beginning to wish I'd done what Bacon did and just stand on it. Our options would be a lot more interesting then.

'I'm going to call Jennie,' I say, 'update her on the Bruce situation, see what she thinks.'

'Good plan,' says Oli, his eyes lighting up, 'put her on speaker and I'll tell her about how I got Bruce to show us the bottom of his shoe.' He really is very proud of that. Disproportionately proud you might say, if you were a little harsher and less supportive than me.

She answers after two rings. 'Anna! How are the little grey cells?'

'Tired,' I answer, 'and confused. We just had Bruce here.'

'Gosh, you're calling in the suspects, are you? Giving them the once-over?'

I explain that we didn't have to call him in, that he just showed up, looking for his keys. I give her the whole story about Bruce not knowing his dad was dead, allegedly, and us having to break the news to him.

'I got him to show us his shoes!' Oli interrupts, before I have a chance to explain.

'Erm, okay, Oli,' says Jennie. 'Why though?'

'Because of the flour!' Oli tries to explain but he's too excited.

'Because of the shoeprint that I found in the flour,' I explain properly, 'so that we could check to see if it had the same chevron design.'

'Ahhh! I see,' says Jennie. 'And did it?'

'No,' says Oli, 'but that's still helpful, isn't it? Eliminating suspects and whatnot.'

'Yes, very helpful. Well done, Oli,' says Jennie, with the voice that I recognise from many, many hours spent in various parks over the years, our children insisting we watch them perform various feats. Oli beams like he's just gone down the big slide backwards.

'That's great then, isn't it?' Jennie continues. 'We can cross him off the list.'

'I don't know,' I say. 'His shoe isn't a match but he clearly knew about this person claiming to be Colin's child. We think that's what he and Bruce were arguing about when Ben saw them.' I tell her about how Bruce had denied even arguing with Colin at all.

'I guess that's kind of natural,' says Jennie. 'If your dad has just been murdered you're hardly going to wave your hand and say "Me! I argued with him just beforehand!" Especially if you didn't do it and you know that what you were arguing about is private.'

'Yeah, I get that, but it wasn't just the row. He lied about having been in the larder too.'

'What do you mean?'

'Oli distinctly remembers seeing him come out of the larder lateish in the evening, but when I asked Bruce – pretty casually I thought – if he'd been in there, he point-blank denied it. He was really quite defensive about it.'

'Even when we mentioned the Pringles specifically,' chimes in Oli.

'What have Pringles got to do with it?' asks Jennie. 'He wasn't stabbed with a tube of crisps.'

'No,' says Oli, 'but when I saw him coming out of the larder he was carrying a tube of Pringles. He did a bit of a thing, trying to be Tom Cruise in *Cocktail*, but missed and dropped them on the floor, which is why I remembered it so clearly.'

'So why on earth would he lie about having been in the larder if he has nothing to hide?' I say. 'He must have been up to something shady or he wouldn't feel the need to keep it a secret.'

'Surely there are all kinds of explanations?' says Jennie. 'He might have felt embarrassed about taking the Pringles when you already had crisps out, or maybe he just needed a bit of quiet time to meditate or something, I don't know.'

Neither of those sound like plausible explanations and I've no idea why Jennie should be trying to defend him. Not that it matters if the footprint evidence is off. It's just so frustrating having all of these loose ends and no idea how to tie any of them together.

'I've got to go anyway,' says Jennie suddenly, 'I promised Matty and Jake I'd FaceTime them before they have tea and it's getting on a bit. Keep me posted!' She hangs up before I have a chance to say goodbye and I'm left staring at my dark phone screen.

'Bye then, Jennie,' I say sarcastically.

I look at the clock on the oven. It's 4.35 p.m. Jennie's right, it is getting on. Apart from making the Christmas starter I've done zero preparation for tomorrow and the sad thing is that I really don't want to. It's funny how finding a dead Santa in your house puts a damper on the whole Christmas spirit thing. Fancy making a festive table centrepiece? Sure! Only wait, we're all going to die some day and it could be today, so, maybe I won't bother. I need to try and get some Christmas enthusiasm going or everybody is going to get here and I'll be sitting in my pyjamas, swigging Buck's Fizz straight from the bottle, bemoaning the futility of life.

I have to say that this whole solving a murder thing isn't as glamorous as I thought it was going to be. I imagined a lot more *discovering of clues* and much less *having no idea*. It feels like everything we deduce is basically just a random stab in the dark, which is ironic given that's what *did* happen to Colin. Where are the cocktails and the cruise ships and the rubies? Why am

I not cycling through a quaint village, hair flowing out in the breeze behind me, on my way to see the vicar to gather important information and take evidence home in my wicker bicycle basket?

Instead here I am in my own kitchen, with potatoes that need peeling, a stupid flour footprint that doesn't match anybody and my ghastly mother-in-law arriving in the morning. It's all rather disheartening, which really isn't represented nearly enough in murder mystery novels.

'What's for tea?' Oli asks innocently, driving the final nail into the coffin that is my day.

'What's for tea? Are you serious?'

'I just wondered,' he says. 'I didn't know if you had anything in mind.'

I loathe this expression. It's the implication that my brain has nothing better to do all day, every day, than plan the next family meal, that I'm constantly thinking about what we're going to eat next. I think I particularly hate this assumption because it's true, I *am* constantly thinking about what we're going to eat next, but I wish I wasn't. I wish somebody else was, so that my brain was free to think about more interesting things. If I wasn't always asking myself what I was going to make for tea, perhaps I would have invented a groundbreaking technology by now, or come up with a cure for Alzheimer's. I swear this is why a disproportionate number of important inventions and discoveries are made by men; it's because all the women are distracted by mental meal planning.

'Funnily enough,' I spit, 'the main thing I've *had in mind* today has been the corpse of my boss, which I discovered this morning amongst the cereal, which I've since learnt may or may not have also been wanked into.'

'Fish fingers and chips then?' Oli offers in a quiet voice.

'Fish fingers and chips is fine,' I huff. 'You put the oven on; I'm going to go and give the upstairs bathroom a quick clean and then collect up Ben's laundry and get another load of washing on.'

I look in on the kids on the way. *Chicken Run* is still on. They are both on the sofa – Lily at one end, Ben lounging the rest of the sofa's length, his feet on Lily's lap. 'Fish fingers and chips for tea,' I call in. They both ignore me. I decide not to press the matter.

Whilst I clean around the bath I keep turning over and over in my head everything we've discovered so far today – the cat GPS, the note in Colin's pocket, his missing phone – trying to fit it all together in a way that makes sense. I think about everyone we've spoken to, how they all seem to have one reason or another to have not been too heartbroken to see the back of Colin.

I scrub around the toilet, remembering how weird Georgie was with me, Bruce's caginess over the larder and Miranda's hysterical outpourings to Jennie. It feels like everyone is hiding something, which is making it very complicated indeed to figure out what's important and what's not. Why can't everybody just tell the truth? *What, like you did to the police?* Okay, *brain*, point taken, we're all capable of the odd lie. It just makes mystery solving annoyingly difficult. I bet I'd find it easier if I was knitting a blanket. Miss

Marple is always knitting a blanket. I wonder how long it takes to learn to knit?

After about fifteen minutes of spraying, scrubbing and lamenting the fact that it isn't 1923 and I don't have a housekeeper, the bathroom is clean enough. Clean enough for me at least. It will never be clean enough for Pamela so there's no point in trying. If Pamela were on that TV show *Four in a Bed* where B&B owners take turns to stay in and rate each other's establishments, I swear Pamela would extract one of her own greying pubes and plant it under a pillow, just so that she could tut loudly about it at breakfast and deduct marks.

I replace the hand towels and the bath mat with the John-Lewis-reserved-for-guests versions and go into Ben's bedroom where I add the dirty towels and mat to his laundry basket and take the whole lot downstairs.

I come back into the kitchen and find Oli just closing the freezer, holding a bag of frozen peas. I have a brief flashback of the imaginary women's heads.

'Are you okay?' he says. 'You look like you've seen a ghost.'

'Oh yes I'm fine, it was just the peas.'

'I'm doing them to go with the fish fingers and chips. Is that okay?'

'You don't have to ask my permission,' I snap. 'I'm not the keeper of teas.' Oli looks hurt and I put down the laundry basket, sighing. 'I'm sorry, love, I'm just freaking out about this whole thing and it being Christmas tomorrow and your parents turning up to find zero Christmas spirit.'

'Come here,' he says, putting down the peas and opening his arms wide. I walk into them and he folds me into a hug. I snuggle in and take a deep breath of his chest.

'There's no tablescape with fresh holly,' I continue, 'no homemade crackers and the gravy is definitely going to be Bisto granules.'

He gives me a squeeze. 'It's all going to be fine. Gravy is gravy, the Waitrose crackers are excellent and wouldn't holly on the table be a bit prickly?'

'I just want to get everything right. I just wish one year your mum would say something nice like: "What a great job you've done, Anna; everything looks delicious," and leave it at that.'

'You have to let it wash over you. It's the only way to do it. How do you think we all got through growing up with her? Smile and nod, agree with her.'

'But I *don't* agree with her,' I protest, 'barely any of the time at all. And you know how much I like everyone to know when I'm right about something.'

'You'll know though, darling, and I know how wonderful you are. You have to accept that's as good as you're going to get. And remember they're only here for two nights and then we can all put our pyjamas back on and eat marzipan fruits for every meal if you like.'

'Okay, okay, I'll do my best. I think I feel a bit silly if I'm being honest, that all my life I've longed for a mystery to solve and now I've got one and I'm not sure I want it anymore.'

'That's not silly at all, Anna,' says Oli. 'Of course it's going to be a let-down when you grow up reading

Nancy Drew. Her mysteries involve a fun trip with friends to a haunted lake where she meets a handsome stranger, finds some hidden jewels and easily catches some obvious smugglers.'

'And she has a convertible,' I remind him, 'and a housekeeper. I do think I might find it more exciting if I wasn't having to think about the laundry and someone was busy baking me a pie.'

'Would you like me to make you a pie?' Oli asks, with a look that says: *Please say no.* 'Or I could toast you a Pop Tart?'

'I'm good, but thank you. I really should get this washing on and then once the kids have had tea maybe we could rope them into decorating the table with the bits we do have. I'm sure we've got more fairy lights in the cupboard under the stairs – let's fling some more of those about too. It's very hard to feel unfestive with fairy lights.'

'Excellent plan,' says Oli, releasing me from the hug and going back to the frozen peas.

I start to unload Ben's laundry basket into the washing machine. Some of the T-shirts are still folded – I swear he just puts his clean laundry pile on the floor and then a couple of weeks later moves it to the basket. It's efficient in a way – cut out the middleman. Why bother putting your clothes away or *wearing* them when you could just set them on an infinite washing cycle.

I'm muttering to myself about gratitude and teenagers when suddenly I stop. I've been mechanically shovelling things in without looking but I'm forced to look now. In my hand is what looks like a white T-shirt and it's covered with a large red stain.

CHAPTER 18

I'm frozen on the spot. Part of me wants to look at the stain but another part of me, a bigger and more powerful part, wants to have never seen it at all. What if it's blood? What if it's Colin's blood? What if it's Colin's blood and my precious firstborn child is a deranged killer? How would I explain *that* to Pamela?

Calm yourself, woman. There could be a perfectly innocent explanation. Let's not leap to conclusions.

I can't help but start running through the logistics though. Will we have to spend every weekend for the rest of our lives visiting Ben in prison, neglecting Lily until she turns to drugs and moves into a squat? I'll have to give up work to start a *campaign*. The mothers always have campaigns. And banners.

'Oli,' I say in a low, quiet voice, 'can you give me a hand a minute?'

'Yeah give me two secs. I'm just going to get the peas on.'

'Leave that for now. I really need you here.'

'It won't take long,' he says, filling a saucepan with water.

'Please come now,' I say with more urgency. Still quiet, but through gritted teeth. Oli gets the message and puts the pan down quickly.

'What is it? Why are you all hunched over and not moving. Is it your back?'

'It's not my back,' I say softly, but with an edge of hysteria, 'I'm staying still in case it means I can go back in time and leave this washing in Ben's room.'

Oli's brows are furrowed. He looks at the washing, then at me, then back at the washing with a double take that would be funny if I weren't still planning out prison visits in my imagination.

'Will you please take whatever this is in my hand and tell me what the stain is. I'm just going to close my eyes.'

'Oka-ay . . .' He takes it from my hands and I scrunch my eyes up tight. 'It's a white T-shirt, but it's not Ben's. It's tiny.'

Oh God, Lily?! Surely not!

'It's from Abercrombie and Fitch, maybe Sasha's? And it's not blood.' I hear him sniff it and squeeze one eye open to peep. 'I think it's red wine.'

'Are you sure?' I say, opening both eyes now and taking it from him. He's right, now that I can see it properly it looks nothing like blood. 'Oh thank God,' I say, letting out the last five minutes' worth of breath. 'I thought it was Ben for a minute there.'

'Thought what was Ben?' asks Ben. He and Lily are standing looking at us. '*Chicken Run* finished so we came to see if tea was ready. What did you think was me?'

He looks down at the T-shirt I'm holding and his face flushes a deep pink. 'It's not what you think,' he starts, thankfully unaware that what I *had* been thinking was that he had stabbed a man in cold blood in his own home and was going to be the direct cause of his sister's lifelong battle with drink and drugs.

Oli interrupts him. 'What I think is that you and Sasha helped yourself to some red wine, snuck it upstairs to your bedroom and then Sasha managed to chuck it all over herself.'

'Oh,' he says, head bowed, eyes to the floor, 'in that case it's exactly what you think.'

I drop the T-shirt back into the laundry, quickly cross the kitchen to him and throw my arms around him. 'I'm so pleased, Ben!'

'I'm really sorry, Mum, it's just that . . . Wait, what?' He leaned back, away from my hug to look at my face. 'Did you say you're pleased?'

'I think what your mum means,' says Oli hastily coming to my rescue, 'is that we're pleased you told us the truth. Isn't that right, Mum?' He nods at me, eyebrows raised.

'Oh yes, that's it! We're just so pleased that you didn't try to lie about it and that it's just red wine and Lily doesn't have to live in a squat!'

'What are you on about, Mum?'

Lily pipes up next to me. 'We learned about squats at school!'

'Did you? That's unusual.' I make a mental note to speak to Miss Henderson.

'Yep, they go like this,' she says, squatting. As she comes back up she farts and laughs. I cancel the mental note.

'We didn't think you'd mind because you'd drunk loads, Mum,' says Ben, rather cleverly I think. It's very hard to give a lecture on the dangers of alcohol when your own child has to go and sit in the garden to avoid you drunkenly attempting a crab on the Twister mat.

'I am over eighteen though,' I point out, lifting my chin a little bit and trying my best to look authoritative.

'It's actually legal for anyone aged over five to drink alcohol at home,' says Ben. 'We googled it.'

Damn Google. The internet has a lot to answer for. When I was a kid my mum and dad could say whatever they liked and I had to just assume they were right. Either that or go to the library, which feels ludicrous now. Who knows what laws they made up. I half suspect that my mum always made up the names of plants and bird calls too.

When I had kids I thought it would be a whole stream of knowledge I would suddenly have access to but no, I still don't have a clue. I think perhaps my mum just said things confidently and hoped for the best. 'Oh that? That's a goldfinch, darling, and that's lily of the valley.' Actually, thinking about it, it does feel like we heard an astonishing number of goldfinches.

'Five years old? Are you sure?'

'Does that mean I can have wine with my fish fingers?' asks Lily.

'Absolutely not,' I say firmly. 'You can have orange squash or water or, as it's Christmas Eve, lemonade.'

She looks thoughtful. 'Do we have any straws?'

'Yes we do.'

'Lemonade then please! And can I have ice?'

'What do you think, Daddy? Can Lily have ice in her lemonade?'

'Ooooh, I don't know about that,' says Oli, looking mock concerned. 'Ice? In December? Won't you be cold?'

Lily laughs. 'No! It will be in my drink, not on me!'

'Well in that case, one lemonade with ice coming up.'

Ben helps himself to a can of Coke from the fridge. He's not saying any more about the red wine incident and neither am I, but both for very different reasons. He doesn't want to talk about drinking in his room with a girl and I don't want to talk about the very clear picture I had in my head of him in black and white striped prison wear. It does get me thinking though.

'What sort of time was it that you took the wine upstairs?' I ask, my voice artificially casual.

Ben shoots me a look as he sits down at the table. 'Why?'

'Just wondering!'

'If you're just wondering because you're trying to establish Sasha's alibi then I've told you, it wasn't her.'

'What's an alibi?' asks Lily, and Ben looks at me apologetically, having forgotten operation 'keep the dead Santa from his sister'.

'It's a type of French cheese,' I tell her. 'You wouldn't like it.' I look back at Ben. 'Is that why you didn't want to tell us? Because you knew it involved the wine and you didn't want to get in trouble?'

He flushes again and looks down at the plate of fish fingers and peas Oli has put down in front of him. 'Sure,' he mumbles. Not that then, something else.

'Is there something between you and Sasha? Is she your girlfriend?' I venture.

His cheeks are almost crimson now. 'Mum,' he says, 'it's not like that nowadays. We don't tie ourselves down to relationship labels and stereotypes.'

'No, no, I get it, fluidity and all that,' I say awkwardly, not getting it at all. 'But you do like her, don't you?'

'Oh my God, Mum, fine, I like her, and I know she didn't, er, eat any French cheese at midnight, because she was in my room and I asked her to be my girlfriend at exactly midnight because I thought it would be cute, okay? HAPPY NOW?'

I am happy. We love Sasha. 'I thought you weren't tied down by labels?'

'It's CHOICE, Mum, okay? You're pro-choice?'

'Absolutely,' I say. 'One hundred per cent choice.' I give him a smile and a thumbs up and he rolls his eyes and helps himself to chips. I handled that very well, I think. I text Jennie. 'Sasha definitely out of it. She was snogging Ben upstairs at midnight.'

Ben eyes me suspiciously. 'You'd better not be texting Sasha's mum or anything grim.' I put my phone down and then turn it face down.

'Definitely not,' I say, smiling again. 'It was an Instagram notification.'

'Wow, did someone like your blurry Christmas tree photo in the dark?'

'That was meant to be *artsy*, Ben. I meant it to be blurry, for the Christmas magic, and actually twelve people have liked it, so there, maybe your mum's cool after all.'

He gives me a look of such pity that I consider checking myself into a retirement home immediately. I might stand a better chance of solving a murder there. I could start a club.

'I was thinking after tea that you could both help me get some Christmassy bits ready for tomorrow – you could be in charge of decorating the table maybe?' They both look at me like it might be a trap.

'Aren't you doing something special from that craft show?' Ben asks. 'What's a called? A tablescape? Isn't that why we were pinching the holly when Dad got scared by the baguette?'

'For the last time,' says Oli, 'I thought it was a bat!' We all laugh. Lily picks up a chip and waves it at his face.

'Are you scared, Daddy?' she asks, making ghost noises and accidentally smearing ketchup on his chin.

'Terrified, although not as scared as if it were a piece of bread and butter.'

'Seriously though,' says Ben, 'I'm not sure Lily and I are up to that level of table decoration, Mum. Are you sure you want to trust us with it?' It's a well-meant question but it stabs me, metaphorically thank God, in the gut as I realise with a start how uptight I've been about Christmas this year. I've been so focused on wanting to show Pamela how effortlessly chic I am that I'd forgotten that Christmas is meant to be fun. Perhaps losing a little of my Christmas mojo might not be a bad thing if it means I back off a bit and stop obsessing about things.

'I trust you one hundred per cent,' I say. 'You're both very creative. I'm sure you can come up with something that will wow us all. We don't have the holly . . .' I purse my lips at Oli and Lily waves her chip again '. . . but you could get bits from the garden if you like. I'll get the crackers out, and the napkins and cutlery, and you use whatever else you like. Go wild.'

They both look genuinely pleased and I'm touched that my two children, eight years apart, can still enjoy a wholesome Christmas Eve activity together. Maybe Ben will discover a love of flower arranging and start nature journalling.

'Let's get as many party poppers as we can find,' says Ben, 'and we can use my Zelda figurines to show people where to sit.'

Okay, maybe not nature journalling.

I think about embracing this new-found relaxed attitude by pouring myself a Baileys and watching *Love Actually* but I should probably at least finish loading the washing machine. And clean the downstairs toilet. And possibly run the hoover around.

'Do we have any Baileys?' I ask Oli.

'In the larder I think. I'll have one if you're offering. Just to keep you company.'

I finish loading the washing machine and go to investigate Baileys supplies in the larder. I open the door and am greeted by the minty-fresh smell of Arm & Hammer. Ergh. The toothpaste.

I spot the Baileys and am momentarily torn. Do I really need to clean the toothpaste up *right now?* Perhaps it's one of those things that's more effective if you leave it for twenty-four hours and I'd be doing myself a favour by waiting. Or perhaps it's the opposite, and leaving it will just mean *baking in* the bloodstains? I think about future me – the one getting up tomorrow morning and remembering the toothpaste is still there – and decide to do it now. I compromise though and have a quick swig out of the Baileys bottle to spur me on.

Oli sticks his head around the door. 'Everything okay in here?'

'Yes, all good,' I say, finishing the swig and wiping my mouth on the back of my hand like a middle-aged pirate. 'I've got to clean up the toothpaste so I was just motivating myself.'

'Would you like some in an actual glass or would that spoil your fun?'

'I think I could manage a glass, and maybe a couple of ice cubes, and a splash of milk.'

'Milk? *In* the Baileys.'

'Yes please,' I say. 'It tastes less alcoholy then, and more like a milkshake.'

'Isn't the point that it tastes alcoholy?'

'Dur no, the point of alcohol is that it gets you drunk, not that it tastes good. Everyone knows that.'

'I think teenagers think that,' says Oli, confiscating the bottle, 'but okay. Milk it is.'

'And can you also bring me a bowl of soapy water, a sponge and a scouring pad please?'

'And a straw?'

'Har har, for the floor,' I say. Oli laughs at what he clearly thinks is his supreme wit and heads back into the kitchen. While I wait I have a bit of a tidy-up, straightening things on the shelves and checking the Coco Pops. It's not that I really think Bruce was jizzing in them, but once you've got a thought in your head . . .

'Here you go,' says Oli, putting a glass of milky Baileys

on a shelf along with the bottle and handing me a bowl of water. 'I'm going to clear up dinner and keep half an eye on the table decorating, just so that it doesn't become a full Zelda battle re-enactment.'

I smile my thanks, put the bowl of water on the floor and get down on my knees to join it. They complain at the idea but I ignore them. I'm not sure what it is about knees that mean at a certain point in life they stop wanting to be knees, but that definitely seems to have happened to me in the last few years.

You'd think the job of a knee would be pretty straightforward – bending, kneeling et cetera – the clue is in the name there, but no. Despite for years having been perfectly happy to let me kneel down to do things, they've now become extremely touchy about the idea. I knew I was entering a new phase of life when I found myself in the garden centre buying one of those floral-patterned kneeling mats that elderly ladies in straw hats have for weeding. I'll have a wicker trug next. Worse, I'll go on a course and make my *own* wicker trug. Actually, that sounds quite fun. I might do that.

Ignoring my knees in a bid to show them their place, I start scrubbing off the toothpaste. The bloodstains are definitely less severe, but I don't think I'll be making one of those promotional garden centre TV ads anytime soon. It's not miraculous by any stretch of the imagination. Still, it's better than it was and there's also the raffia mat option. Come to think of it, there's probably a workshop for that too.

Twenty minutes later I've removed all of the toothpaste and a lot of the blood from the grout and I'm just giving the whole floor a final wipe-over. That's the trouble with any kind of stain – you might do a brilliant job on it, but it inevitably then highlights how grubby everything around it is. I move a polythene-wrapped twelve-pack of cat food to get into one of the corners and my eye is caught by something shiny lying on top of one of the tins.

I look more closely and recoil, rocking back on my knees, much to their disgust. I lean in again, pick it up and place it in my left palm. I use my other hand to lever myself up off the floor, reach for my Baileys and drink the whole thing down in one.

I shudder, replace the glass on the shelf and look back at my hand and the single gold hoop earring.

CHAPTER 19

I feel sick, and not just because of the Baileys. I know exactly who this belongs to. I'd have known even if she hadn't been asking me about it this morning, because it's one of a pair I bought her for her last birthday. This earring belongs to Jennie.

My mind whirs. All of this time I've not even thought about Jennie as a suspect, so sure was I that all of those years of friendship meant that she couldn't possibly have done it, but have I been wrong all along? Jennie specifically told me that she hadn't been into the larder all night and yet how would her earring have found itself here otherwise?

I'm panicking. Perhaps I'm remembering it wrong? There has been so much to take in today; perhaps it's quite innocent and she popped in at some point to get something. I mustn't jump to conclusions. Putting the earring into one pocket I take my phone out of the other and message her.

'We're getting nowhere fast here,' I write, 'so we're

doing a recap of who we know was in the larder at any point in the evening. I was obviously, and Oli, and we're pretty sure Sav and Toby as they were helping with drinks and food. Just double-checking if you were in there for anything?'

I hit send. I can see that Jennie is online and the ticks turn blue, meaning she's read it. She starts typing, then stops, then starts again.

'Nope, I didn't go in at all,' she says. 'Send me a pic of the list when you're done, though, and I'll add it to the murder board!' She includes a knife emoji, which right now feels a little bit in poor taste. I give the message a thumbs up and put my phone back in my pocket.

Fuck.

I try to think of a logical explanation for it. Perhaps the earring has been there since before the party? No, because she told me this morning that she'd lost it last night. She could have lost it somewhere else and somebody picked it up and dropped it there later? Technically possible, but hardly likely. Or is she being framed? That's a stretch. If you were going to go to the effort to frame someone then wouldn't you wipe away your own footprint? And make the earring more obvious?

No matter how I try to reconcile it in my head the only way this makes sense is if Jennie simply lost the earring while she was in the larder herself. It's not the solution I want though because there's only one conclusion to draw from that – Jennie lied to me.

Fuck fuck fuck.

I need to think about this properly. My glass is empty so I take another swig from the Baileys bottle. It doesn't help. Okay, think, woman, think. Don't get caught up in the emotion of it; take a step back. What would Poirot do here? He'd look at the facts. I compile a mental list of facts:

Jennie was here at the party at midnight, the time of death.

Jennie's earring was found at the crime scene.

Jennie claims she wasn't in the larder all night.

Jennie disliked Colin.

It doesn't look great, honestly, written down in my head like that, but it's far from conclusive and there's plenty to argue the case for the defence:

Jennie might not have liked Colin, but did anybody like him? Not liking someone is hardly reason to kill them.

The shoe print in the flour isn't a match for Jennie's shoes.

She knows how much I love those Sabatier knives.

While that last point might seem small, she said herself that if she was going to kill him she'd have bashed him on the head with a Kilner jar. Unless that was a double bluff to mislead me? No, I just can't imagine it. I can't picture Jennie, my practically lifelong friend, as a killer. Jennie who taught me how to do French plaits *and* French kissing. Jennie who was there for me when my mum and dad got divorced. Jennie who *helped me cover up the demise of the school hamster.*

Nope. I can't. Not Jennie. I feel almost worse about this idea than when I thought it was Oli. There's something almost cliché about a husband being a secret serial killer, because as much as you might love them, they are a man after all, and you never *really* know what a man is thinking. True, most of the time it's probably food or sex or just a brain-tumbleweed situation, but you can never be sure.

Not with Jennie though. I've known Jennie for forty years. We've spent endless nights talking in detail about our thoughts on everything from how to tell if our crushes liked us to what we'd look for in a sperm donor if we'd had to go down the solo parent route. I *know* Jennie.

Or at least I thought I did.

I need a second opinion, but Jennie is my second opinion and I can't call her. Not yet anyway. She's already lied to me; I don't want to force her into a corner. I'll have to talk to Oli about it. I don't want to, because it was him who said we should have kept Jennie on the suspect list and this is going to be his moment to give me the I-told-you-so look, but I'll have to suck that up.

I gather up my cleaning stuff and the Baileys glass and take everything back into the kitchen. Ben and Lily are still in the dining room decorating the table – I can hear them squabbling about who gets to sit next to Toby and Sav. Oli is unloading the dishwasher.

'I found this in the larder,' I say, taking the earring out of my pocket and holding it out for him to see. He glances at it and carries on putting plates away into the cupboard. 'What should we do about it?'

'Um, put it back in your jewellery box?' he suggests.

'It's not mine,' I say, 'and I found it just now, *in the larder.*'

It takes him a minute and then I see his eyes widen as his brain catches up. 'Oh I see!' He puts the plate he's holding away and comes over for a better look. He picks it up and examines it. 'Whose is it?'

'I don't want to tell you,' I say quietly.

'What do you mean you don't want to tell me? Whose earring is this, Anna?'

'It's Jennie's,' I whisper.

'Who?'

'Jennie!' I say more loudly. 'But she told me she didn't go in the larder at all, all night, and so she must be lying to me, Oli!' He starts to make the I-told-you-so face but I burst into tears and he thinks better of it.

'She's my best friend!' I wail. 'She helped me bury the hamster!'

'I don't know what the hamster means,' he says gently, giving me a hug, 'but just because we found her earring doesn't mean she killed Colin. There could be any number of explanations for how her earring got in there.'

'Like what?'

He's silent. 'I'm not sure right this second,' he admits, 'but I bet there are plenty. Like maybe she hugged you and her earring got caught in your hair and then you went into the larder for something, stumbled about a bit and it fell onto the floor?'

Stumbled about a bit? That's a bit rude. He's right though, that does sound like it could just about have happened. 'Do you really think that's what happened?' I ask.

'I mean, no, not really,' he says with brutal honesty, 'but it *could* have happened – that's the point, isn't it?'

In theory yes, that is the point, but I do not feel reassured. Whenever a killer in stories is caught because of a lost button or a hatpin no one says, 'Oh but that hatpin could easily have become dislodged when Lady

Such and Such hugged her and then perhaps it just happened to get caught in Lady Such and Such's hat, and then later on came loose on exactly the spot that the murder occurred.'

It sounds lame. I may have had a lot to drink but I think I'd have noticed, or Jennie would have noticed, if I'd been walking about with a large gold hoop dangling from my head.

'I guess it's *possible*,' I say, 'but it doesn't feel probable.' I sniffle some more and then rub my hands across my face and give my cheeks a gentle slap. 'God, having one of your friends commit murder in your own house is *stressful*, isn't it?'

'Yes.' Oli sighs. 'It's a lot less exciting than I thought it would be from listening to podcasts.'

My eyes light up. 'Isn't it though? I felt so ashamed of myself earlier for thinking that, but it's so true. Although maybe it's context? This is our first investigation and we do have two kids in the house and the imminent arrival of in-laws. Perhaps it's more exciting if you're on a Nile cruise or lounging on the Riviera.'

'I expect so,' agrees Oli. 'If we weren't having to do laundry and unload dishwashers we might be able to make it a bit more dynamic. So what are you going to do about Jennie?'

I scrunch my eyes up tightly and sigh. 'I don't know. I could just confront her, but if she's already lied she could just lie again. I feel like I need something more to go on, you know? Primarily we're lacking a WHY. Why would Jennie want to kill Colin? Yes she thought he was a dick, but she thought that about a lot of people and a lot of people thought it about Colin. It doesn't feel like reason enough on its own, so is there something we don't know about?'

'Could you talk to Michael?' Oli says.

'To Michael? As in call him and ask, "Is there any reason why your pending-ex-wife might want to stab my boss?"'

'Well I might phrase it a little more subtly than that, but basically yes. We're still good friends with him; we've both known him for years. Couldn't we just ask?'

I think about it, but every part of me squirms at the awkwardness of the idea. 'I don't think I could,' I admit. 'Apart from anything else it would feel like a betrayal, like I was going behind Jennie's back.'

'Well, you would be.'

I sigh and put some glasses from the dishwasher back in the cupboard.

'What if I spoke to him?' suggests Oli. 'I could even say that I found the earring and didn't know what to do about it. I could keep you out of it completely, ask Michael not to mention it to Jennie.'

'Would you do that?' I ask.

'Of course,' he says. 'I don't think it can be Jennie – there's the shoe print apart from anything – but if it helps to reassure you and helps us gather a bit more useful evidence then of course.'

'Thank you, darling,' I say, leaning up to give him a kiss on the cheek. 'That would be brilliant.'

He smiles. 'No problem. I'll do it now.' He picks his phone up off the kitchen table. 'I'll do it in the garden in case Lily pops out from anywhere. That child is a menace. Remember that time she hid under our bed and we almost did the dirty with her six inches below

217

us?' He shudders and goes out through the back door into the garden.

While Oli goes out into the garden to make his call I peel some potatoes and mull things over. I don't strictly need to peel any potatoes, but I find it comforting. It reminds me of when I was little and we used to go to my gran and grandad's house in Swansea for Christmas.

My gran used to keep her potatoes in a cardboard box on the floor of her little larder cupboard, which always smelled of old Tupperware and plastic picnic cups. It would be my job to get the potatoes out from the box and then I'd stand on a stool next to her at the sink while she peeled them and cut them into chunks. She'd do this on Christmas Eve and then stand them in water in a pan on the stove, covered with a metal lid, ready to cook the next day. She did the same with her sprouts, but judging by the texture she may well have switched those on the night before too.

There's something soothing about doing such a mechanical job with your hands. It frees you up to think clearly somehow. I make the most of the feeling by running back over our suspects in my head. My favourites for it are Bruce and Miranda. Everyone knows that it's more often than not someone very close to the victim, like a partner, and both of them have the best motives – love and revenge for Miranda and money for Bruce.

There's Sav, who has a plausible motive and was certainly talking earlier as though there was a plan to 'take care of things', but is an investment gone wrong really a reason to commit murder? I could understand more maybe if it was his whole livelihood, but Pup's Pantry is really just a hobby that makes a bit of cash. Did Sav see it as something more perhaps? Did Colin ruin his chance to make it big in the doggy biscuit world?

What about Marcus? We've not given him much thought because he didn't know Colin as far as we know, but it is only that – *as far as we know*. He was at the party at the time, he had access to the larder, and we don't know what shoes he was wearing, so maybe it's time we dug a little deeper for a connection? He was so relaxed though when I spoke to him this morning about Georgie's phone, unlike Georgie, and he didn't even flinch when I made the quite obvious references to Colin's death.

And then there's Jennie, but I'm on the last potato and so I'm spared having to think about it. I cover the potatoes with water and a lid, move them to the stove and look out the window into the back garden. Oli is still on the phone, sitting at the patio table, his long legs stretched out in front of him, crossed at the ankles. Please, baby Jesus, let there be absolutely no reason that Michael can possibly think of why Jennie would wish Colin dead.

As I watch, Oli hangs up the phone. He doesn't move at first; he just stares at the blank screen. After a while he stands up, turns to come back to the house, sees me at the window and forces a smile.

I'm waiting when he comes through the back door. 'Well?'

'Well,' he says, 'I don't know what to say, Anna; it's mixed news.'

'What do you mean mixed news?'

'Michael is adamant that Jennie wouldn't have had anything to do with it – that's the reassuring part.'

'Of course he'd say that. *I'm* adamant she had nothing to do with it, but that doesn't make it fact.'

'No, true, and I didn't want to push it too hard and make it look like we properly suspected her. I didn't want to make it into a *thing*.'

'I mean, it *is* a thing, but okay.'

'But he did tell me about something that happened a couple of years ago after a Christmas party – not ours, a work one that Jennie went to with you?'

'The one where Colin made a pass at Jennie and she threw a glass of punch on him? I know all about that. That's hardly grounds for murder, and it was ages ago.'

'Apparently that wasn't the end of it though. Michael said that Colin didn't take kindly to being doused in Christmas cocktail and he started dropping unsubtle hints to guys at the golf club that he and Jennie had been having an affair and that he'd broken up with her, and that was why she'd thrown the drink.'

'He did what?!' I say. 'The utter bastard! I could kill him, honestly . . . oh, well no, not actually kill him.' Oli raises his eyebrows. 'But surely that can't be true. Jennie would have told me – she never said anything about it!'

'Michael said it all happened just as things were starting to go wrong for their marriage, and that he heard one of the rumours from a friend and although he didn't believe it, it all kind of fed into the general mood of things for them at home. He said that they were going through marriage counselling at the time and the counsellor had advised that one way to help the relationship might be to create better boundaries, help them unite as a couple.'

'As in not blab about your marriage to your friends all the time?' I ask.

Oli gives me a half-smile. 'Yes, I think it is something like that, love, sorry.'

'So Jennie could potentially hold Colin responsible for the failure of her marriage?'

'I don't think it was the deal-breaker, but by the sounds of it, it didn't help, so yes, maybe she could be holding a grudge, for that and for the rumours generally.'

I think about it. Jennie can be fiery for sure, but I don't know. 'Two years ago though, Oli – surely you don't sit on something that long and not say anything?'

Oli agrees it seems unlikely. 'Unless this Christmas was a trigger – first Christmas without the kids, maybe Colin makes some sly remark and she sees red?'

'Maybe, but I'm sure she'd have just chucked another drink at him in that case, not written him a secret note luring him into the larder.'

'That is definitely much more Jennie's style,' Oli agrees. 'But there you go – that's the information. What do we do with it, that's the question.'

I sigh heavily. I know the answer. 'I have to talk to her,' I say.

'I think so,' says Oli, 'although carefully. Michael told me all of that in confidence, so we don't want her to think we've been looking for dirt. Give her a call, tell her you found the earring and take it from there. Hopefully there's a perfectly reasonable explanation.'

'About why she lied to me, her best friend, about being at the scene of a murder?' I take my phone out of my pocket. 'I really hope so.'

CHAPTER 20

Before I have the chance to call Jennie, Ben and Lily burst into the kitchen. Well, Lily bursts; Ben follows behind looking pleased with himself but in a decidedly less bouncy way.

'Mummy! Come and look at the table! It's so beautiful!' She grabs my hand and drags me towards the dining room.

'I'm coming! No need to drag me.' She lets go of my hand but keeps looking back over her shoulder as we go, just in case I try to make a break for it. Oli follows me.

She stops at the dining room door. 'Don't look,' she commands. 'Close your eyes.' I close them. 'Both of you,' she barks, and I imagine Oli closes his too. I daren't look. I hear her open the dining room door.

'Walk forward,' she says. I walk into the doorframe and she laughs. 'Careful, Mummy!' We shuffle forward a few more steps until I can tell that we're inside the room.

'Okay,' she says, 'open your eyes!'

I open them and the first thing I see is her beaming face and her arms flung wide. 'Tada!'

I look at the table, its flaps extended, ready to seat six of us for dinner tomorrow. Rather than bring in a couple of extra chairs from the kitchen to add to the usual four, they've got Ben's chair from his desk upstairs and Lily's dressing table stool to make up the numbers. The placemats and cutlery are set out neatly, although backwards, and every place has a Zelda figurine, a hand-written name card and a glass – some are wine glasses, some are the pink glass tumblers with the strawberry decorations.

There are crackers and party poppers and the centre of the table has a line of cork mats set amongst piles of evergreen shrubbery from the garden.

'I wrote the name cards,' says Lily proudly, 'with all the grown-up names and a Christmas picture.' I look at the one closest to me. It says *Pamaler* and there is a small pencil drawing of what looks like a pig wearing a Christmas hat.

'It's absolutely perfect,' I say, beaming back at them both, and I mean it. This is so much better than any ludicrous tablescaping. Plus Pamaler can hardly turn her nose up at something her own grandchildren, spawn of her precious son, have crafted by hand.

'Do you really like it, Mum?' asks Ben. He's smiling. I wonder how my boy can have gotten so tall and yet still look about ten years old.

'I really really do,' I say. 'It's way better than anything I could have done.'

'Can we decorate something else?' asks Lily. I look at Ben, expecting him to protest, but he's looking at me keenly.

'Sure! Of course you can. We've got lots of vases in the cupboard next to the sink if you want to make any arrangements with more bits from the garden, or have a look under the stairs and I'm sure we've got fairy lights lying around. Help yourself to anything you like.' Keeping them busy while I talk to Jennie seems like a good idea.

'I've got to make a quick phone call,' I say, 'so I'll do that in my bedroom out of your way. Ask Dad if you need anything.'

They toddle off, happily bickering about what to do first. 'Good luck,' says Oli, giving me a reassuring smile as I head upstairs.

Sitting on the bed, I try to think through how I'm going to approach this. It's not every day you have to interrogate your best friend, after all. I decide on FaceTime for transparency – it's much harder to lie to someone when they're looking you dead in the eye, and I know Jennie well enough to be able to read her face and her body language better than she likes to think.

Enough faffing about. I open the app and call Jennie.

She answers quickly. I can tell from the angle of the living room behind her that she's sitting on her favourite armchair. She's holding a large glass of wine, which I see because she waves it at the screen as she answers.

'Cheers, babe! Happy nearly Christmas! How is it going chez corpse?'

'Hi, Jennie, not too bad. I've sort of given up, to be honest. Well, not given up, relaxed a bit maybe. I let the kids do the dining table. That should give you an idea of my state of mind.'

'Whoa! You relinquished control of the tablescape? Bravo, Anna! Here's to delegation! I have to say, I was dreading this Christmas, being without the kids for the first time, no stockings to wrap or potatoes to peel, but you know what, it's not that bad if you lean into it.'

I can imagine she's right. Wouldn't we all like a Christmas on our own secretly? Just one, just to do whatever we want, no one to cater for, no emergency runs for Sellotape, no marzipan fruits to worry about.

'I have a tray of M&S nibbles in the oven – the Indian selection – and I'm currently watching a made-for-TV Christmas film, which is the biggest ever pile of shite, but if you can get over the ludicrous storyline and horrible misogyny it's a fucking festive delight!' She gives me another cheers.

'Jennie,' I say. My tone is obviously sombre. She notices the shift and puts her glass down. 'I need to talk to you about something.'

'Shit, Anna, what is it? Are you okay? You look awful, no offence. Is it Oli?'

'No, it's not Oli. It's about you.'

'Me?' Her eyebrows shoot up and she leans closer to the screen. 'What's wrong, hon? Seriously, what's the matter?'

'I found your gold hoop earring,' I say dramatically.

'What the fuck? Is that it? Thanks! Bloody hell, you made it sound like you'd just found out I had a week to live or something.'

'I found it in the larder,' I add. She doesn't say anything. 'You told me you didn't go in the larder all night.'

'Shit,' says Jennie, 'I suppose the game is up then?'

226

'The game?' I exclaim. 'It's not a fucking game, Jennie!'

'Okay okay, I know, I never meant for anyone to get hurt, especially not Bruce.'

'How could you imagine for a second Bruce would *not* be hurt?' I splutter.

'I don't know, he just puts on that cocky act, like nothing gets to him, but then it turns out deep down that he's pretty insecure and sensitive. I didn't know, I thought he'd just think it was a bit of fun.'

A bit of fun?! I can't speak, I can't believe she's saying this.

'It's been such a tough couple of years, breaking up the family, wondering if anyone would ever fancy me again. I guess I just wanted a bit of excitement, something to make me feel alive again.'

What the actual fuck, Jennie? I don't know what to say. I feel like I'm looking at a stranger. This cannot be the same person who hid with me in the oak tree in the park to watch Andrew Thompson playing football.

'I don't think you need to be classed as insecure or sensitive to be a bit cut up about your dad dying, Jennie,' I say coldly.

'Yeah obviously, not ideal timing from me as it turns out, but obviously I didn't know it was going to turn out like that. I feel bad about it now, of course I do, but it was only meant to be fun and Bruce was well up for it at the time.'

'Wait, Bruce was *in on it?*'

'What the fuck, Anna? What are you talking about? Of course he was! I didn't drug him or anything!' She's laughing now, but it's her usual Jennie laugh, not an evil genius laugh. I don't understand.

'Hang on,' I say, 'I think I need to take a minute here. Can you start from the beginning?'

So she does, and it's not what I was imagining. She tells me about how unsettled she'd been feeling since Michael moved out, how she's suddenly started looking at herself objectively, realising how much you take for granted when you're married, how little you notice the passing of time. She tells me how old and undesirable she's been feeling without that one person always there to make you feel wanted.

She tells me that after a few drinks at the party she got chatting to Bruce, and how flattering and exciting it felt to be flirting with an attractive man so much younger than her. She says there was something so simple and fun about him that she'd thought why not just go with it, recapture some of that lost youth?

'So we shagged in your larder,' she says. 'Sorry!' She doesn't look sorry at all, she looks positively smug.

'Nooooo! The Coco Pops!' Oli was basically right, there could well be jizz in the cereal after all. 'Jennie, you didn't! With Bruce?'

'Yes with Bruce! He's hot in case you hadn't noticed. Not the sharpest sandwich in the picnic maybe, and a bit awks that now he could be a killer, but it was just a bit of fun, an ego boost if you like. And it worked. Bloody hell, Anna, I felt amazing afterwards, because it means everything's okay!'

'What do you mean everything's okay?'

'I mean it all still works! I haven't forgotten how to have sex or, more importantly, how to have fun! It was liberating and exciting and just what I needed, honestly. We should be celebrating, Anna – I've still got it!'

228

I want to be happy for her but my head is spinning, mostly with all of the new information but also with the thought of Bruce shagging in my larder. It's not a mental image I ever wanted to have.

'You look confused. What's wrong? Isn't this what you were calling me about?'

'Sort of,' I say.

'What do you mean sort of? You said you'd found the earring in the larder, and I know Bruce told you he wasn't in the larder when you knew he was, so I figured you'd put two and two together?'

'I may have made five,' I say, sheepishly.

I watch as the pieces fit together in her brain. 'Wait,' she says, eyes wide, 'did you think I *killed Colin?*'

'No! I mean maybe, but not really, Jennie. That's why I was so confused and upset. I knew you'd lied about being in the larder and I couldn't think why you'd lie to me. I didn't know what to think!'

I look at her pleadingly, I don't want this to be the thing that ruins years of friendship. 'Please forgive me,' I say.

She doesn't say anything, she just looks at me, stony-faced. I'm about to start begging when her expression cracks and she lets out a raucous laugh. 'Forgive you! I'm thrilled! You really thought I might be such a woman of passion that I'd plunge a knife into someone! How thrilling!'

'I don't think it's really a compliment,' I say, not wanting to upset her but not sure she appreciates the gravitas of the situation. 'Plus someone *did* plunge a knife into someone, you know. It is kind of serious.'

She waves away my protestations. 'Oh I know but, Anna, please don't worry. I'm going to take it as a

229

compliment because I am now the sort of woman who has sex in cupboards at Christmas parties just because they want to. But come on, I know how you feel about those knives. Did you honestly think I'd do that to *you*?'

I can't help but smile. I'd thought her jubilant mood today was because she had a mystery to solve, but it turns out there was more to it than that. She has a glow about her that I realise now I've not seen for a long time, and if my Coco Pops had to suffer in the pursuit of her happiness then I guess that's okay with me.

'So that's why Bruce came out of the larder looking so pleased with himself,' I say, 'but why did neither of you say anything if you were both so cool about it?'

Jennie sighs and pulls a face. 'Well,' she says, 'I thought we were both cool about it, but it turns out Bruce thought that it could be the start of something wonderful and as attractive as he is, I'm really not looking to get into a relationship anytime soon. Afterwards he kept trying to be all boyfriendy around me, so I had to nip it in the bud and tell him that wasn't what I was looking for, and he got upset and it was all a bit awkward.'

'Oh God,' I say, 'he didn't cry did he?'

'Yes, he was a bit snivelly, which put me right off him. He's very snotty.'

I shudder at the memory.

'I suggested to him that we should probably keep it to ourselves and try to enjoy it for what it was. I guess I felt guilty initially, and I wasn't sure how you'd react – I was going to tell you, just maybe not in the middle of all of this murder stuff. After Christmas and face to face maybe.'

'I wish you had told me,' I say. 'It would have saved

me a lot of stressing about how on earth my best friend could be a cold-blooded killer. And now we know too why Bruce lied about being in the larder.'

'I'm sorry, Anna, you're right. I should have said something, but then I got panicky too about DNA evidence. We used a condom but . . .'

'STOP! I don't need to think about *fluids*, not in an area with so many foodstuffs. Let's just brush over that bit okay?'

She laughs. 'That's fair. I will spare you the details for now. So how's the sleuthing going?'

'God I don't know,' I say, sighing heavily. 'I'm back to square one now, I guess. At least when I briefly thought it might be you I had a solution. I'm just going round in circles. I've no idea of the motive; I can't seem to put anyone at the scene and that bloody shoe print, I wish I'd never seen it, honestly.'

'Well I might be able to help you with an alibi,' says Jennie, 'not for me, by the way. I wasn't shagging *during* the murder.'

'Who then?'

'Miranda. She texted me just now to tell me about her Instagram live.'

'Why's she texting you? I didn't even know you were friends – I thought you said she was exhausting?'

'She was, but she had just found out her husband is dead, so you'd be a bit highly strung wouldn't you? She's actually quite fun I think, when she's not hysterical with grief and rage. We swapped numbers and we're going to go out for a drink.'

'You're going out for a drink with one of our suspects? Is that even allowed?'

'Well first of all yes, because I'm not the police and she's not technically *my* suspect, plus I already shagged one of them so it would be a bit rich of me to say no to a drink with another based on principles. Also I don't think she did it, but even if she did it would be quite dramatic and fun to have a friend go to trial for murder, wouldn't it? I could go with her and wear daring outfits and shout "I object!" at pivotal moments.'

'I think you'd get thrown out, but okay. What's her alibi?'

'That's the thing: she claims it's an alibi, but I don't know if it counts. She says that after her row with Colin she went and had a bit of a breakdown in your downstairs loo, and once she'd stopped crying she did an Instagram live telling everyone what a scumbag he was.'

'She did an Instagram live from the toilet?'

'She wasn't actually peeing I don't think, just sat on the toilet, lid down.'

'Right, so we can go and watch it and it will give us the time?'

'No, that's the trouble. She says she went straight to the toilet after the row, had some time to calm down and then did the live, but you can't actually see the exact time, so she could have done it later I guess, or earlier. Anyway, I'll send it to you. Have a watch — it's hilarious — and then see what you think. I'm sending you the link now.'

A notification appears at the top of my phone. A WhatsApp from Jennie. 'Got it,' I say. 'I'll go and watch it now and let you know. And, Jennie, I really am sorry for suspecting you.'

'Honestly, darling, please don't apologise. If you can't

accuse your very favourite lifelong best friend of murder occasionally then seriously, who *can* you accuse? Love you lots!' And she's gone.

I sit for a while. Jennie has been in my life for as long as I can remember, but it's been a long time since I stopped to think about what that means and what an important person she is to me. The thought of her being someone I didn't recognise has shaken me. That and the shagging if I'm honest. Not the act of it, I'm not a prude, but in *my* larder? Sure, most things are in tins or packets, but even so, is it even hygienic?

I go into a bit of a spiral, imagining *splatter*, and then have to remind myself that a bit of loose jizz is, sadly, not the worst thing the larder has seen in the last twenty-four hours. I'm going to have to take everything out, aren't I? I'm going to have to bleach the whole lot and start again.

It *could* be a good excuse to get some more Kilner jars though. I'll show Oli all of the TikToks I saved of beautifully organised larders with everything neatly in colour-coordinated clip-lid boxes. *Then* I'll show him the fridge tour videos where you open the door and it's just a tub of grapes, a vase of fresh flowers and a framed picture of a cat. With those for context, the larder tubs will look like the sane option.

I remember that I'm meant to be watching Miranda's Instagram live to figure out if it serves as a reliable alibi, whereas what I really want to do is have a little nap. I tap my phone so that the screen lights up: 6.17 p.m. Today feels like it has been about ten years long at this point. I could just close my eyes, just for five minutes.

I lie back on the pillows, close my eyes, and start a virtual tour of the kitchen storage section of HomeSense, picking out exactly what I'll need if I'm going to create the Larder of Dreams and become the efficient, serene woman I know I can be, deep, deep down.

I imagine fetching myself a wholesome snack from one of my many larder tubs to take down to my artist studio at the bottom of the garden, where I'm working on an abstract nude self-portrait in acrylics. I had a boyfriend briefly when I was a teenager whose mother painted abstract nude self-portraits. Their house was full of them, which was rather disconcerting for fifteen-year-old me, but I've never forgotten them. They were full of colour and life and my boyfriend's mother would waft about in her batik kaftan, waving a hand casually at one as she passed, saying things like: 'That was when I came back from India, darling – I had *such* a strong urge to connect with my inner peace and translate that onto the canvas.'

I find myself on the verge of falling asleep, and I could swear I briefly dream about connecting with my own inner peace when I'm awakened by Lily bursting into the room.

'Mum,' she says, breathless from running up the stairs, such is her excitement, 'you've *got* to come and see the living room. We've made it into an actual magical wonderland and you're going to love it!'

It looks like my inner peace will have to wait.

CHAPTER 21

I follow Lily downstairs, running my sleeve along the edge of the banisters as I go to pick up the dust. I look at the grubby smudge I've left on my jumper and remember that I've not actually showered today. Oli was in the shower while I discovered Colin, and then with the rush to get everyone out to Starbucks and out of the way, and then the tiny issue of trying to figure out who ruined my party by *knifing* a man to death, I've not got around to the small matter of washing. I sniff discreetly at my armpit. Yep, rank.

We go through the same rigmarole of me having to close my eyes and be led, blind, to the living room door, although this time I manage not to walk into anything. When I open my eyes I'm met with what genuinely does seem to be a magical wonderland. There are strings and strings of fairy lights adorning just about every surface you can see and vases filled with so many different shades of green.

The very best bit though is the mantelpiece, which

has been swagged to within an inch of its life with large clumps of holly and mistletoe.

'Where on earth did you get that?' I say, clapping my hands over my mouth, tears welling up in my eyes.

'Steve's garden!' says Ben, his eyes twinkling. 'The car had gone from the drive and so we snuck over in the dark with the secateurs.'

'Dad was very brave,' says Lily, giving him a little pat on the arm.

'The mistletoe was in the tree at number 17,' says Ben, 'but we looked it up and mistletoe is a parasite so technically we were doing the tree a favour.'

'We're basically environmentalists,' adds Oli. 'Do you like it?'

'I love it! It's beautiful. Thank you so much, guys. What an awesome job you've done!' I look around at the three smiling faces and the swathes of badly arranged fairy lights and I feel a flash of contentment. I can't believe I've let myself get so bogged down in Pinterest boards and Instagrammable table decorations this year when all I need is right here.

I check the time: 6.45 p.m. In previous years I've made a big deal out of getting everyone ready for bed nice and early on Christmas Eve, normally so that I can work myself into a frenzy getting everything perfect and making the kids' Christmas stockings into works of art, but in my current state of emotional exhaustion mixed nicely with familial fondness and a large dollop of 'fuck it all, let's just have fun while we're alive', I realise that all of that effort was only ever for ME.

It's an odd feeling. I've convinced myself for so long that I make such a ridiculous effort at Christmas for other people, but it hits me hard that I've been kidding myself all of this time. Perhaps I genuinely thought I was doing it for everyone else, but really, if I'm totally honest with myself, whether or not we have a Christmas table centrepiece or homemade gravy or wrapping paper made from the recycled birth certificates of orphans or whatever nonsense we're made to believe is essential, it doesn't make a bloody bit of difference to anyone.

The whole charade is just that, a game. An act to try and prove to myself that I'm a good enough parent or a good enough daughter-in-law or a good enough PTA member, when I am already all of those things. If Pamela can't see it then more fool her, because my family can see it, and all they want from me at Christmas is to be there and, in Oli's case at least, to chill the fuck out.

I let the realisation sink in and decide to embrace it.

'Right then,' I say loudly, clapping my hands, and for a split second I see the kids' faces fall as they prepare themselves for me to usher them into pyjamas. 'Who wants to play a game and eat the chocolate decorations from the Christmas tree?'

'Me!' squeals Lily.

Ben looks confused. 'I thought we couldn't eat them until after Christmas so that we could all *appreciate and admire the artistic arrangement?*' He says this last bit in a high-pitched, patronising voice, which I assume is meant to be me. Rude.

'Fuck it,' I say, accidentally out loud. Lily's eyes are wide. 'Not fuck it,' I say. 'Shit, not that. Ignore that, everyone. Start again. What I mean is, it's Christmas! Let's have some fun, shall we?'

I don't need to worry about apologising for myself

as everyone has lost interest in me and is swarming around the Christmas tree picking off the best-looking chocolates. Ben might have been taking the piss but they *were* artistically arranged and I have a pang of regret that Pamela won't get to see the effort I went to, to source vintage-style foil-wrapped Father Christmases, just like the ones Oli said he used to have when they were children.

Looking at the mini Santas though, it's hard not to see Colin on the larder floor, so perhaps eating them and getting them out of sight isn't such a bad idea.

'What shall we play?' asks Ben, mouth full of chocolate.

'Monopoly?' I suggest.

Ben groans. 'Boring! How about Twister?' He gives me a wink.

'Can we play Cluedo?' Lily asks.

I flinch and Oli and I exchange a glance that says *too soon?*

'I don't know about Cluedo,' says Oli, trying his best to sound soothing and persuasive, 'how about Dixit? We all love that one.'

Her bottom lip starts to quiver. 'But we all love Cluedo too! We haven't played Cluedo for ages and it's my favourite, and you promised we could play it at Christmas and that I could play all by myself and not have to be on a team with Daddy!'

We did say that. She's only seven years old and logic isn't really her strong point yet. Neither is being able to show someone a single card in your hand without all of the others falling on the table.

Ben joins in, clearly loving the idea of double

Christmas homicide. 'I vote for Cluedo too! Lily, you can sit next to me and I can help you.'

Lily looks delighted with the offer, not realising that Ben's idea of helping is just to look at all of her cards.

I look at Oli and he shrugs. Cluedo it is then. We give in and Lily goes off to fetch it from the games cupboard. I gather the rest of the Christmas tree decorations and take them through to the kitchen where I put them in a bowl and on the kitchen table. Oli takes a bottle of red wine out of the rack and holds it up, eyebrows raised.

'Yes please,' I say, smiling and disrobing a chocolate Santa. I bite off its head as Oli hands me a glass of wine and puts a bowl of peanuts down next to me.

'Can I have another Coke, Mum?' asks Ben.

'Go for it,' I say, and hold my glass up to cheers the can he takes out of the fridge.

Ben senses weakness. 'Can I have vodka in it?'

'Absolutely not,' says Oli.

Ben seems unperturbed. 'Gin?'

'Still no,' says Oli, 'plus gin and Coke sounds grim, mate. You can have one of the little bottles of beer from the fridge if you like?' Oli is clearly picking up on my *fuck it it's Christmas* vibe.

'Can I seriously?'

'Yes seriously, but just one.'

Ben grabs a bottle, opens it and takes a swig, staking his claim before Oli can change his mind. Lily comes back in with Cluedo, sees Ben's beer and gives him a disapproving look.

'Daddy,' she says, in her primmest voice, sounding like an elderly lady in a Miss Marple novel, revealing to the vicar that she has just seen two young people canoodling behind a gravestone, 'Ben is drinking beer and he's only a *child*.'

'I'm fifteen actually,' says Ben, as though that isn't technically still a child, 'and no need to dob me in, Dad said I could.'

Lily transfers her look of disapproval to Oli and calls on me to impose decorum. 'Mummy, Daddy is letting Ben drink beer when alcohol is very dangerous and bad for you.'

Ben snorts. 'I don't think Mum is the one to lecture me on that, Lils.'

I try to look affronted and like I might have some claim on the moral high ground but we all remember the amaretto. I opt for distraction instead and go in with a high-value bribe. 'Would you like a Fruit Shoot?' I ask Lily.

She narrows her eyes, her arms folded across her chest. 'Fine,' she says, although I know that this will be going in the bank for her to bring up at a later date, probably at an especially inopportune moment like a parents' evening or in front of a GP.

Lily has a talent for revealing your most personal secrets casually, in front of the very people you don't want to know about them. Like the time she told Camilla, the then chair of the PTA, how funny it was that she had the same name as the lady from school that *Mummy always says is a pompous twat,* or when she told an entire bus full of people that I had thrush.

Oli gets her a blackcurrant Fruit Shoot and Lily starts to unpack Cluedo. Ben takes the cards and starts organising them. I set out the players onto their starting squares and put the murder weapons into the rooms on the board. I realise I've put the dagger in the kitchen and hastily move it to the ballroom.

'I'm Miss Scarlett,' announces Lily. She knows that Miss Scarlett always gets to go first. 'Mummy, you can be Mrs White because you like cooking.' I baulk at the idea of being seen by Lily as what is essentially a servant, tasked with providing meals for and cleaning up after the family.

'Can't I be Mrs Peacock?' Mrs Peacock is old, but she has a bit of glamour about her at least with her tiara.

Lily looks at me for a moment and considers. 'No,' she says simply.

'I'll be Colonel Mustard,' says Ben.

Lily looks at Oli. 'You are Reverend Green, Daddy, because he doesn't have much hair either.'

'And because of my dedication to the church of course,' says Oli, taking a large swig of wine. I raise my eyebrows. 'Blood of Christ,' he says, waving his glass and taking a handful of peanuts.

'Oh yes, of course,' I say, matching his swig. 'Cheers to the baby Jesus on his nearly birthday.'

Ben has sorted out the cards by this point and is dealing everybody out their hand. Lily disappears from the table and returns with *Why Mummy Drinks at Christmas* and *Why Sex Doesn't Matter* – it doesn't take a genius to figure out whose shelf she picked those from.

'What are you doing?' I ask as she opens *Why Sex Doesn't Matter* at what I hope is a relatively inoffensive page.

She stands it up on the table and then opens *Why Mummy Drinks* and stands that up next to it. 'I'm making a shield,' she explains, 'so that I can lay out my cards and nobody can see them.'

She reaches for the dice, nudging her shield in the process. *Why Sex Doesn't Matter* falls over, revealing the library and the lead piping. She stands it back up and we all pretend not to have noticed but cross them both off on our sheets. She throws the dice.

'Six! I get to throw again!'

'You do,' I say, 'but do you want to move your six squares first?'

'Oh yes.' She counts out six and moves seven squares. Oli moves her back one while she throws again. She gets a five and moves triumphantly into the dining room.

'I'm in the dining room,' she says. We all wait. She looks at us expectantly.

'You have to have a suspect and a murder weapon.' Ben sighs.

'Okay,' says Lily, looking at her cards. 'I'll have the rope and Mrs White.'

'Remember to not just pick all the things you have already,' I say. She looks at her cards again.

'I want to change my mind,' she says, and I put a question mark on my sheet next to the dining room, the rope and Mrs White. 'I'll have the dagger and Colonel Mustard. Ha! Now you have to go to the dining room, Ben!'

She likes the idea of Ben having to do what she tells him and doesn't register the fact that it means that Ben gets to move off his starting point right away.

'You all have to show me your cards now,' she says.

'We don't have to show you our cards,' says Ben. 'We just go round until someone shows you one card, starting with me, and I don't have any.'

I show her Colonel Mustard and she writes something down behind her screen. It's Ben's turn. He stays in the dining room with Professor Plum and the dagger. Neither I nor Oli have anything to show him but Lily shows him the dining room. We all know this because *Why Mummy Drinks at Christmas* falls over while she does it and she puts the dining room down face up while she stands it back up again.

Ben groans and looks at Oli and me appealingly, but I just shrug. He takes a sip of his beer and Oli tops up our wine glasses.

We go around the table a few more times. By this point we all know all of Lily's cards and I'm pretty sure it's Miss Scarlett in either the kitchen or the study, but I don't know the weapon. I've just finished my second glass of wine though and it has been a long day, so I don't think I'm at the top of my sleuthing game.

I was sceptical about playing Cluedo just hours after stumbling upon a real-life murder, but there's something very comforting about it, working through each suspect in turn, using logic and a process of elimination to come to the indisputable truth. There are no grey areas in Cluedo, no maybes, no stupid shoe prints that refuse to fit in with any theories.

I wish we could apply the same logical thinking to Colin's murder. It feels like it should be so simple as we already know it was the Sabatier in the larder. All we need is the *who* part. In my mind I assign each of our suspects a Cluedo character.

Miranda would definitely be Mrs Peacock – I could picture her wearing a tiara to Tesco for sure. She has the right glamorous vibes, even if she is bonkers. Bruce I'll have to put as Colonel Mustard as there's no way he could be a professor. Colonels are always a bit buffoon-like in the stories.

That leaves Rev Green for Sav, which leaves a bit to be desired ethnically, but Sav *is* a teacher, and you could say that a vicar is teaching the word of God. Who do we have left then? Mrs White and Miss Scarlett. I guess Mrs White could be Jennie, as apparently mums are essentially just housekeepers, even though I'm ninety-nine per cent sure she's off the hook, and I'll give Miss Scarlett to Georgie, just to make up the numbers.

It's Ben's turn and he's been twitchy for the last round, so I suspect he is ready to make a guess. I suspect right. He picks up the envelope ready to check his guess just as Oli's phone starts ringing.

'It's my mum,' he says, looking at the screen, 'I'd better get it.'

I vaguely hear Ben and Lily bickering about the game – Ben saying he was right but Lily saying that she should be the winner too because actually she did know the answer; she just hadn't guessed it. I'm not listening properly though, as I'm watching Oli. He's not speaking – not an uncommon phenomenon while on the phone to his mother – but his brow is furrowed and he's biting his bottom lip.

'Okay,' he says, 'if you're sure. That makes sense I guess.' Another pause. 'No of course, and it's no problem.

You don't need to bring anything extra; we've honestly got everything covered.'

I raise my eyebrows questioningly but he half raises a hand at me and turns away.

'No honestly, Mum, it's fine. Yep. No, please don't stop, we have enough potatoes. Yes, and the low-alcohol beer Dad likes. Anna remembered everything.' Another pause. 'Yes, even chestnuts. She's very well organised, Mum.' I think I hear a loud and derisive cackle from the other end of the phone but that could be my subconscious. 'Okay,' Oli says, 'see you soon,' and he hangs up.

He sighs and looks at me with trepidation and sympathy.

'What is it?' I say. 'What's wrong?'

'I don't want you to freak out,' he says.

'Of course I won't freak out!' I say, freaking out.

'They're on their way.'

'What do you mean on their way? I know your dad likes to leave plenty of time for traffic but they're not due until tomorrow, so that seems overcautious even by his standards.'

'They're on their way now,' Oli says. 'Mum said the forecast was looking iffy for tomorrow and that Deirdre next door had left early to stay with her daughter in Bourton-on-the-Water, so they thought they had better do the same.'

'But we're nowhere near Bourton-on-the-Water,' I say. 'That's in the Cotswolds, isn't it?'

'The forecast says light rain tomorrow for Shropshire,' says Ben, looking up from his phone. 'That's where Grandma and Grandpa are, isn't it?'

'I don't understand,' I say. 'When are they getting here? Not tonight?'

'Mum says she just checked the sat nav and according to that they'll be here in thirty-two minutes.'

CHAPTER 22

I can't do anything for a few seconds other than stare at Oli, open-mouthed.

'They left three hours ago, Mum says, so yeah, they'll be here in about half an hour.' He grimaces apologetically.

'Half a fucking hour?!' I shout, oblivious to Lily's tuts. 'What the hell?'

'I think Mum worries about Dad driving in bad weather since the cataract operation,' says Oli.

'Sure, I get that,' I say; I'm not a fucking monster, 'but *light rain*, Oli? LIGHT RAIN?! And surely the dark is worse?'

'I don't know what to say, Anna – maybe they were excited to see us?'

'PAH!' I spit. 'Hardly.' I look at Ben and Lily. 'Not you guys obviously. I'm sure they are very excited to see you. Why don't you go and get changed into your pyjamas and do your teeth?' They both look disappointed that the unchill version of Mum has reappeared so quickly, but I will not have Pamela arriving at 8 p.m.

and making comments about how late it is for them to be up.

They reluctantly head upstairs and I turn back to Oli. 'You know what this is,' I say. 'It's a test?'

'A test?'

'Yes, a Christmas test. Your mother is trying to catch me out.'

'Honestly, Anna, I really don't think it's that.'

'Don't you?' I hiss, eyes darting. 'Then why the hell did they not call and let us know that they were planning to come this evening instead? When they were worried about the weather – *allegedly* – why didn't they call then, and talk about it, or at least let us know they were leaving? Isn't that what any sensible person would do?'

'Well, I guess it would have made a bit more sense to let us know.'

'A *bit more sense?* Damn right it would have made a bit more fucking sense, but then it wouldn't have been a test. No, I see what's going on here, your mother wants to catch me out. She wants to get here unexpectedly, with as little notice as possible, in the hope of finding me lounging around and unprepared.'

Oli takes a deep breath. 'Anna,' he says, 'even if that's what she's doing, which I highly doubt, does it really matter? Because we *are* prepared, and she'll see that and it will all be fine.'

'But I'm NOT prepared!' I cry. 'I'm not even WASHED!' I raise one arm and advance my armpit towards him. 'See? Smell this!'

Oli backs away, horrified. I can feel tears beginning to well up and I do everything I can to push them back down again. The last thing I want when Pamela turns up is to look blotchy.

'And what about the larder?' I add. 'I haven't even thought about what we're going to say to them about all of that! Your mum is going to go nuts when we tell her. I expect she'll refuse to stay here. We should have made a plan!'

The tears have started now. All of the stress of the day and the two large glasses of red wine have provided the perfect foundation for this final brick of stress. Oli comes towards me and hugs me.

'It's going to be fine,' he says. 'Whatever my mother says or does, does not need to define our Christmas. We can still have a perfectly nice time; we just have to let it go over our heads. And as for Colin, maybe we just don't say anything?'

I ease myself partially out of the cuddle and look up at him. 'Just not tell them?'

'Just not tell them.'

'But won't they find out?'

'How?' Oli asks. 'We'll keep them here for a few days, in a Christmas bubble. If they do happen to see something on the local news then no one is going to be giving away the exact location of the murder, are they? So we just don't tell them. And if they find out at a later date, well, we cross that bridge when we come to it.'

I think about it. It does make sense. So long as the police don't come round wanting to examine the crime scene or anything. But would they really do that on Christmas Day or Boxing Day when they were so keen to get out of here today? It feels unlikely.

'If you really think we can get away with it?' I say.

'I do,' says Oli. 'Now,' he says, sniffing, 'you are a teeny bit stinky, so how about if you go shower quickly and I'll have a whizz round and tidy up down here and make sure everything is good for the spare room. Mum says she and Dad stopped and got sandwiches in the M&S at the services, so they don't need dinner or anything, so nice and simple, we get them here, a drink and some snacks and we can stick the TV on for a bit or play another game.'

'Okay,' I say, feeling slightly less hysterical. 'I'll put the Cluedo away, get showered and try to recapture my laissez faire Christmas spirit.' I collect up the cards, gather up the pieces and put them in the box with the board and put the lid on. As I tuck it under my arm to put away in the cupboard, I realise that I didn't check and see what the solution was. Bloody typical. Looks like that investigation went the same way as our live one.

Oli hands me a third glass of wine. 'Take this with you,' he says, giving me a reassuring smile. 'It will help with the Christmas spirit.'

Ten minutes later I'm getting out of the shower to the noise of my phone ringing. I wrap a towel around me and trot into the bedroom to answer it. It's Jennie.

'Hey, Jen,' I say, sitting on the bed and taking a sip of wine. It tastes weird after just cleaning my teeth so I take another sip to take the taste away.

'Word up, Holmes! How goes it?'

'Awful,' I say. 'Pamela is going to be here in twenty minutes.' I take a third sip for medicinal calming reasons.

'I thought they weren't coming until tomorrow?'

'So did I until they called ten minutes ago to say they'd decided to come early because of the weather and Deirdre, and would be here in half an hour.'

'Half an hour?! Why didn't they call sooner? And who the hell is Deirdre?'

'Deirdre is their neighbour, who has left early to get to her daughter in Bourton-on-the-Water.'

'Bourton-on-the-Where? I didn't even know we were expecting bad weather.'

'We're not,' I say. 'Anyway, I had to shower because I stank and now I'm just getting dressed and trying to regain my chill.'

'Blimey,' says Jennie, 'so what's the deal with the mystery solving? Will you be getting a second opinion from Pamela and Martin, giving them a tour of the crime scene and all that?'

'Absolutely not, my plan is to not tell them anything about it. Can you imagine if Pamela knew her precious chestnuts had witnessed a murder? No, we're going to keep it to ourselves, which might mean the detecting has to go on hold.' I realise as I say this that I'm disappointed. Perhaps I was actually enjoying it a little more than I'd thought.

'Noooo! You can't put it on hold! I've just got the printer working and the murder board is looking ace. Plus, you might be interested to hear about a call I just had from Miranda.'

I take Jennie briefly away from my ear to check the time. I have about fifteen minutes until Oli's parents arrive. I weigh up my options.

'I do want to know,' I say, 'I'm just putting you on

speaker so I can get dressed and put some make-up on at the same time.'

'Saucy, I like your style. Do you want to switch to video?'

'Absolutely not,' I say, giving myself a quick towel-dry and rummaging in my underwear drawer for a clean bra.

'Spoilsport,' she says. 'I'm sitting here all alone at Christmas and you won't even give me a flash of your boobs.'

'It's really a gift *not* to see me naked these days. Honestly, Jen, I avoid mirrors as much as possible.'

'Nonsense! You are a gorgeous creature, Anna, a thing of beauty, a sexual being to be adored! Just because Instagram keeps showing you those ads for neck cream and face yoga – you need to stop watching them and it will lose interest.'

'All right, just because you shagged a thirty-something-year-old in my larder. It's different for me – I don't have your confidence.'

'It's all in the mind,' she says, 'you just have to manifest it. Say it out loud enough and it becomes true. I think that's how it works. It's not really about Bruce anyway. It was an ego boost for sure but I truly think that as long as you're naked, men literally can't see anything else. All you have to do is take off your bra and they are blind to age or weight or anything else that women are taught to obsess about.'

'Even if when you take off your bra, your boobs drop a good six inches?' I ask, hoisting mine into my clean bra, leaning forward and shaking them into place.

'Even then, Anna, they just don't notice it. They just see a *naked woman* and a switch flips.'

I pull my jeans back on. 'What was it you wanted to tell me about Miranda anyway?' I ask.

'Ooooh it's great gossip,' she says, 'and could make all the difference to our motive situation. She called me about half an hour ago, having had, I would guess, one or two small gins, and started going on about how much she'd enjoyed talking to me earlier, how refreshing it was to really feel listened to and all that. I am a very good listener; she's right about that.'

I try to interrupt to tell Jennie to hurry up as the in-laws will be here soon but she doesn't seem to notice and ploughs on with her story.

'She told me that she'd been going through all of Colin's correspondence – his filing cabinet and his emails. She said it started off as bitterness, trying to discover who he might have been having an affair with most recently, so she could get in touch with them, but she hadn't found anything interesting. There were the emails between him and the estranged child, but nothing that useful there, just a bit about how they'd moved to the area about eighteen months ago from Yorkshire, realised he was local and decided to reach out, nothing to give away who they were.'

I pull on an olive green roll-neck T-shirt – the nice one from Boden that covers up the worst of my neck – and brush my wet hair. I don't want to put the hairdryer on while Jennie is on the phone so I towel it as dry as I can while she carries on.

'The interesting bit though is when she started looking into his work stuff. We've been working on the assumption that Bruce's motive was money and the business right?'

'Right,' I say, moving on to foundation and then mascara.

'But there is none! Miranda says the business has been haemorrhaging money for years, that he's remortgaged the house without her knowing, and that he's on the verge of bankruptcy! She reckons he's been keeping it going as long as possible out of pure vanity because he loved the idea of being the "respected local businessman" and didn't want to lose his spot at the golf club.'

I freeze with the mascara wand in mid-air, eyes wide, my mouth in the classic 'O' shape for when you're putting on eye make-up.

'Isn't that exciting?' says Jennie. 'It puts a whole new perspective on things, doesn't it?'

I put the mascara wand back in the tube and screw it in place. 'Potentially,' I say, 'but it has other consequences too, doesn't it?'

'What do you mean?'

'As in my job?'

There's a silence.

'Oh fuck, Anna, shit, I'm so sorry. I got so caught up in the whole murder motive thing I didn't think about that. Fuck.'

'If Colin really was on the verge of bankruptcy, that means I'm going to lose my job. And probably without a pay-off if there's no money left.'

'God, I'm so sorry, Anna, I just didn't think. I'm going on about Bruce and you're the one who's going to be up shit creek.'

'It's not your fault. It's okay, it's just a bit of a shock, but to be totally honest it's probably a good time to find out because I don't think my brain has the space to take it in right now. It will just have to percolate while I deal with Oli's parents.'

I try to think about the concept of losing my job, what that will mean for us as a family, but I'm right about my brain: it just can't compute. It appears to be playing 'Last Christmas' to itself and humming along.

'I'm not sure about the Bruce angle though,' I continue. 'If Miranda is only just finding out now about it all, including the fact of having her house remortgaged from underneath her, doesn't that imply that he's been keeping it to himself? I've never had the impression from Bruce that he thinks the business is in trouble.'

'That's true, I hadn't thought of that. Could Bruce have worked it out for himself, do you think? Would his role have given him more of an insight than Miranda would have got?'

'I honestly don't think so. His job, if you can call it that, definitely wasn't on the financial strategy side of things and you know him now, Jennie, does he strike you as the sort of man who'd have an insight into anything much at all?'

'Not really,' Jennie admits. 'I picture him more in a blue-sky-thinking type of job – the sort where you don't actually know much about anything but you like wearing a nice suit.'

'Exactly that,' I agree, 'which brings us back to where we started. If Bruce was as in the dark as his mum about the state of the business finances, then his motive still stands, even if he is going to find himself sorely disappointed.'

I check the time and feel a wave of panic. 'I need to go, sorry, Jen. They're going to be here any minute and I still need to dry my hair.'

'Of course, crack on and make yourself look beautiful. I'll have a think over things. I'd offer to get in touch with Bruce, see if I can find anything out from his side, but I don't want to give him the wrong impression.'

'Yes don't do that. He's a bit of an idiot but I don't want you to break his heart or anything. Just keep me posted if you have any brainwaves.'

'Will do,' says Jennie, 'and good luck with Pamela. Just remember you are fabulous and Oli is very lucky to have you!'

I smile ruefully and she hangs up. I immediately switch on the hairdryer on the top heat setting and blast my hair until it's bone-dry. I don't want Pamela to think I'm only just showering at nearly bedtime. I brush my hair through, check my make-up, grab my wine and phone and head downstairs, taking some deep breaths as I go. I get a flashback to this morning, stopping on the stairs for deep breaths to try and quash the hangover, Colin still lying happily undiscovered downstairs. It feels like an awfully long time ago.

Downstairs everything is the picture of suburban Christmas Eve bliss. Oli has put on some Christmas music, which explains 'Last Christmas' and makes me feel marginally less deranged, and he's sitting in an armchair, glass of red wine in hand. He smiles at me as I come in, and I get a little butterfly moment. Even after all these years I still quite fancy him. Ben and Lily are both in their Christmas pyjamas, watching TV and drinking hot chocolate.

'You look lovely and clean,' he says, always the romantic.

'Thanks,' I say, doing a twirl, 'I brushed my hair and everything.'

'The kitchen is spotless,' he says, 'and I double-checked all the toilets in case anyone had been in since we cleaned them.' He gives a sideways look at Ben, who is paying him no attention.

My tummy butterflies give a happy flutter. Someone should really make it much clearer to men that hearing things like 'I've cleaned the toilets' is much more attractive than a six-pack or a full head of hair. Ask any woman, especially a mother, about their preferred style of foreplay and I bet plenty of them would say 'having my partner wash up without being asked'.

I'm about to go and sit down in the second armchair when we're interrupted by the noise of the Ring doorbell. I open the notification on my phone even though I know only too well who it is. The video footage shows Pamela in an unflattering fish-eye view. She appears to be running her finger along the top of the doorbell and then checking her finger for dust.

Oli gets up. 'I'd better let them in, I suppose.'

'Must you? Couldn't you pretend we're out?'

'I'm afraid not, darling,' he says, kissing me on the cheek on the way past. I put my wine down on the coffee table, careful to use a coaster, and follow him into the hallway.

CHAPTER 23

'Darling!' says Pamela, pulling Oli into an embrace as soon as he opens the door. 'So wonderful to see you!' She releases him from his hug, but holds him at arm's length by the shoulders. 'You look thin. Has Anna been feeding you properly?'

'Lovely to see you too, Mum, and I'm really not thin, and also I'm a grown man and it's not Anna's job to feed me. Why don't you come in and sit down?'

She moves past him and into the hallway. 'Hello, Pamela,' I say, doing my very best to sound enthusiastic, 'we're so pleased to see you. What a lovely surprise to have you here for Christmas Eve!'

She gives me a lukewarm smile and hugs me, sniffing as she does. 'Your hair smells lovely and clean,' she says quietly in my ear. 'You didn't need to shower especially for us.'

I laugh as though at a fond joke between friends and not a passive-aggressive dig. She laughs too, dismissing me with a sly smile as she wafts past me into the living room, leaving me with Martin.

Martin I have no problem with. If anything there is a sense of camaraderie between me and Martin, an understanding of what it is to endure the sort of woman who actually put 'no riff-raff' at the bottom of the sign for entry to the church summer fete and had to be discreetly moved by the vicar from her position at the gate to serving teas inside.

Martin is of course carrying all of the bags and so we settle for a kiss on the cheek. 'Hello, Anna love,' he says warmly, 'sorry for the early arrival. I tried to talk her down but once Deirdre decided she was leaving early to get to Elizabeth in Bourton it was a fait accompli, I'm afraid. They've been trying to outdo each other since the nonsense at the flower show.'

Oli takes a small suitcase from him and I relieve him of a second overnight bag and a bag of potatoes.

'I told her she should have stuck to "fruit pie with shortcrust pastry" and let Deirdre have "glass jar of pickled produce" but you know what she's like.' He rolls his eyes but he's smiling and there is a genuine fondness there, which I'm sure must make Pamela a lot easier to bear.

'It's no problem at all, Dad,' says Oli. 'It's always a pleasure to see you both and we're all set here, just having a regular relaxed Christmas Eve, spot of *Chicken Run*, that sort of thing. It's no bother at all. Come in and have a drink.'

'Thanks, son,' says Martin, 'but there are a few more bags in the car, presents and whatnot.'

'I'll get those, Martin,' I say, 'if you give me your keys. I'll just put these potatoes in the kitchen with all of the other potatoes that we already have and then I'll pop out and get everything in for you.'

'You're a gem, Anna, thank you, love,' he says, handing over the keys and following Oli into the living room.

I go into the kitchen, scowling at the bag of potatoes. It's the gestures like this that infuriate me because you can't say anything. You can't get mad with somebody for bringing you a bag of potatoes, can you? Pamela would just say she was trying to be helpful, 'Oh it was just in case, Anna. I know how overwhelming Christmas can be with a family!' and then I'm the petty bitch if I make a fuss. At least I have the smug pleasure of already having peeled my potatoes and put them in water. There will be no getting away from the fact that I clearly *already had potatoes.*

Not that that will stop her from saying something ridiculous. I can picture her now. 'What a good job I brought potatoes, Anna, as it looks like you've used yours all up!' I could escort her into the larder and show her the huge box of potatoes I have in reserve, but she'd be sure to notice the smell of toothpaste. I have learnt over the years to just smile and nod. Smile and nod and inside you're allowed to picture accidentally pushing her down the stairs.

I decant the potatoes into the box in the larder, muddling them all together to make a point. I don't know *what* point, but it makes me feel better. Straightening up I catch a glimpse of the remaining Sabatier knives in their wooden block. We'd kept them on the higher shelf in the larder ever since Lily was smaller and got hold of one of them from the kitchen counter. Just four of them now, looking silly without their fifth member. Like Take That without Robbie. Everyone knew they couldn't survive that.

While I'm hiding in the larder, I have a quick look at the John Lewis website. I bet you can get replacements. There must be professional chefs who need replacements because they get mad deboning a salmon and fling their knives at the wall in a fury. I'm sure that's the sort of thing that happens. I've never deboned a salmon, but it sounds maddening.

The knife that's missing is the carving knife, which is fitting as it's the most brutal-looking of the set. You can buy it on its own, but it's £85, which is probably why Oli denied all knowledge of it; £85 is way too much to spend on a single knife, especially if I'm about to be out of a job.

I'm disconcerted by one of the reviews that describes it as 'simply sliding through the meat'. Poor old Colin. Apparently this reviewer has arthritis in her hands and the knife has given her back her joy of cooking, so effortless is it to use. It makes me think for a moment about Margaret. We discounted her early on based on assumptions we'd made about her age and physical strength, but if the knife really is that easy to use and slides through 'difficult to carve joints' then perhaps we were too hasty?

I often wonder who the people are that have both the time and the inclination to leave reviews like this. I loved that knife, but there is no way I'd ever have deliberately gone onto the John Lewis website, created an account and left a review calling it 'delightfully sharp'.

The larder door opens and I'm interrupted by Oli.

'Hello,' he says, 'is it that bad already?'

'Potatoes,' I say, holding up the empty bag and shoving my phone back in my pocket.

'Right,' he says, 'potatoes. I've come in for crisps. I'm doing drinks and snacks. Do you want anything?'

'I'm okay, I'm going to go and get the stuff out of your dad's car. Then I'll come and do my best daughter-in-law Christmas chat.' I pass him a large bag of the fanciest crisps and we close the door behind us.

I've got my head in the boot of Martin's car, gathering up the gift bags, when I hear a rustle and Margaret appears next to me. I jump, banging my head.

'Crikey, Margaret, where did you spring from?' I suspect she rustled her way through the hedge.

'Next door, Anna. Are you okay?'

'I'm fine, Margaret, it's just been a long day.'

'Well I know, dear – that's why I came to see you. I saw the car pull up and I wondered if the police were back and if there was anything I could do to help.'

'What would you be able to do?'

'Oh you know, teas maybe.'

'That's very kind of you, Margaret, but it's just Oli's parents come for Christmas, not the police.'

She looks disappointed.

'Talking of police though,' I add, with not a small amount of perverse pleasure, 'did you get on okay at the Co-op earlier? They haven't charged you for shoplifting, have they?'

'Certainly not!' Margaret visibly ruffles at the accusation. 'It was a simple misunderstanding. We sat down in the office over a cup of tea and once they appreciated my connections with the local Neighbourhood Watch and how active I am on South Medling Matters they were extremely apologetic and even opened a packet of custard creams.'

'That's great,' I say, shutting the boot and locking the car. 'I'm going to head back in now with these bags but I'm glad to hear we're not going to have to look after your garden while you're in prison.'

She narrows her eyes at me. 'It was actually because of you, Anna, that I was stopped. I was trying to tell you something that I thought might be of significance and you dashed off, forcing me to give chase!'

'What was it you were trying to tell me?' I ask, looking unsubtly towards the front door.

'Perhaps I won't tell you as you're clearly not interested,' says Margaret, rather petulantly.

'I do really want to know, Margaret. It's just that Oli's parents have just arrived and I've got all these bags in my hands, you see.' I lift the bags up to make my point. 'Plus it's pretty chilly out here and I've not got my coat on.'

'That's exactly my point!' Margaret exclaims.

'What is?'

'That you're not wearing a coat!'

'I'm sorry, Margaret, is that what you wanted to tell me? That I'm not wearing a coat? Because I do know that already.'

'Don't be ridiculous, Anna, why on earth would I come out here in the dark just to tell you you're not wearing a coat? It's no wonder you didn't make it onto the Neighbourhood Watch steering committee.'

'It's not that I didn't *make* it. Oh never mind, I'm confused then, Margaret – is it about the coat or isn't it?'

'It is and it isn't!' She folds her arms across her chest and smiles triumphantly, giving me an excellent opportunity to practise my 'smile and nod and imagine pushing them down the stairs' technique.

'It's not your coat I'm thinking about per se, Anna, although you would be wise to think more carefully about your outerwear in the middle of December, but I'm glad you agree that it's not the most auspicious choice to be loitering in your driveway in the dark without one. It's all very clear, don't you think?'

It is not clear at all. I wonder for a moment if Margaret has had a stroke.

'Look, I really do need to get back inside,' I say. 'Everyone will be wondering where I am.' This is only partly true. I do want to go inside but I doubt anyone has even noticed I'm not there. Pamela probably just thinks I'm in the kitchen, where I belong, if she has thought of me at all.

'So you agree that it's very odd behaviour? Good, I'm glad!' She turns to leave, muttering to herself now. 'And such a young slip of a thing too. You should just go back inside if you're that cold.'

'Yes, thank you, Margaret,' I call after her. 'Very useful information. I will go back inside. Happy Christmas!'

Jesus, that woman, she gets worse and worse. She did call me a young slip of a thing though, so I don't feel like we can discount everything she says *too* quickly. What that was all about though, I have no idea, and no time to think about it because Ben appears at the front door.

'Grandma sent me to check on you,' he says. 'She said you'd been a long time and perhaps you were struggling with the key fob.'

'That was kind of her,' I reply. Fucking witch. I know how to work a key fob, thank you, Pamela. I take a deep breath and remind myself that I am a calm and competent woman, a calm and competent woman. In through your nose, out through your mouth. Calm and competent.

'Watch out, Mum!' shouts Ben as I trip up the front doorstep. He steadies me and takes some of the bags from me.

'Sorry, darling,' I say, 'it's a bit dark out here.'

We make it into the hallway and I close the door behind me. I kick off my shoes and carry the presents through into the living room where Lily falls on them with squeals of excitement.

'Can I get the presents out and put them under the tree?' she asks, eyes sparkling.

'Of course you can, Lily darling,' says Pamela. 'All the ones in the penguin paper are for you and the blue paper is for Ben. Daddy has two presents in that shiny paper there and that big one is for Mummy.'

My heart sinks. What on earth has she got me this time? Every year I go out of my way to find something tasteful and expensive and every year she returns the favour by choosing me a gift that is simultaneously generous, thoughtful and hugely insulting.

One year when Ben was a baby she got me an incredibly expensive electric toning belt, managing to imply that not only was I fat, but also too lazy to do anything about it. Last year she got me a voucher for a cookery class. Now you might think that's a perfectly lovely gift, and maybe it would have been if the course wasn't called 'Basic Cooking Skills'. It promised to teach things like 'how to work safely and hygienically in the

265

kitchen', 'how to dress correctly for the kitchen' and 'safe knife use' which, ironically, was the opposite of what I was thinking when I thanked her for it.

'That's very generous of you, Pamela,' I say, watching as Lily puts my large gift under the tree. 'You really shouldn't have!'

'Oh I really think I should have,' she chuckles. 'I've seen Oli's shirts remember!'

Oli's shirts? I look at the box. Has she bought me an IRON? For fuck's sake. I want to point out that Oli irons his own shirts, what with him being a grown man with working hands, but I can imagine how shocking that would be to Pamela – poor Oli, being forced by his degenerate wife to do his own ironing.

Oli must see the metaphorical steam coming from my ears (not the iron) as he jumps up and starts fussing around everyone, offering drinks and passing around the crisps. His mother looks circumspectly into one of the bowls.

'They're Tyrrells!' I say shrilly. 'I know what a crisp connoisseur you are, Pamela – only the best for you!'

'I can see that, Anna. You're right, I do have an eye for a superior snack. You can just tell from the crunch and the distribution of seasoning. You don't organise as many WI luncheons as I have without realising the importance of attention to detail.'

'Oh absolutely,' I agree, enjoying a very happy moment with the knowledge that they're actually Aldi own brand.

'I was wondering though, Anna, if I might trouble you for a marzipan fruit?'

I'm not sure what to say. Is this is a test?

'A marzipan fruit?' I repeat.

'Yes,' she says, raising her eyebrows and tilting her head slightly to one side. 'Only if you have any.'

This is definitely a test, but I don't understand the rules.

'I didn't think you were especially fond of marzipan fruits, Pamela?' I ask. 'I thought you felt they were a little common?'

'Oh I've always loved marzipan fruits, dear, so delightfully quaint. I said as much to Lady Eleanor when she was kind enough to host the Ladies' Embroidery Circle for their Easter afternoon tea. Every table had some as part of their tea. It was really delightful. Three tiers and not a crust in sight.'

Okay, now it makes sense. When I offer marzipan fruits it's akin to me fishing the cat food scraps out of the bin and serving them to her on a bed of Findus Crispy Pancakes, but when Lady sodding Eleanor does it then it's the ultimate in sophistication.

'I didn't actually get any this year,' I say. 'I didn't think you liked them.'

'Oh what a shame, Anna! You must have misremembered. What a pity. I do appreciate, though, that at your age it can be hard to keep your memory quite as sharp. I have my daily Wordle of course, and the lovely Richard Osman and his fabulous teatime trivia. Have you thought about adding a puzzle to your morning routine?'

Funnily enough no, I hadn't thought of adding a fucking puzzle to my morning routine, my morning routine being currently fairly saturated with about forty-seven other jobs that I don't want to do either. Perhaps she imagines I just sit quietly on my balcony (I don't have a balcony), sipping hot water and lemon juice, chanting positive mantras and aligning my chakras for the day.

'I can offer you a Bendicks?' I say.

She wrinkles up her nose. 'I don't approve of chocolates you have to unwrap. You're not presenting me with the bill at an Indian restaurant.'

'How about some After Eights, Mum?' Oli offers. 'They're in those little envelopes, but it's not really unwrapping.'

'I'll stick to the Tyrrells,' she says. I smile.

Lily chimes in. 'I'll have some After Eights!'

'I think it's bedtime for you, Lils,' says Oli, 'now you've got all those presents so nicely organised under the tree.'

Lily flops herself down on the floor in protest. 'I don't want to go to bed though! It's not fair. Everyone else is staying up and eating After Eights!'

'Nobody is eating After Eights,' I reassure her. 'We'll save them for tomorrow so that you don't miss out. But Daddy's right, it's time to go to bed now.'

'But I'm not tired,' she says, yawning.

'Let's go and get a mince pie and glass of milk for Father Christmas,' says Oli, 'and then maybe Mummy will take you upstairs and read you a story.' I'm about to bristle at this, but I catch his eye and he gives the faintest of nods to his mother and I realise he's giving me an escape route.

'Absolutely,' I say quickly, 'perhaps even two if you're a good girl. You go with Daddy and I'll go and get your bed all cosy.'

Oli and Lily head off into the kitchen and I make my excuses and go upstairs. In Lily's room I realise the bowls of crisps and wasabi peas are still in a neat line under her duvet, so I gather them up, brush out as many of the crumbs as possible and give the duvet a good shake. I'm straightening her pillow as she comes into the room.

'Don't look under there, Mummy!'

'Under your pillow?' I ask, immediately lifting it up to look underneath. She claps her hand over her mouth. Under her pillows is a box of Bendicks mints. I open the box. It's only half full.

'What on earth are you doing with these?' I'm a little cross if I'm honest. Scavenging for leftover crisps is one thing, but it isn't like Lily to pinch an entire box of chocolates.

'It's a secret,' she whispers.

I look at her sternly. 'You know that you don't have secrets from Mummy.'

'But Uncle Toby and Uncle Sav said it was a secret!'

'What do you mean? What's going on here exactly?'

'We were having a midnight feast,' she confesses. 'But it was meant to be a secret. Uncle Toby brought the chocolates and Uncle Sav got us lemonade and then we sneaked up here and ate them in bed.'

That makes more sense. I expect it was their way of getting Lily up to bed during the party. Perhaps I hadn't been quite as on the ball last night with the whole parenting thing as I could have been.

'Well that *does* sound exciting! You stayed awake all the way until midnight!' This part is doubtful. I remember when Ben was younger and would have sleepovers. I'd make a big deal of organising a midnight feast, usually at around 7.30 p.m.

'I actually did,' she said. 'Uncle Sav showed me the time on his phone and we all ate a chocolate when all the numbers said zero, so it was actually top secret. You honestly can't tell anyone, Mummy.'

'I won't tell anybody,' I say. 'It can still be a secret. Now, into bed and let's read a story.'

She chooses a book from the shelves and we both get into bed and under the covers. I'm disappointed to see it's one of the fairy books again, the dreadful ones where they are seeing how far they can push the boundaries of fairy naming – Valerie the Vegan Fairy, Tilly the Tonsillitis Fairy, that sort of thing.

I'm halfway through the story when I stop. Lily gives me a nudge but I don't notice because my brain has finally processed the last ten minutes and presented me with its findings. A midnight feast.

If Lily was up here eating Bendicks mints with Sav and Toby at exactly midnight and, we can safely assume, a good few minutes either side, then neither Toby nor Sav could have been downstairs murdering Colin. Lily was specific about all of the numbers on Sav's phone showing zero – making it exactly midnight. Unless it's an elaborate fake alibi that's so subtle it rested on me finding a box of Bendicks under Lily's pillow and questioning her about it, then my brother and his partner couldn't have done it.

CHAPTER 24

It only takes a few more pages after I restart the story for Lily to be fast asleep, but I don't get out of bed. Instead I carefully get my phone out of my pocket and text Jennie.

'I have an update for the murder board.'

I wait for her status to flash up as online and see her typing.

'Oooh what?!' she replies, with three magnifying-glass emojis.

'We can definitely discount Toby and Sav. They were upstairs with Lily in her bedroom having an actual midnight feast. Lily told me Sav showed her his phone and it was all zeros.'

More typing. 'And we're happy that's accurate?'

'It's pretty specific, isn't it? She wouldn't have made that up.'

'Could Sav have changed his phone though? Maybe they were trying to establish an alibi?'

'Maybe, but in that case why not mention it? When I

spoke to them earlier they didn't say anything about having a midnight feast, and Lily said that they'd all agreed it would be a secret. That's not what you'd do if you wanted everyone to know you had an alibi is it?'

'No, true,' Jennie types back. 'Also the whole dog biscuit motive was the weakest, plus it's Toby and Sav – you just can't picture it can you? They go on litter picks for Christ's sake. Murderers don't go on litter picks.'

'So we take them off the list of suspects?'

'Agreed. I never asked you what you thought about Miranda's live?'

Shit. I didn't watch it. I meant to, and then Lily had disturbed me and I'd completely forgotten about it. I really am the worst detective.

'I'm watching it now,' I type. 'I'll let you know.'

I scroll back to find the link in the chat and click to open it. Drunk Miranda blares loudly and I quickly turn the volume on my phone right down. Lily has stirred, but resettled. If I hold the phone very close I can just about see and hear her at the same time.

It's quite difficult to follow. She's had a lot to drink and is obviously very angry. There's a lot about Colin being a cheat and having drained her cosmic essence, which I don't really understand. She has about three solid minutes on her as a spiritual being and then around halfway in she must clock the time as she makes a comment about it now being officially Christmas Eve, and how pathetic it is for her to be crying in someone else's downstairs toilet. She has a bit of a turning point then, seems to rally herself, and finishes up a few minutes later vowing that she is a strong and independent woman who is going to

272

manifest only positive and nurturing things for herself in the new year.

I feel like *my* cosmic essence has been drained by the end of it, but it seems fairly conclusive – as it turned midnight, Miranda was in my toilet having a spiritual epiphany. Unless she's an exceptional actress, which I very much doubt. Unless she's made her money in those Spanish telenovelas, then Miranda couldn't have killed her husband.

I put down my phone, lean back against the headboard and try to let all of this new information sink in. On the one hand we're making progress and eliminating suspects, but where does it leave us? If Toby and Sav were having a midnight feast, Miranda was live on Instagram, and Bruce was in the happy afterglow of his shag fest with Jennie, then we don't have any viable suspects left with any reason to kill Colin.

There's no getting away from it – we've detected ourselves into a dead end.

I try to go back over it all in my head but it's too much information and my timelines are getting muddled. I concentrate on the people who don't have concrete alibis – are we discounting Bruce based on his emotional reaction or could he still be in the running? And what about Marcus? We've not looked at him because of how relaxed he was with me on the phone this morning, and the fact that he didn't know Colin at all, but what if there's a motive or a connection we don't know about?

We've got all of the people who left before midnight – could they have come back later on? I feel a wave of panic as I wonder if we've discounted dozens of people for no reason but then I remember the doorbell footage, plus the fact that the back gate was locked from the inside.

So then who was it?

When you think about how many people are accounted for at midnight, were there even any people left at the party? I work through everybody in my head and where they were and I'm left with just me, Oli, Jennie, Bruce and Marcus – not exactly a thumping party, but we had been going for a *long* time by midnight.

It occurs to me that there's one thing I have completely failed to check – my photos. I know I had my camera out at various stages of the evening. Maybe I have inadvertently caught the killer on film? I'll be pissed off with myself if it turns out that I've had clear evidence in my hand this whole time and just not thought to look.

I scroll through my photos and it's obvious that I am not going to crack the case this way. There are a lot of blurry-looking selfies with Jennie, some compromising shots of Marcus playing Twister and about a hundred close-up shots of Lily, where she must have pinched my phone. There are no photos at midnight of anybody tiptoeing in or out of the larder, splattered in blood and holding a knife.

Okay, I think, just because I don't have any, doesn't mean somebody else might not. I text Jennie back.

'Miranda looks in the clear to me,' I say. 'You were right there. Do you have any photos from the night? I only just thought to check but all I have are things like this.' I attach a particularly drunken-looking photo of the two of us, cheersing with shots of amaretto.

She types back. 'No, I already thought about that but I didn't take any at all, sozzles.'

No luck there then, but maybe Oli has some? I look at Lily snoring quietly next to me and back at my phone. It's 8.42 p.m. and I must have been up here for about twenty minutes. I can't drag it out any longer; I'll have to go back down. I reluctantly extract myself from under the duvet and climb inelegantly over Lily to reach the floor. I tiptoe to the door, the floorboards creaking.

'Santa?' Lily mumbles. I freeze. I stay still as a statue for about thirty seconds but I don't hear anything else so she can't have really been awake. I make it onto the landing and close the door behind me. Pamela's voice wafts up from the living room in horsey peals.

Back in the living room it doesn't look like anyone has missed me. Martin is snoozing quietly in an armchair and Ben appears to be showing Pamela something on TikTok. She's looking intrigued and appalled in equal measure, but seems to be enjoying herself. Ben in her eyes is like a young Oli and so can do no wrong. Oli is in the other armchair on his phone. He looks up when I come in.

'Everything okay, darling?' Oli asks.

'Yes, she's asleep, all good. Do you want to come and help me make some tea?' I ask significantly.

He jumps up. 'Sure,' he says, following me to the kitchen. Pamela looks up as we pass. 'We're just going to make some tea, Mum, if you'd like one?'

'Only if it's decaf,' she says, and Oli gives her the thumbs up.

In the kitchen I catch Oli up on all of the developments. He's pleased to hear that Sav was upstairs with Lily at the time and agrees that Miranda's live rant makes for a good alibi.

'It doesn't ultimately help though, does it? Because we still don't have a suspect with the means, motive *and* opportunity.'

'I keep thinking perhaps someone came back in when we weren't looking,' I say, 'but there's the doorbell, and Ben went through that really thoroughly. Unless someone snuck past it somehow?'

'I don't see that they could,' says Oli. 'It goes out quite wide on each side, almost to the welly rack on one side and to the hedge on the other. Even if they came in commando style and shimmied across the tarmac on their stomach I think we'd have still seen them. And the only other way would be through the back and I checked the back gate before I went to bed – that was locked.'

'It's clutching at straws I know, and if they'd come in from the front door through the living room we'd have seen them, but I just can't see how it can have been *anyone*. I suppose it couldn't have been suicide? Up to his neck in debt, no way out?'

Oli scoffs. 'I really can't see it. If I wanted to top myself I can think of much better ways to do it than by dressing up as Father Christmas, going to someone else's house and stabbing myself. Surely that's a bit dramatic. No, I don't think it's suicide.'

'An accident maybe?'

'Seriously? You're one of the clumsiest people I know, Anna, but even you wouldn't pop into the larder for something and *accidentally* pick up a knife and plunge it into your own stomach.'

'He could have been startled by something? Perhaps he took out the knife to admire it and then the cat jumped on his back and he flinched? They are really nice knives.'

Oli shakes his head. 'Even if he did take out a knife to admire it, which is highly unlikely, no matter how nice they are, there's flinching at a cat and grazing yourself and there's stabbing a knife deep enough into yourself to kill you. Plus if you'd done it accidentally then you'd stumble out of the larder and shout for help, wouldn't you? This must have been deep and powerful enough to immediately knock him backwards and put him out of action.'

I sigh heavily. 'Well I don't know then, an act of God? Divine retribution?'

I remember then about the photos. 'Can I see your phone?' I ask Oli. He hands it over and I put in the code – Ben's date of birth.

'What are you looking for?'

'Photos,' I say. 'I checked mine but there wasn't anything useful and Jennie didn't take any. It's a long shot but I thought it was worth checking. I remember you taking some, I think?'

'Oh good idea, yes I did.' He comes round and stands looking over my shoulder. There are a lot of me attempting a crab. I am not doing it well.

'I can *do* a crab,' I remind him. 'It was just the mat.'

I carry on scrolling until they change from Twister to shots on the sofa. There's me and Jennie deep in conversation, and then a selfie of Oli and Marcus. I check the photo details: 11.58 p.m.

'This might be something,' I say, pointing at the timestamp. 'Marcus was in the living room with us at 11.58 p.m.'

'It could be,' says Oli, 'but it could still have been possible, couldn't it, for him to have gone straight to the larder after that? I don't remember the photo being taken or what happened next. Are there any more?'

I carry on scrolling but there are no more photos with Marcus in. There are none with Bruce either, or Miranda, and none with Toby and Sav until about half past midnight.

'No more of Marcus,' I say, 'so I don't suppose we can rule him out on that, but it still comes back to motive. And his attitude this morning was just too relaxed.'

'And he doesn't look like a man *about* to commit murder in this photo,' Oli points out.

'What does a man *about* to commit murder even look like?' I ask. 'Should we be looking for an evil glint in his eye?'

'I don't know, just a bit more tense maybe? Although I guess he might not have realised at this point how murderous he truly felt. He'd have still known he was planning on confronting Colin about whatever it was that the note was about though.'

'It's too hard, Oli!' I wail. 'I can't figure it out! And there's still that fucking shoe print! Bloody hell, my brain can't take it.'

'Changing the subject then,' says Oli. 'Toby messaged to see if we wanted them to bring anything else with them tomorrow – emergency drinks or anything – but I said we were good. I told him Mum and Dad were here already and he said he'd bring an extra bottle of crémant just in case. Are we going to tell them about Colin?'

I grimace. 'What do you think we should do?'

'I think we should probably say something. I don't think they'll have an issue with it like Mum and Dad most definitely would, and they'll probably appreciate the honesty?'

'Yeah, I think you're right,' I say, 'but I don't want to tell them while they're here. Maybe I'll give him a quick call now. It's not too late, is it?'

'He was only just texting me so no, I think you're okay. Maybe go out in the garden though, just in case anyone overhears you?'

'Good idea,' I say. 'I want my coat though. It's freezing out there. Margaret sprang up while I was getting the presents out of the car and gave me a lecture about it.'

'About what?'

'I'm not even sure exactly. She kept saying she had something significant to tell me but then just kept going on about me not wearing a coat and how you shouldn't be loitering in the drive in the dark. I'm a bit worried about her, to be honest. She nearly got done for shoplifting earlier.'

'Shoplifting? What the hell? Where? How?'

'It was when I was in the Co-op. She was in there getting this sad-looking chicken dinner for one and she came out of the shop after me without paying for it.'

Oli laughs. 'That's hilarious. I'd love to see something in the South Medling Facebook group about Margaret being done for shoplifting. Can you imagine her indignation? Why did she follow you out though?'

279

'To tell me this *very important thing*, which seemed to just be about coats, although I was actually wearing my coat at the Co-op so who knows, honestly.' I get up and fetch my coat from the hall. 'I'll go and call Toby now.'

Oli kisses me on the cheek and goes to fill the kettle. 'I'd better actually make tea,' he says, 'or Mum will wonder what we've been doing out here. Do you want one?'

'Go on then,' I say, opening the back door. The cold hits me and I shiver. 'I'll have it out here please.' I step into the garden and close the door behind me.

CHAPTER 25

Toby is more than a little surprised to hear our news. He puts me on speaker and I tell the whole story to him and Sav. They ooh and aah in all the right places and ask lots of questions about everything we've discovered so far.

'It sounds like the police were appalling,' says Toby, when I tell him about their visit. 'Seriously, what the fuck? Standing in the shoe print like that. I hope they were wearing gloves at least when they were examining the scene.'

I think back to this morning. I think they did have gloves on.

'Did you notice any fingerprints on the knife?' Toby asks. 'If the flour could have left a shoe print it might have shown up a fingerprint too.'

I admit that I didn't look at the knife. My mind was all over the place when I first found him and by the time I'd decided to look for clues after having called the police I only had a short amount of time. I hadn't thought about fingerprints though. If our theory about it being a spontaneous crime is true then would the murderer have thought to wear gloves? They could of course have wiped the knife clean afterwards, but that would rely on them not panicking and trying to get out as quickly as possible.

'I wonder how long it would take to match a fingerprint?' I wonder out loud. 'Do you think the police would even tell me if they found anything?'

'I think it's more likely they've forgotten who you even are, or left the fingerprint on a bus or something,' says Sav. 'I think you should put in a complaint. It sounds awful.'

'With any luck they'll be able to find a fingerprint match,' says Toby, 'if not on the knife then from somewhere else in the larder. The murderer is bound to have left some DNA. You can't do anything these days without leaving DNA.'

'The trouble is that loads of people were in the larder at some point,' I say, 'so how do you know which prints come from the killer and which are from innocent people looking for crisps?' And it's not just fingerprints is it? I shudder at the thought of Jennie and Bruce and their liberal sharing of DNA.

'I'm just so glad we were upstairs with Lily at midnight,' says Toby. 'Sorry about the Bendicks by the way. I hope you weren't saving those especially for Oli's mum.'

I tell him it's fine, that Pamela has developed an aversion to wrapped chocolates and is now all about the marzipan fruits.

'But wasn't there that whole fuss where she said that people who ate marzipan fruits . . .'

282

I interrupt Sav before he can finish his sentence. 'Don't,' I say, 'just don't. I've given up trying to apply logic to the woman. Needless to say that however she previously felt about them, since she was given them at some fancy Easter afternoon tea she thinks they're God's gift to treats. Of course I don't have any.'

'Well of course not,' says Toby, 'not after what she said about . . .'

'Enough marzipan fucking fruits! I just can't think about that right now. I want to get everything straight in my head but I can't make everything fit. It's infuriating. It can only have been one of a certain number of people and yet somehow it wasn't any of them. It's maddening. I feel like we're so close and yet at the moment none of it makes sense.'

'It solves our problem at least,' says Sav. 'We can stand down the solicitor.'

'Oh yes of course, Pup's Pantry!'

'That's what we were talking about this morning when we said we'd taken steps – we've had some legal advice and we had a plan to put Colin in his place.'

That makes a lot more sense than the assumptions I had leapt to and I make noises that I hope convey that I had assumed that was what they'd meant all along.

'I might have some bad news about that actually, Sav,' I say. 'I don't know what the deal is in terms of Colin owing you money, but I wouldn't bank on getting anything – it turns out he was pretty much bankrupt.'

'That's fine by us,' says Sav. 'I didn't want anything more to do with him anyway. I just wanted him to stop trying to bully me into compromising the brand and tarnishing Bianca's legacy.'

Toby starts to say something else just as Oli appears at the back door. He has a mug of tea in his hand.

'I got distracted making Ben another hot chocolate,' he says. 'Do you still want this out there or are you nearly done? I think everyone might be wondering where you are.'

'I'll come in now,' I say to Oli, my hand over the mouthpiece. He smiles and takes the tea back inside. 'Sorry, guys,' I say to Toby and Sav, 'I need to get back inside and put in some time *en famille*. People are asking after me. If you suddenly remember seeing one of the guests sneaking furtively out of the larder just after midnight then let me know.'

They both promise to share any revelations that come to them during the evening and I reluctantly hang up and go back inside. Martin has woken up and is talking animatedly to Ben about the best way to tow a caravan – how they got onto that I have no idea, especially as to my knowledge Martin has never owned a caravan. Oli is patiently listening to his mum as she tells him in great detail about how Deidre's daughter Elizabeth has started her own soy candle business using aromatherapy oils and flowers she dries herself.

'Have you heard of Etsy, Anna?' Pamela asks me as I sit down on a cushion on the floor next to Oli's legs.

'Yes, I've heard of Etsy,' I say.

'Well Elizabeth has done ever so well on it. She's opened her own Etsy shop would you believe! I'm not sure where, Deirdre wasn't entirely clear on that bit, but last week she sold three candles. Deirdre is so proud of her. Elizabeth has always been the creative type, just like my Oli.' She smiles at him.

284

'I wouldn't say I'm that creative, Mum,' he says.

'Nonsense,' says Pamela, 'of course you are. I've still got the certificate from when you won that national writing prize.'

'I think it was a slogan about not flying kites near pylons, Mum,' says Oli.

'Well there you go – if that's not writing then I don't know what is.'

'And I think it was just our school, or maybe the town at most.'

'But if it *had* been national you'd still have won, darling, it was superb. And don't forget you can play the oboe.'

I look at him in surprise. He's kept this very quiet over twenty-plus years of us knowing each other.

'I cannot play the oboe, Mum. I had a *go* on an oboe. You remember when Aunty Lizzie had that boyfriend who was in an orchestra? I had a go on his, that's all.'

'And what did he say? That you're a natural. A natural oboe player doesn't need lessons. You just picked it up and you were away. Sheer talent. You remember, don't you, Martin?'

'Remember what, dear?' asks Martin.

'Oliver playing the oboe.'

'Oh yes dear, a natural,' he replies without hesitation.

'The fact is, darling,' she says, turning back to Oli, 'that if you're a *creative type* then there's no getting away from it, whatever you turn your hand to, you can't help but accomplish it with elegance and flair. And if you're not—' she looks pointedly at me '—then you're better sticking to the more practical things. Not that there's anything wrong with being a little more homely and

285

sensible. Every creative genius needs somebody to feed and clothe them and book their dentist appointments. It's the great circle of life.' She waves her hands dramatically and I nearly choke on my tea.

Oli gives me a good pat on the back and I compose myself. The idea of Oli as a creative genius is a bit much even by Pamela's standards. She has had a sherry though.

'Have you ever towed a caravan, Dad?' Ben asks.

'No,' says Oli, 'but if we had one I think that would probably be your mother's area of expertise. She's much more practical than me.' His mother narrows her eyes at him.

'How about a game of something?' I suggest.

'Cards Against Humanity?' Ben offers.

'I'm going to go ahead and say no to Cards Against Humanity,' I reply.

'We could play normal cards? You promised me you were going to teach me how to play poker. You said we could play for cash.'

I laugh awkwardly. Pamela is frowning darkly at me. 'Just pennies, Ben, remember? Not real money.'

Ben looks confused and goes on, not getting the hint. 'What? You said we could play for real money and that you'd take me for all I had?'

'I think Mum was only joking about that, Ben,' says Oli, and then quickly, before Ben can say anything else. 'How about we teach you Black Maria?'

'What's Black Maria?'

'It's a card game, but too complicated for Lily and better with a few more people. Also Grandma just happens to be rather good at it, aren't you, Mum?'

'Well,' she says, puffing up her chest a little bit, 'I am

286

something of a legend at The Shuffle Squad for my winning streak of 2012. Of course Ken made a fuss about having the sun in his eyes but we all knew he was just bitter.'

'Okay, fine, Black Maria then,' says Ben, 'but can we play for money?'

'No,' Oli and I say simultaneously. 'But we can have After Eights,' I add. 'If you go and get the cards.'

We all decamp to the table in the kitchen. Ben shuffles the cards while I go to the larder for the After Eights. Pamela appears behind me, as if by magic. I jump.

'I wondered if you had any more Tyrrells,' she says, eyeing the bag of Aldi's finest ready-salted.

'No sorry, just these Aldi ones.'

'Ah well, not to worry.' She stays in the doorway though, sniffing the air. 'It smells very minty in here,' she says, eyeing me suspiciously and looking around carefully.

'That'll be the After Eights,' I say, taking them down off the shelf and wafting them about in front of her nose. 'See?'

'Yes thank you, Anna, you don't need to brandish them at me. I can see them perfectly clearly.' She turns and leaves the larder. I shut the door firmly behind us. We're all sitting down and Oli is dealing out the first hand when my phone pings with a text. It's Toby. I open it.

'I was just thinking about everything,' it says, 'and I know you said that everyone with a motive has an alibi, but what if someone left and then came back later?'

Oli is still dealing so I write a quick reply.

'No good,' I write, 'we've checked the doorbell video footage and no one came back.'

Another message appears.

'I was thinking of someone coming in the back through the garden? The back door is right next to the larder, so they could get in and out without anyone seeing?'

'Yeah we thought of that, but the back gate was bolted from the inside, so I think that's a dead end too.'

Oli has finished dealing and is explaining the rules to Ben. My phone pings again.

'No it wasn't.'

'What do you mean? What wasn't?'

'The gate wasn't locked.'

'Yes it was, I checked this morning and Oli checked before we went to bed last night.'

'Maybe it was then,' Toby has typed, 'but that's because I locked it at about 1 a.m.'

CHAPTER 26

'Are you ready, Mum?' I look up from my phone and see everyone around the table watching me, their cards ready in their hands. Mine are still in the pile in front of me where Oli dealt them.

'Oh right,' I say, 'we're starting, are we?'

'Dur, Mum, yeah we're starting. Dad has explained it and it sounds simple enough.'

'A minute to learn, a lifetime to master,' says Pamela, her face deadpan.

'Isn't that Othello, dear?' says Martin and immediately wishes he hasn't as Pamela shoots him down with a look that could turn small animals to stone.

'Everything okay?' Oli asks. 'You look a bit lost there.'

'Sorry,' I say, picking up my cards, 'everything is fine. I just had a bit of a strange message from Toby.' My head is spinning. What does he mean he locked the back gate? Had he been out of it? Was I wrong to discount him? Or was he saying that it had been open

289

all along, that anybody could have come into the garden, into the house, at any time?

Oli looks concerned. 'Is everything okay with them?'

'Yes yes, everything's fine,' I say again. 'Toby just told me something about, um, Father Christmas, that throws a bit of a new light on things.'

Pamela interrupts, impatient to get started and show off her enviable Black Maria skills. 'About Father Christmas? Anna, are you quite all right?' She turns to Martin. 'It's the 5G, I expect. We saw that mast on the way in, remember? Stella from Knit and Knatter told me all about it. It interferes with brain waves,' she adds in a stage whisper.

'My brain waves are fully functional, Pamela. My brother just had a bit of news for me and I'm not sure what to make of it.'

'About Father Christmas? You do realise, Anna, that he's *not real* don't you? Oliver hasn't been doing the stockings all this time and simply not telling you?'

'Mum, Anna's not an idiot, of course she knows Father Christmas isn't real.'

'Wait,' says Ben, in mock surprise and hurt. 'Santa isn't *real?*'

'I think perhaps you'd better play this hand without me while I give Toby a quick call back,' I say, my chair scraping on the floor as I stand up.

'But, Mum! Dad has dealt the cards already!'

'I can deal again, Ben. It only takes a minute.' He collects everyone's cards back up and starts shuffling. I flash him a grateful smile and take my phone into the living room.

I close the living room door and take a minute to pace up and down a few times, hyperventilating and flapping my hands about. It is all very un-Poirot. Finally I catch my breath enough to call Toby.

'Oh hey,' he answers casually, 'everything okay?'

'Um, not really,' I say. 'I think part of my brain might have just exploded?'

'Why, what's wrong?'

'The back gate,' I say, 'tell me what you meant in your message.'

'Oh that, well just that I locked it. Sav and I went outside about 1 a.m. for a bit of fresh air and a Christmas Eve snog. The garden lights were on and Sav noticed that the back gate was ajar, so I popped across the lawn to shut it and slipped the bolt across it.'

'What do you mean ajar?'

'Well just that really, not wide open or anything, just not quite shut. Enough to make us think we should probably shut it for you. Does it make a difference?'

'Fuck me, does it make a difference?! We've been working all day on the assumption that our murderer had to be one of a very small and finite group of suspects and now you're saying that literally anyone could have just come in off the street and bumped off Colin. Christ. Why didn't you mention it before?'

'Whoa, steady on, Anna, you only just told us what happened, so until now we had no idea it was even relevant.'

'I know, I'm sorry. I didn't mean to snap at you. I'm just freaking out a bit here, Tobe. It was horrible enough when I thought it had to be someone I knew, but now I'm thinking a stranger could have been inside my home, with my children in it, *killing someone*, and I had no idea and have no way to figure out who it is.'

'Okay, calm down, Anna. Are you pacing?'

'Maybe.'

'Right, sit down and let's think about it logically.'

I sit down.

'Yes, the back gate being open does put things in a different light, but I don't think it means that any random killer was swanning about in your larder.'

'You don't?' I say in a small voice.

'Definitely not. Think about it. You're in a cul-de-sac right? At the end of a cul-de-sac no less. How much passing footfall do you get?'

'None,' I admit. 'Unless it's cars turning around because they got our road muddled with the entrance to the cricket ground.'

'And can you even see your back gate from the street?'

'No.'

'So, how likely is it that a random murderer happened along your road, thought they'd have a look around the back of your house, found the gate open, thought they'd take their chances even though there were clearly a lot of people about, and happened upon Colin in the larder?'

'Not very at all,' I say.

'Plus there's the note, isn't there, asking Colin to be in the larder at midnight? That was written from inside your house. It still has to be someone you know, Anna; it just doesn't make sense otherwise.'

I'm breathing more normally now. Toby is right – the

facts don't fit it being a stranger, so we're back to it being someone who was at the party. The back gate could have nothing to do with it at all.

Unless.

'You're right, Toby, sorry for being a bit mental. I don't know what happened there,' I say, standing up again.

'Don't apologise. It sounds like it's been a bit of a bonkers day. I'm not surprised you feel on edge. Just try to stay objective, okay?'

I hear Bianca barking in the background.

'I've got to go, Anna. We were just about to take Bianca out. I think she ate too much doggy popcorn. Call me though if you need me, okay?' I hear him say 'coming, poppet' before he hangs up and I'm left holding a silent phone. My brain is far from silent though. Things have started shifting and I'm beginning to see what I think could be an answer. It's the Swindon escape rooms all over again.

I send a quick WhatsApp to Jennie.

'Are you okay to drive? If so, get here asap. I'm on the trail.'

It only takes a few seconds to get a reply.

'On my way, Batman!'

I stick my head around the kitchen door. 'I've just got to pop out,' I say, desperately thinking of an excuse to leave. 'Toby said that he's sure he saw some marzipan fruits in the Co-op, so I thought I'd nip out and get you some, Pamela.'

'Anna, it's late. We've got plenty of stuff here, and I doubt the Co-op is even open now. It's Christmas Eve, remember?'

'I know, Oli, but I want to check,' I stare at him, willing him to get the message. 'It's *really important* to me to give your mum the Christmas she deserves.'

He must know I'm lying now.

'Do you need any help?' he says. 'Will you be safe?'

Pamela looks bemused by the whole thing. 'I'm sure she doesn't need help getting a bit of marzipan, Oliver.'

'I'll be fine,' I say. 'I've had a couple of drinks so Jennie is coming over to drive me there. I won't do anything stupid.'

'What on earth are you talking about?' Pamela asks. I ignore her.

'I'll call the police if I need to,' I say to Oli. 'We'll be careful.'

Pamela puts her cards down. 'What sort of Co-op *is* this?'

But I've left.

I go into the hallway, grab my coat and put my trainers on. It should only take Jennie about five minutes to get here, just enough time to talk to Margaret. I walk up her front path and knock on the door gently. It's getting late and I don't want to wake her if she's already in bed. She answers in her slippers, a cardigan pulled tightly around her.

'Margaret,' I say, before she has a chance to even say hello, 'I need to ask you something about when I saw you at the Co-op and when we were talking on the driveway earlier. You remember?'

'Of course I remember. I'm not senile.'

'You weren't trying to tell me that I should have been wearing a coat, were you?'

294

'What? Of course not. I'd hardly come running out of a shop after you to tell you to wear a coat. You're a grown woman.'

'Exactly! You were trying to tell me something else, weren't you?'

'What are you talking about, Anna? I thought we'd already had this conversation. I was telling you about that young girl, out on your driveway at all hours, freezing herself half to death.'

'Thank you, Margaret,' I say, 'I'm sorry I wasn't listening properly earlier.' I can feel my heart pounding in my chest as the pieces of the puzzle start to slot themselves together. 'Would you like to come to Christmas dinner tomorrow, Margaret?' I ask, high on a surge of adrenaline. 'We'd love to have you and you might just have helped me solve a very serious crime!'

Margaret is stunned into silence, which makes a change. Then her sense of self-importance takes over. 'Well,' she says, 'if it's a very serious crime, then I feel like it would be my duty to come to lunch, thank you very much.'

'See you tomorrow, Margaret!' I call over my shoulder, leaving her on the doorstep looking baffled.

I see headlights turn in at the end of the road. I've just got time to check one more thing – my wellies – upside down in the welly rack, just out of the range of the Ring doorbell. There it is, the chevron design that has been haunting us all day, right there under our noses. There's a small round stone stuck in one of the ridges. I run my finger along the sole through what I'd thought earlier was dust, but now realise is *only* on my wellies. Flour.

Jennie pulls into the drive, turns off the engine and jumps out of the car. She runs over to me, eyes gleaming in the porch security light.

'What's the big news?' She's breathless with excitement.

'Jennie, I've done it! I really am Agatha Raisin!'

She looks me up and down – shapeless winter coat and muddy trainers. 'You might need to work on your outfits a bit but okay.'

'All right, not the accessorising bit, but the detecting!'

'Have you found a new clue?'

'Even better,' I say and I pause, mimicking her earlier reality TV-style tension-building technique.

'Well spill the fucking beans then,' she says.

I bite my lip and give a little clap. I feel like I'm nine years old and on the final chapter of a Famous Five book. 'I've solved it,' I squeal. 'I know who killed Colin!'

CHAPTER 27

Jennie stares at me.

'Well?' she says eventually.

'Well what?'

'Who was it? Dur, Anna.'

'Oh yes, that! I'm not going to tell you,' I say.

'That's a bit mean, isn't it?' She frowns.

'I'm going to do better than that,' I say. 'I'm going to *show* you. We're going to catch them ourselves!'

Jennie's eyes go wide and she tips her head back and laughs loudly. 'Yes, Anna! I knew you had it in you to go rogue! How are we going to do it? Lure them to an underground gambling den and extract a confession by electrocuting their nipples?'

'I was just going to go to their house,' I say, 'and confront them.'

'Boring! Can't we do the gambling den thing?'

I raise my eyebrows. 'Do you know of any gambling dens in South Medling?'

'Minor flaw in the plan,' she concedes. 'But still, are

we seriously just going to show up and they're going to let us in and say, "Oh yes it was me?" They'll not open the door to us, surely?'

'I'll figure that out when we get there,' I say, 'I'm ninety-five per cent sure we can do this.'

'And what happens if it goes the five per cent way?'

'It won't. Are you with me?'

'Hell yeah I am! This is the most exciting twenty-four hours I've had in years! Where are we going?'

'Get in the car and I'll give you directions,' I say.

A few minutes later and we're pulling up outside the Co-op. Jennie switches off the engine and I open my door.

'Wait, what are we here for?' Jennie asks. 'Did someone at the Co-op do it?'

'We're here for marzipan fruits,' I say, getting out. Jennie scampers behind me. At the door is the same officious-looking security guard who called out Margaret for her chicken dinner theft attempt. He stands in front of me as I try to go into the shop.

'We're closed,' he says.

I look past him and can see two people at the checkouts. 'No you're not,' I say. 'I can see people inside.'

'They're completing the purchases that they started shopping for *before* we were closed,' he explains slowly and aggressively, 'and then I'll be closing the shutters.'

'But I only want one thing,' I say. 'Couldn't I just run in really quickly? I'll be out again before you know it.'

He stares at me. 'We're closed.'

'Hang on a minute,' says Jennie, screwing up her eyes and peering at him, 'weren't you in our year at school?'

'No,' he says, without looking at us.

'Yes you were,' says Jennie. 'Stuart Lambard. I remember you! You thought you were God's gift, swaggering about with your hair in curtains and streaked orange with Sun-In. You used to bully Nick Franklin about wearing shorts all year round. How the mighty have fallen! Is this how you get your kicks now, bullying respectable women on the steps of a Co-op on Christmas Eve?'

'I'm just doing my job,' Stuart Lambard snarls. 'I've no idea what you're talking about. Now get lost.'

'Ha! Get lost? We're not scared of you, Stuart Lambard!'

Stuart Lambard growls.

'We don't even *want* to come into your stupid shop,' says Jennie.

I nudge her. 'We kind of do, Jen,' I whisper, 'for the marzipan fruits?'

'We'll go somewhere else for them,' Jennie whispers back.

Stuart Lambard is unimpressed. 'Are you ladies going to move along or do I have to call for back-up?'

'Back-up?' Jennie laughs. 'This isn't a drugs bust, Stuart; you're not in the SAS. You're a security guard at a local convenience store. Not even big Tesco! I don't imagine you even *have* back-up!'

I feel like we might be getting off track a bit here. 'Jennie, can we just leave it? We have more important things to do, remember?'

'Oh fuck yes,' says Jennie, 'I forgot about that. Lucky for you, Stuart Lambard, we actually have important crime-busting work to do.' I drag Jennie away. 'Tosser!'

she shouts over her shoulder. Stuart snarls and takes a step forward and we both run back to the car.

'Sorry about that,' she says, clicking her seatbelt into place. 'I got a bit carried away. Do you remember him though? Everybody at school fancied him even though he was a complete idiot and mean too. That was the Nineties for you though. The bigger the twat, the bigger the crush. Not like nowadays where it's all kindness and inclusivity. Did I tell you that Susie at work was telling me that there's a kid in her son's class who gets bullied for *not* being neurodiverse or having a diagnosed mental health condition? Bonkers.'

She looks at me and I raise my eyebrows. 'Finished?' I say.

'Yes sorry, I'm focused now, I promise.'

'Good,' I say, 'because we are about to casually call on a murderer and confront them about their crime, so I think we should probably have our heads in the game.'

'Absolutely,' says Jennie, 'head in the game. Got it. What are you doing?'

I have my phone out, making a call. I hold one finger up to Jennie while I wait for an answer. Six rings and then it goes to answerphone. Bugger. I leave a quick message, including an address, and really hope somebody picks it up soon.

'Is that the address we're heading to?' Jennie asks as I hang up.

'Yep, that's the one. Are you ready?'

Jennie starts the car and revs the engine, smiling. 'I was born ready.'

Five minutes later we pull up outside a row of large

Victorian terraced houses, most of which have been turned into flats. We get out and look up at number 12. My heart is pounding. I feel like I did standing at the end of the aisle at the church, about to get married. *That* turned out to be a decent decision, but is this? What if no one picks up the answerphone message?

'What's the plan then?' Jennie asks, burying her hands into her coat pockets. 'Are we just going to ring the bell and wait for someone to let us in or are we climbing through a window? I'm not sure I have the hip flexibility for anything too adventurous.'

'I'm not sure,' I say. 'Do you think we're doing the right thing?'

'What do you mean? Are you not sure it's the right person?'

'I'm sure about that bit, but are we being stupid confronting them ourselves? What if they kill us too?'

'Is that likely? You're in a better position to judge than I am – you're the one who knows who it is.'

'No, I don't think it's likely, but maybe they'll panic? Perhaps we should just get back in the car and drive home and play Black Maria.'

'Black Maria? What are you on about, Anna? Look, we're here now, and if you reckon that odds are we *won't* get murdered then I say that's good enough and we should go for it. How often do we get to do something like this, something *actually exciting?* Aren't you sick of life being a never-ending cycle of packed lunches and changing sheets and deciding what to have for dinner?'

I admit that yes, meal planning is tedious, but perhaps

there's a middle ground between that and capturing killers in their own home? Jennie is unperturbed.

'Don't you get it, Anna? This is our chance! Our chance to be something other than mums and wives, or soon-to-be ex-wives in my case. I'm not saying I don't love my kids, of course I do, but let's be honest, they can be pretty boring. This is something for us, something for those ten-year-old versions of us, obsessed with mysteries, desperate for one of our parents to let us have the shed as our detective clubhouse. If you look at it like that, this is really just us healing our inner children.'

I look at her sceptically. 'Do our inner children *need* healing?'

'They *always* need healing,' she says confidently, 'every woman I see on Instagram is healing her inner child. Either that or they're on a juice cleanse or discovering they're bisexual and I don't fancy either of those.'

I feel frozen on the spot. Because Jennie's right, as much as I love Oli and Ben and Lily, sometimes I feel myself getting lost in the midst of all of the roles I play every day. Today has been an emotional rollercoaster and there have been moments when I wished it had never happened, death of an innocent(ish) man aside obviously, but then there have also been moments, those escape-room moments, where I've felt that rush of something new and challenging. It's been in those moments that I've had a flash of how we used to feel as children, before we got bogged down in laundry and housework and World sodding Book Day.

'Plus,' says Jennie, 'you don't want to end up like Stuart Lambard.'

That does it.

'I don't think we can just ring the bell,' I say. 'That's too easy to ignore. But it's flats, so we could ring a different bell to get let in and then go straight to the front door, catch them unawares?'

'Sounds like a plan,' says Jennie, 'and easier than the window idea.'

We walk up the front path. There's a panel of four doorbells, each with a surname written next to it. I look at them in turn. One has a little flower drawn next to it. 'Let's try this one,' I say pressing the flower bell. 'It looks the friendliest.'

The intercom crackles and a woman's voice answers. 'Hello?' she says.

'Oh hello, is that Miss McKenzie?' I say, reading her name from the doorbell label. 'I have a Christmas flower delivery.'

'Ooh, how exciting! Yes that's me. I'll buzz you in and I'm right at the top of the building.' The door buzzes and we pop it open.

'That was easy,' says Jennie, manoeuvring past the bike in the hallway, 'although I feel bad that she's not actually getting Christmas flowers. She's going to be disappointed.'

'Bring her back a bouquet tomorrow if you feel that bad about it,' I suggest.

'Maybe I will,' says Jennie indignantly, knowing she won't.

She follows me up the first flight of stairs and stops behind me on the landing in front of the door to flat 2. I lift my hand up to knock, and then change my mind.

'We are doing the right thing, aren't we?' I ask Jennie.

'Yes,' she says, 'absolutely. Besides, we have to get inside whoever's flat this is or the nice woman from upstairs will come down looking for her flower delivery.'

I take a deep breath and try again but I still can't do it. I turn to Jennie again for reassurance but before I can stop her she's got impatient and has knocked on the door herself. She moves to one side, out of sight of the peephole, and gestures for me to do the same. A few seconds pass and then we hear movement on the other side. A pause, and then the sound of the door latch and finally it opens to reveal the killer.

I smile. Jennie gasps. The killer says nothing.

'Hello, Georgie,' I say. 'Can we come in?'

CHAPTER 28

The first thing I see is the flash of fear on Georgie's face. It's the same look I saw when I came round earlier to bring her phone back and I can't believe it didn't scream at me at the time. The brain is a funny thing, I guess, only seeing what it wants to see. We'd discounted Georgie from the beginning because we knew she'd left the party early and so we didn't notice the clues that turned out to be staring us in the face.

Georgie composes herself. 'It's pretty late, Anna, and I'm still not feeling great, to be honest. Is it important?'

In my imagination I've only ever done the dramatic confrontation and confession, so I'm temporarily unsure about what to say next. Jennie steps in. Literally, squeezing past Georgie and into the kitchen.

'So sorry! I must have a wee! Where's your toilet?'

Clearly Jennie and I are going to have to collaborate a bit more in advance if we do this again. Using the toilet was my excuse for coming into Georgie's flat last time. She's going to think we met at an incontinence support group or something.

'Perimenopause,' I say, by way of an explanation, and I step into the flat too before she has a chance to stop me. Once inside, I make myself at home, taking a seat at the kitchen table.

'I'm not meaning to sound rude, Anna,' says Georgie, 'but what exactly are you doing here at nearly ten o'clock on Christmas Eve? Shouldn't you be with your kids?'

We hear the toilet flush, running water, and then Jennie emerges, patting her hands dry on her jeans. 'Sorry about that,' she says, 'weak pelvic floor. I blame the children. Of course I could have done the pelvic floor exercises like the health visitor told me but seriously, who actually does pelvic floor exercises, other than for the thirty seconds after someone mentions them?' She gives me a knowing look and I unclench guiltily.

Jennie sits down at the table too. Georgie looks like she wishes she were anywhere else in the entire world.

'Have a sit-down, Georgie,' I say, patting the seat of the chair next to me. 'I think we need to have a chat.' I sound like her mother, about to tell her all about periods, which I'm sure she really doesn't want to hear about after my last visit and the Mooncup fiasco.

She hesitates and then sits down, unable to come up with a reason not to.

'You're right, Georgie, I do have kids that I should be with on Christmas Eve, but it's been a funny old day, one way and another.'

'A very funny day,' repeats Jennie.

'It all started off okay, apart from the hangover,' I continue.

'A very nasty hangover,' says Jennie, leaning back in her chair and folding her arms across her chest.

I look over at her and sigh. 'Jennie, do we really need the dramatics? This isn't *The Bill*.'

She unfolds her arms and sits normally. 'Sorry, Anna, I got carried away again. I'll be quiet, I promise.'

I turn back to Georgie, who is looking frankly terrified, whether of what she knows is about to come, or of Jennie's 1970s bad-cop vibe, I don't know. 'The day started to go wrong, Georgie, when I went into my larder to get some bin bags to clear up the party mess and instead found a dead Father Christmas.'

She flinches. 'What, what do you mean, a dead Father Christmas?' she stammers.

'I think you know what I mean,' I say quietly. I look at her closely. She must be barely thirty. Could she be closer to Ben's age than mine? I suddenly feel incredibly sorry for her.

'I don't know what you're talking about,' she protests, 'really I don't.'

'I think you do, Georgie,' I say, 'and it might be sensible to talk to us about it first, otherwise you're going to be telling your story to the police in an interview room and they may not be quite as sympathetic as us.'

She looks from me to Jennie and back again, tears welling in her eyes.

'Honestly,' says Jennie, 'we didn't even like him.'

'Jennie!' I scold her. 'You can't say that about a dead man.'

'It's true though! He was an utter creep. No one liked him. Can you honestly think of anyone who isn't better off without him?'

'Bruce seemed pretty cut up about it,' I point out, 'what with Colin being his dad and everything.'

A stifled sob reminds us that we're here to confront Georgie, not to bicker between ourselves.

'Shall I tell you what I think happened,' I say, 'and then we can see where we are?'

'You're wrong though,' says Georgie feebly, 'whatever it is you think.'

'I think you did leave the party at 11.15 p.m., just as the Ring doorbell showed us, but I don't think you went home. You couldn't, because you'd already given Colin a note, telling him to meet you in the larder at midnight. Perhaps you meant to come straight back in, maybe you just went outside for some fresh air. But you ended up deciding that you wanted to sneak back in without anyone seeing you – you didn't want us to know that you were meeting Colin.

'I'm not sure what you did initially,' I go on, 'maybe you went for a walk, tried to calm yourself down. What I do know is that Margaret saw you on the driveway, without a coat on – *loitering* in the driveway she called it.'

'I dropped my phone,' says Georgie. 'I was looking for it.'

'You did drop your phone, but I don't think that was why you were loitering because I don't think you realised. It wasn't well hidden – Toby and Sav stumbled across it easily enough in plain sight. I think perhaps it fell out of your pocket when you were putting on my wellies.'

Her eyes are darting now and she's chewing her lip.

'I think you'd noticed earlier that the back gate was unlocked, maybe you even had an idea in your head of what you were going to do and had unlocked it yourself. You realised that the back door was right opposite the larder door and that would make it easy to come in through the back door and pop into the larder for your rendezvous without anyone being any the wiser. You don't want to mess up your heels though, crossing the lawn, so you pop my wellies on. The welly rack is out of the sightline of the doorbell camera so we wouldn't have seen you.'

'Just before midnight you sneak around the back, through the gate, into the house and into the larder. Colin is there waiting for you. Did he know why you wanted to see him, Georgie?'

Georgie whimpers. 'You can't prove any of this. You don't know what you're talking about!'

'I do I'm afraid, Georgie, and I can. I have Margaret as a witness, seeing you waiting in the driveway. I have my welly with traces of flour on it and the print in the flour in the larder. And I have this website address you wrote down for me about the Mooncup.' I take a scrap of paper out of my pocket and lay it on the table. 'The handwriting matches the note to Colin asking to meet him.'

She's crying now, silent tears spilling down her face.

'I also know that in your panic to cover your tracks, you took Colin's phone with you. We couldn't find it on him or anywhere in the house, but when I came to bring you back *your* phone, I noticed one on the table already. That was Colin's, wasn't it?'

Her eyes dart to the table now, just behind me. I follow her gaze and there it is, the phone that disappeared on my first visit. She reaches across me to try and get to it, but Jennie darts out a hand and snatches it first. She taps the screen and it lights up. The picture shows Colin in black tie, his arm around the mayor, his face the picture of smugness.

We all look at the picture, then Jennie and I turn slowly to Georgie, who has crumpled.

'I didn't mean to,' she sobs. 'You have to believe that. I never went in there with the intention of hurting him. I just wanted to talk to him. It all happened so quickly, I can't even remember picking up the knife, and then there was all this blood. It was like I was watching it all happen to somebody else.'

'Hang on a minute,' says Jennie, 'catch me up here. I don't understand – why did you want to meet him in the first place? Were you having some kind of fling?'

'God no!'

'Because it's okay if you were – we're not here to judge. You wouldn't be the first person to fancy a bit of festive fun in the larder.'

'Jennie,' I say, 'shut up.'

'What? I'm just saying, we're all women, all sexual beings.'

'Georgie was not having an affair with Colin,' I tell her.

'Well what then? I don't get it.'

I look at Georgie. 'Do you want to tell her or shall I?'

'I'll do it,' she sniffles. 'I wasn't having an affair with him. He was my dad.'

Jennie's mouth drops open. 'What the fuck? YOU'RE the secret child?' She looks at me. 'And you KNEW?'

'Only just before I called you,' I admit, 'only when everything started to fall into place. I couldn't figure out the motive. Why on earth would Georgie want to meet my boss Colin in secret? I didn't buy the love affair, so what was the reason? And then I remembered something you'd said, Jennie.'

'Me? What did I say?'

'It was two things actually. First it was in your background checks. You said you hadn't been able to find anything much about Georgie other than the report about her adoptive parents dying in the car accident two years ago. You said they lived in Leeds. Then later on when you were telling me about what Miranda had found out about Colin's child – you said that they had moved down from Yorkshire eighteen months ago.'

'It was my parents dying that made me think about looking for my real dad,' Georgie says. 'They were the best parents you could ask for and when they died I was just devastated. I thought perhaps if I could find my biological dad that it would go some way to filling the gap.'

'Ohhh, okay, I get it,' says Jennie, 'so you found out he lived down here and moved down to be closer?'

'Yes, but it took me a while to pluck up the courage to get in touch. In the meantime I met Marcus and started a new job and I was just beginning to feel human again. Marcus was so supportive too about me making contact with Colin. He didn't know who he was though. I wanted to keep everything very private until I knew a bit more about him and had decided if I wanted to open my life to him, but Marcus thought it was a good idea.'

'Wait,' says Jennie, 'I actually don't get it. Colin was your dad, and you wanted him in your life, so why did you kill him?'

'I didn't mean to kill him! I just wanted to talk to him. I was so surprised to see him there at your house, Anna – I was just going along to a party with Marcus. I didn't know that his neighbour, you, would turn out to work for Colin. I didn't know what to do. Colin didn't know who I was of course – we hadn't got that far yet – but I knew who he was, and watching him I couldn't help but think that he was pretty different to the picture he'd painted of himself in emails. He'd told me he was very reserved, low-key – a real family man, he said.'

'It must have been a bit of a shock to see him as an outsider,' I say.

'It was a massive shock! At one point in the party he tried to get me to sit on his knee and tell Santa I'd been a bad girl. I was horrified. Was this the same man? Was this really my dad?! I didn't want to make a scene at your party, Anna, but I had to speak to him, I had to get some answers, so I slipped him the note so we could talk more privately. Then as soon as I'd done it I started spiralling. I didn't know whether it was the right thing, whether I should tell anyone. I went outside to try and pull myself together, but then Marcus called and I panicked and told him I wasn't feeling well so had gone home. I couldn't then come back without it looking suspicious, which is when I came up with the plan to come in the back.

It wasn't meant to be sneaky; it was just to spare myself any embarrassment.'

'And what did Colin say when he saw you in the larder?' I ask.

'At first he thought I'd come to proposition him, which was horrific, so I had to get straight to the point and I told him I was his daughter. And he laughed, he actually laughed! He didn't seem at all concerned about his behaviour, just gave me this weird slap on the shoulder and said it was great to meet me and all this stuff about me being a chip off the old block. He wasn't taking it seriously at all.

'I was frustrated, I wanted him to realise how important it was to me, but also how his leaving my mum had impacted me. He'd not wanted anything to do with her when she told him she was pregnant; he'd just left her. She'd always given him the benefit of the doubt because she loved him, said he was too young and free and she shouldn't have tried to pin him down, but it broke her heart. Literally. She had congenital heart disease and when Colin left I think she must have stopped looking after herself properly. She died when I was eighteen months old. My parents – my adoptive parents – told me all that they knew, which wasn't very much – and I've filled in some of the gaps.'

'I'm so sorry,' I say, 'I'm so sorry you lost your mum at such a young age. That must have been such a traumatic thing to go through, even if you don't remember it.'

'I tried to tell Colin a little bit about my life and my adoption, but I could tell he wasn't really interested.

When I mentioned my mum, do you know what he said? He said he was never even sure at the time how many men she'd been sleeping with, that she was a *bit of a goer*. "My type of girl" he called her, but not "marriage material".'

Jennie and I both wince.

'That's when I saw red. I started crying, trying to tell him about her dying, how she'd loved him, but he just laughed. I could hear the music from outside the larder but it was like it was a million miles away. I just kept picturing my mother, how she must have felt when he left her all alone, pregnant with me, loving him, this awful man who would never have been worthy of her. It just made me so sad.'

I reach out my hand to Georgie's and give it a squeeze. Jennie gets up and gets some toilet roll from the bathroom and Georgie blows her nose. 'I just wanted him to stop laughing and listen to me,' she says, so quietly that we both have to lean forward to hear her. 'I saw the knives on the shelf, so I picked one up and held it up, as a warning. As a way to make him take me seriously. I stood in the way of him and the larder door and asked him if he even cared at all that he was my dad. But again, he just laughed, with a glint in his eye like this was all some big joke to him. Some hilarious anecdote to tell at the golf club. My hand holding the knife was shaking. He lunged over to push me out of the way, and then before I knew what was happening my hands felt wet. It felt like slicing through butter . . . the knife just slid straight into him.'

'God, those Sabatiers really are good . . .' Jennie whispers. I kick her under the table.

'He just fell to the ground. As soon as I saw the blood, I panicked and ran.' Georgie begins to cry, all over again. 'He was a bastard, but I didn't mean to kill him. I just wanted him to listen . . .'

I squeeze her hand again, just as the front door bursts open. Detective Sergeant Bacon stumbles in, closely followed by Simons.

'Aha! We've got you!' He regains his balance as Simons steps out from behind him, taking on what looks like a karate pose.

'Don't try anything funny now,' she says.

'All right, Simons,' says Bacon, 'that's enough, thank you.'

'There's no need for theatrics from either of you,' I say calmly. 'No one is trying anything in the least bit funny. Georgie has been very honest with us and told us exactly what happened. She's not about to make a run for it, are you, Georgie?'

'No,' she says sadly, wiping her eyes with her scrunched-up handful of soggy toilet roll. 'I'm not going to make a fuss. I did it. I didn't mean to kill him, but I know that I did and I'm very sorry about it.'

'Right,' says Bacon, 'I'm very glad to hear it.'

Simons drops her arms to her sides and straightens up. 'A very wise decision, a very wise decision indeed, as I am trained in the art of Feng Shui and I am not afraid to use it.'

'What are you going to do,' asks Jennie, 'rearrange her furniture to flow her into jail?'

'That's enough from you,' Bacon says, waggling his finger at Jennie. 'I could have you for perverting the course of justice.'

Jennie stands up and waves a finger back at him. 'Having sex in someone else's larder does not make you a pervert! I am a sexual being!'

'I don't think that's what he means, Jen,' I whisper. 'I think he's saying we're interfering.'

'Interfering? Ha! You couldn't have solved this case without us, Inspector Sausage! It's only thanks to my brilliant detective colleague here and my invaluable research into the suspect's background that you're here at all!'

'Please ignore my friend,' I say, hoping to avoid more than one person being arrested. 'What she means to say is how glad we both are that you got my answerphone message and were able to get here so quickly. It's perfect timing and we're really very grateful for you being so efficient.'

'Well, quite,' blusters Bacon, 'it was all men to the pumps when we got the message.'

'And women!' Simons pipes up.

'Yes thank you, Simons, and women of course. We're a very modern police force obviously, plenty of jobs nowadays that women can have a good go at. What I mean is that a quick response is the name of the game, the meat of the pie as it were. And very good pies they were too.' He looks around, confused. 'Now, where were we?'

'I think you were about to arrest Georgie,' I say helpfully.

'Ah yes, that's right, you're coming with us Miss, er . . .'

'Jones,' offers Georgie.

'Correct! Now off we go – no nonsense now.' He

walks her out of the flat, Simons trotting along behind like an obedient spaniel.

'I guess we go too then?' I say, looking around at all the evidence left on the table. 'Should we tell him about Colin's phone or the handwriting sample?'

'Nah,' says Jennie, 'he'll figure it out. Bright as a button that one.'

I leave Georgie's flat through the still-open front door, looking back over my shoulder for Jennie. She's not there. 'Jen?' I call.

'Just coming!' She appears at the door, slightly flushed, and pulls it shut behind her. 'Let's go then.'

'What is it? What have you done?'

'Nothing! Why are you looking at me like that? Come on, let's get going.'

'Fine,' I say, leading the way across the landing and down the stairs, 'but you better not have done anything stupid.'

We get back in the car and sit for a minute, letting the last ten minutes sink in. We did it. We actually solved a real-life mystery. It feels pretty damn good.

Jennie sums up my thoughts. 'That was fucking awesome, wasn't it? She just crumbled! You were amazing, Anna. I mean, I feel sorry for her too. Fancy finding out your dad, your only remaining living parent, is an utter cock, but still. Bit much to stab him for it.'

'It *was* fucking awesome, Jen. We smashed it.' I let out a deep sigh and lean my head back against the headrest.

'The cherry on the cake though – you'll never guess what I spotted on the side in Georgie's kitchen?'

'What?'

She rummages under her coat and pulls out a box. 'Marzipan fruits!'

'Jennie! You stole them from a murderer?'

'Well she's not going to need them, is she? So it seemed a shame to waste them. No point in them just sitting there.'

'I guess not, but it feels a bit weird. Two wrongs don't make a right and all that.'

'Two wrongs don't make a right? Are you kidding? She stabbed your boss to death and I pinched a box of cheap marzipan. It's hardly an eye for an eye.'

'I know, you're right. I'm sorry, it's been a bit of a day, hasn't it?'

'Damn right it has,' she says, taking the plastic film from the outside of the box and helping herself. She bites into it, and pulls a face. 'Gross, I forgot how disgusting marzipan is. Who eats these things?'

'I do,' I say, taking a marzipan strawberry and putting the whole thing in my mouth. 'Now let's go home.'

EPILOGUE

'Cheers to family and friends,' I say, raising a glass of crémant and beaming happily at everyone squashed around the table, 'because that's what Christmas is really all about!'

'And cheers to living for the moment,' adds Jennie, slurring slightly, 'because we really never know when it might be our last and we should all embrace every minute!'

'Yes, thank you, Jennie,' I say, giving her a look.

'Seriously, guys, we need to live life! Be grateful for everything we have, find joy in the wonder of Mother Earth! We're all sexual beings!'

I cough loudly over the last bit, give a final loud cheers and clink glasses with as many people around the table as I can reach. It's not all of them, as our table for six has evolved somewhat over the last twenty-four hours.

When Jennie dropped me home last night, I made her promise to come over for Christmas lunch so that we could debrief discreetly at opportune moments in the kitchen. She confessed she'd been actually pretty sad about the idea of Christmas Day alone, but hadn't wanted to feel like she was intruding. I then remembered that I'd invited Margaret, and Jennie said that if I was having any old waif and stray around for dinner then she was definitely coming.

It was Jennie's idea to invite Marcus too. I wasn't sure at first, but I sent Oli over first thing this morning to talk to him man to man, i.e. awkwardly and briefly, and he'd allowed himself to be persuaded. It was a bit strange at first, knowing that it was kind of our fault that his girlfriend was in jail for Christmas, but we plied him with drink and he seemed pleased to have the distraction.

I'd also called Toby and Sav once Pamela and Martin had gone to bed and insisted that they come for the whole day and not just for early evening nibbles. I played the 'I've had such a traumatic day and just want my family around me for Christmas' card and they relented on the condition that Bianca could come and have her own seat at the table.

And so here we are, twelve of us, including the dog, sitting down for Christmas lunch in what can only be described as 'intimate' conditions, as the table is really only cut out for ten people max. Bianca is sitting between Toby and Sav to minimise turkey swipage and Jennie is next to Marcus, practising her new-found flirting skills. I've told her it's too soon, but she says she's just cheering him up and I should stop being such a prude.

I made the bold decision to sit Pamela next to Margaret. It could have gone either way putting two such strong personalities next to each other, but it has paid off. Pamela told Margaret all about the flower show and Margaret said Deirdre sounds like a 'sore loser' and has promised to share her mother's pickled egg recipe with her for next year.

Without the context of yesterday, Pamela and Martin were a bit surprised by how many extra guests were suddenly invited for lunch, but I think we've managed to convince them that we are just being neighbourly. We made sure that Toby, Sav and Marcus were on board with keeping the murder of Father Christmas for over twelves and under sixties only. Margaret was problematic as I'd said all the stuff about her helping me to solve a very serious crime, and she'd seen Georgie in the driveway, but I told her that Georgie had been caught as part of a South Medling ring of criminals stealing recycling boxes and that she must keep it top secret. She'll discover the truth soon enough, but for today at least we can relax.

Clinking concluded, I take a seat and we all tuck in to our main course. There wasn't enough starter to go around, especially given the cats had the leftover smoked salmon, but we bulked it out as best we could with a couple of extra avocados and everybody has been very accommodating.

The main course was easier as we just did masses of extra vegetables and will have to forgo anything with turkey leftovers. Pamela had her moment in the spotlight when it turned out we *did* need her extra potatoes after all, and I conceded that she had been right to bring them just in case. It stuck in my throat a bit, but I am trying my best to not always see the worst in everything she says and does, and I think she might be cutting me a bit of extra slack. She was very restrained earlier when she answered the door to Margaret and found the rubber gloves still where I had hidden them from the police in the hallway plant pot.

Oli leans over to me and touches me on the arm. 'How are you doing, love? This is all fantastic. We're all very lucky to have you.'

I smile at him. 'It was a team effort,' I say, and it really was, the whole lot of it, not just the lunch. I look around the table at everyone relaxed now, enjoying themselves, and I feel a wonderful lightness. It seems like an odd feeling given that a man has just died in our house, but there has been a shift in the last twenty-four hours and I think we've all felt it. Has it really taken someone else's death to make me feel more alive? Is that wrong to even think? It's true though. Solving Colin's murder has made me realise that there is still more to me than parenting and the PTA.

I have a big glug of wine and look around the table. It's my third glass, possibly my fourth, but everyone knows that wine drunk whilst cooking doesn't count. Everyone is eating and chatting, and I'm so pleased that I made them all come, even if it means that we're having to use a few of the plastic picnic plates and Margaret had to go next door and get some extra forks. Everything is about as far from a Christmas tablescape as you can get, and yet it's perfect. I think I might love every single person around this table, even Pamela.

'Oli,' I whisper, as I top up my glass for the fourth or maybe fifth time, 'next Christmas shall we all go away somewhere?'

'Just us and the kids you mean, get away from everything?'

'No! I mean all of us, everyone here. We could rent out a big mansion or something – a castle maybe. Oooh, a castle on a loch! Maybe there are more people we could invite? People who don't have friends or family to spend Christmas with?'

'Like who?'

'Don't you have that cousin no one likes?'

'Ian?' says Oli, looking sceptical. 'The one who stole money from the Scouts to pay for prostitutes? I don't think you'd get Mum sharing a castle with him, even if it *was* loch-side.'

'Okay, not Ian, but you know what I mean, people who just need someone to reach out to them.'

He doesn't look convinced. His dad asks him to pass the potatoes, much to Pamela's delight, and so I turn to Jennie instead.

'Jennie,' I say, 'what do you think about next year spending Christmas in a castle by a loch?'

'I'll have the kids next year,' says Jennie.

'Even better, the more the merrier! I am embracing the magic and messiness of Christmas and I thought it might be nice.'

'Yeah maybe,' she says, helping herself to more cranberry sauce, 'although you might need to find a new job before you splash out on a castle.'

She's right. There's going to be the small issue of me probably not having a job after Christmas, but I'm not worried about that right now. 'Perhaps we should start a detective agency,' I say. 'We could be consultant detectives and make our fortune solving mysteries.'

323

'Are there many mysteries in South Medling? Apart from stuff like who keeps painting those penises on the clothes bank in the library car park?'

'That's not even a mystery,' says Ben. 'That's Darren Bailey from school. He thinks he's hilarious but he's a massive dick. They're basically self-portraits.'

'We'd have to go international,' I explain, 'probably Monaco, the French Riviera, that sort of thing.'

'Obviously,' says Jennie, 'keep it classy. I'll be the jewel heist specialist.'

'Do you know anything about jewels?' I ask. 'Or heists?'

'No, but everyone knows it's all about confidence, Anna. Do you think men actually know anything about half the stuff they do? Of course not, they just talk in a loud voice and use jargon. I'll learn a few key heist phrases and Bob's your uncle.'

She says it with such confidence that I almost do believe her.

A little while later and I'm clearing the table, ferrying empty dishes from the dining room to the kitchen. Pamela follows me, bringing an empty vegetable bowl and the gravy boat.

'That was lovely gravy, Anna – you'll have to give me the recipe.'

I look at her, wondering for a minute if it's a trick, but I don't see any malice in her eyes. Perhaps it's the crémant that Toby has been casually keeping her topped up with, but I swear she almost looks happy.

'It's just Bisto, I'm afraid,' I say.

'Well it was lovely,' she replies, rinsing the gravy boat under the tap before putting it in the dishwasher. I'm still standing, stunned, when Oli comes in carrying a stack of plates.

'Every okay?' he asks.

'Your mum just complimented the gravy,' I say, 'and it was Bisto.'

'There you go, see. I told you she was fine with you.'

'I think she's drunk,' I say. 'Or maybe it's a tumour.'

'Let's go with drunk,' says Oli, dumping the plates on the side by the sink. 'Now what were you thinking for pudding?'

What was I thinking for pudding?

I take a few seconds to seethe inwardly before remembering that I'm new, relaxed Anna now.

'What were *you* thinking for pudding?' I ask.

'I'm thinking we open another bottle of crémant, gather up all the sweets and chocolates in the house and dump them all on the table for people to help themselves.'

It sounds perfect. How simple he makes it sound – this not giving much of a toss about things.

'I love it,' I say, 'just don't forget the marzipan fruits.'

ACKNOWLEDGEMENTS

I'd love to be able to paint a picture of myself as a struggling writer, wrestling daily with my inner critic, finally committing pen to paper after months of angst, but in all honesty, writing *Happy Bloody Christmas* has been an absolute joy. I loved writing it, getting to know my characters and feeling so at home with Anna and Oli. I guess I have to say thank you first of all then to my brain, for being the sort of brain that just lets me enjoy things without over-thinking them.

A massive thank you to the wonderful Rachel Hart who took a chance on me and gave me the trust and the freedom to just get on with things, whilst always being there to offer guidance and support. Thank you, Rachel, for your belief in me and for letting me show you my pets over Zoom calls. I couldn't have asked for a better editor to work with.

Thanks to my family, especially my daughters Bee and Belle for their encouragement and for showing their support by letting me regularly drive them through

Starbucks. Thank you to my sister Annabel for laughing at my jokes and not asking me to drive her through Starbucks.

Thank you to me lovely friend Gill Sims for all of the hours we've spent imagining ourselves as refined lady detectives, bicycling through the countryside, our wicker baskets full of Important Detective Equipment, baguettes and love letters from admiring gentlemen. Our shared imagination and longing to solve a murder was an excellent foundation for this book.

Thank you to my dog Mako for helping me to see the joy in everything around me and for the daily reminder that I'm not too good to pick up poop.

Loved *Happy Bloody Christmas?*

Don't miss Jo Middleton's next hilarious
murder mystery, coming soon...

Not ANOTHER
Bloody Christmas

When Anna decides to take her family away for
Christmas to avoid a repeat of the 'dead man in the
larder' debacle, she finds herself plunged into another
festive fiasco when a body turns up in the library of
their supposedly 'idyllic' rural retreat.

With a dubious double booking, an unexpected
snowstorm, secret tunnels and the mysterious Mrs
Haddock to contend with, can Anna and her unlikely
allies save Christmas or will this holiday be their last?

Available to pre-order now!